Gray

By
Richard G Austerman

Table of Contents

Chapter 1

My eyes popped open due to a pounding in the back of my head. I was going to move, but it dawned on me: it was not my bed. Too warm and soft. Mine is a hard bedroll. I took a sniff, and Lola came to mind. It was her perfume that I was smelling. Lola owns Lola's Place, a saloon and, for lack of a better word, a brothel.

I had only been in town for an hour when Lola and I became friends if you want to call it that. When I got to town, I stopped at the Livery and stored most of my gear there. I took my bedroll, saddlebags, rifle, and scabbard.

Then I got a room at the only Hotel I saw. For an extra dollar, I got a hot bath. The tub was out behind the Hotel in a flimsily built shack. The lady who takes care of the tub was outside the hut and said, "I'll wash your clothes for a dollar. The clothes will be dry before the sun is down."

The clothes I had on were my cleanest set, so I said, "Let me run up to my room and get my other set of clothes. Then we got a deal."

With a shrug, the lady said, "Sure, I'll be here."

When I returned to the shack, I gave the lady my clothes and two dollars, saying, "That second dollar is for you having to wait for me to get my other clothes."

After my shower, I went back to my room and shaved. Then I went in search of a drink and some grub. I stepped out of the Hotel and asked no one in particular, "How did I miss that?"

Lola's Place was across the street from the Hotel. As I crossed, a few riders came down the road, and I slowed down to let them pass. I was about to walk into Lola's Place when two drunk cowboys came busting out the swinging doors.

In a Texas drawl, one of the drunks decided he didn't like me and said, "Mister, you're in my way. I don't like that, or you, for that matter."

"I'll get out of your way," I said. "I don't want any trouble."

"Fuck you!" the cowboy said and started to draw down on me. I was quicker and put the business end of my revolver in his mouth. Of course, that busted his lips and knocked out some of his teeth. I looked at his partner and said, "Touch that iron, and your friend is dead, and so are you. Now, you two back up against the wall."

Both of them quickly did as I said. I took their pistols and tossed them out in the street. "You boys need to take yourselves over to the Doctor's office. Have him fix this dumbass's lips and teeth if he can. Then come back here and stand against this wall for one hour."

The second cowboy nodded, and the first tried, too, so I took my pistol out of his mouth.

I said, "If you don't come back here, I'll come and find you. And let me tell you, you won't like that at all. You can get your hardware after the hour is up. Understand, boys? Oh, one other thing. You will die if you step one foot in this bar again. Now get out of my sight." Those boys were sober when they walked away.

I turned to go into the bar and found I had an audience. The doorway and windows were crammed with heads. I grinned at the ones in the door and loudly said, "BOO!" I never saw men and women move so fast. The doorway was clear of all but one woman.

Lola.

"Cowboy," she said, "the first drink is on me. Was the end of your six-shooter in Pete Rawlings's mouth?"

"Yes, Ma'am, it was. I told him I would get out of his way, but he went for his gun. Fortunately, I was quicker. He lost a few teeth, and his lips got cut up some. Those two are lucky; I usually shoot first and talk later."

Lola laughed and said, "What's your handle?"

"Gray, and yours, Ma'am?"

"Lola. I own this establishment and a good deal of town. How good are you with that six-shooter?"

"I ain't dead yet."

Lola snorted at that and walked into the saloon. I followed in the wake. She headed for the bar, and the customers got out of her way. As we reached the bar, Lola asked, "What are you drinking, Gray?"

"A shot of whiskey. Something other than Rye Whiskey. For some reason, that kind of whiskey bothers my stomach."

"James," Lola called out, "bring me my bottle. Let's go sit at my table, Gray."

I followed Lola to the far corner and saw many eyes on us. People didn't know who I was, and they were curious. Lola sat behind the table, and I took a chair where I could see the swinging doors out of the corner of my right eye. A wall was to my back.

We had barely sat down when one after the other, three scantily dressed ladies, came over and hugged Lola. While squeezing each other, they whispered, and Lola shook her head. By the time the last one left, I was grinning.

"What are you grinning for, cowboy?" Lola asked as she grinned at me.

"I would be willing to bet they all wanted to know who I am and when would they get to fuck me."

Lola laughed, saying, "Yeah, right on the first guess. So, which one do you desire?"

The bartender brought Lola a bottle and two glasses. As he set them on the table, Lola said, "James, this is Gray. I'm thinking of hiring him as a bouncer. What do you think?"

James smiled and stuck out his right hand, saying, "Nice to meet you, Gray. Are you the guy that settled that rustling problem in Santa Ana, New Mexico?"

"Yep, I am."

James said, "I heard there were six dead, and you didn't get a scratch. What are you doing in Holbrook?"

"I'm Passing through on my way to California. James, what kind of problem does the town have that Lola feels she needs a bouncer like me for?"

"A few local ranches sold out to big money from east Texas. We got some Texans coming into town, and they don't mix well with us Arizonians."

Lola said, "You just met two of those Texans."

With a grin, James said, "The foreman, and I don't know how many guns he'll bring, will come looking for you."

I nodded and said, "Thanks for telling me what's happening here. A man should know what he is facing. Where can I get a decent meal here in Holbrook? And, by the way, Lola, that whiskey you drink is good and smooth."

"Why, thank you, Gray. I like it too. The best place in town is Simpson Café. Their food is good," Lola said. "It's on this side of the street and in the fourth building further into town."

I stood and said, "Then, Lola, that's where I'm going. I'll consider the job offer and get back to you after eating. It was nice to meet you, too, James."

Chapter 2

I left Lola's and walked to the cafe. The walkway was covered, so I didn't have to watch out for any horse patties. I stopped at the edge of the front window of Simpson Café and looked. I counted ten tables, but there may have been two more out of my sight. There were two couples and a few single men having dinner.

On opening the door, I saw the waitress pouring a refill of coffee to the man at the table to my right. She said, "Be with you in a sec."

Turning her attention to me, the waitress asked, "Dinner for one?"

I nodded and said, "Do you mind if I take the table against the back wall."

"No problem. Most folks sit at the first table they come to," the waitress said as she looked me up and down. "You're not one of them Texans, are you, cowboy."

I shook my head, saying, "No, Ma'am, but I met a couple. Didn't care for them at all."

I ordered a special dinner and coffee. As the waitress turned to leave, I said, "Ma'am, will you please take two of the chairs away from my table?"

The waitress turned back and said, "Yes, sir. Are you expecting someone for dinner?"

"Not expecting anyone. There is, however, a possibility of three ladies coming here real soon. If three chairs are at my table, they will come over here. I don't think either you or I want that. When they see one chair, the ladies won't be able to agree which one sits with me, and they will leave."

The waitress grinned and said, "You mean ladies from Lola's Place, don't you, sir?"

I grinned and said, "Yes, ma'am, I do. Do you know how many ladies work at Lola's Place?"

With a chuckle, the waitress said, "The last I heard, there were ten ladies of the night at Lola's Place. And that is not counting Lola. Now I have to get your order in so that you can eat. You might need the food before the night is over." A few moments later, loud laughter came from the kitchen.

The waitress was still chuckling when she brought me a big cup of coffee. She had the coffee pot with her and shook her head as she poured my cup full.

As I took my second sip of coffee, the three ladies from the saloon entered the Café. They looked around, and one said, "He's at the back wall." They started my way, then stopped and had a little powwow. With one last look at me, the ladies left the café.

The ladies were looking at me when the door opened. They bumped into two cowboys who were on their way into the restaurant. After some laughing, the five of them headed back up the street. More people came in, and the place was starting to fill up.

I wondered where my food was when the cook brought it to me. "Mister," the cook said, "I want to thank you for stopping a ruckus before it started. How did you know those ladies were coming to see you?"

"Well, I had a little altercation outside Lola's Place."

"I heard about that."

"Lola offered me a job as a bouncer, and we went to her table. As we sat down, those ladies came over, hugged Lola, and said something. Lola said no."

"What did the ladies say, do you know?"

I grinned and whispered, "Do you want to know?"

Cook whispered, "Yes!"

"They wanted to know when they would get a chance to fuck me."

"Shit, I knew that was what they were saying. Enjoy your dinner, Cowboy."

I finished eating and paid the waitress. Then I asked, "Do you or Cook mind if I go out the back way?"

Cook heard me and waved for me to come back. As I walked by her, I stopped and said, "Your food is as good as Lola claimed it would be. It was as good or better than any I had in Saint Louis. The only way to know if yours is the best is to return another time. I'll have another meal. I bet your meal will win. See you later, Cookie."

The cook was still laughing when the back door closed behind me.

I slowly made my way to the back door of Lola's Place. I did not want to find any of those three ladies waiting for me. Opening the door, I found myself in a storage area. I heard a lot of noise coming from the central part of the saloon. There was light from the cracks around a door in the far wall. I carefully made my way to that door. I felt around on the door and found the handle. Then I opened the door just enough for me to look out.

I saw Lola, or at least her back, and she talked to the most beautiful lady I had ever seen. I think I was struck dumb. I blinked hard to clear my head and scanned the main floor, looking for any of the three ladies.

A commotion outside the swinging doors caught our attention. A lady loudly said, "But, Mister, he is not in there. He was just down at Simpson Café having dinner."

A male voice said, "Lady, I don't believe you. Pete, take those two. I got this one."

A cowboy nearly as tall as me came through the door, arms around two of the ladies I was looking for. They had come to the café. Behind him was another man holding on to the third lady. Both men had their guns in their hands.

"So, Betty, what's going on?" Lola said in a smooth, calm voice.

Chapter 3

I saw the light reflected off a gun barrel through the window to the right of the swinging door. I quickly went out of the way that I came into the building. Moving to the corner of the building closest to the street, I stepped onto the boardwalk. The two cowboys I encountered earlier looked into the saloon and did not see me. Both men had their guns out and held them up by their shoulders.

Keeping my eyes on the men, I reached down and pulled my second gun out of my boot. I straightened up and drew my revolver. Stepping up to the men, I shoved my pistols into the small of their backs and said, "Let's…."

That's as far as I got because one of the cowboys was so nervous that he pulled the trigger on his pistol. The shot hit the second cowboy in the head and came out the other side.

I heard boots running as the tall cowboy and the one he was with came through the swinging door.

"Don't," was all the cowboy in front of me got. The tall guy shot the man in the chest. My first shot caught the second guy in the throat, and my second shot hit the tall guy in the heart. Both men crumpled to the boardwalk. One dead and the other holding his neck and trying to breathe.

Lola stuck her head out of the swinging door and asked. "Gray? Is it okay to step out?"

"Sure, but I don't think the guy who got shot in the neck is dead. Might send somebody for the Doc."

"No need for that. I'm right here," a skinny man said as he exited the saloon behind Lola. The Doctor knelt by the guy holding his neck and shook his head. Then he checked the tall guy. Same head shake. When he stood up from studying the last guy, the Doctor looked at Lola and said, "Both are goners."

Lola looked at me and asked, "Gray, what is it with you and this walkway? You had to draw your gun out here for the second time." Lola waved at Sheriff Jack Brownie as he walked up to Lola's Place, saying, "Sheriff Brownie, why don't you and Mister Gray come on in so he can tell us what the hell just happened."

The sheriff looked me up and down before saying, "Gray, you are the man who handled that problem over in Santa Ana, New Mexico."

"Yeah, and a few others along the way."

The Sheriff nodded and asked, "Lola, do you know if those cowboys are part of the new Broken Arrow Ranch?"

"Yes, Jack, they were. The tall one was the foreman."

Sheriff Brownie shook his head and said, "Well, what do Texans expect when they come here and wave their guns around? Gray, next time you want to shoot someone, how about you come and get me first? If I can't talk them out of a gunfight, then have at it."

I nodded and said, "Sure thing, Sheriff. If I have time, I'll do that."

Sheriff Brownie kissed Lola and said, "I need to finish my rounds, but knowing what happened here is more important. Gray, let's talk, then I'll check the rest of the town."

The Sheriff and I followed Lola to her table and sat down. No one bothered Lola while I told them what had happened. Neither the Sheriff nor Lola said a word until I finished talking.

Rubbing his chin, Sheriff Brownie looked me up and down and finally said, "Not your fault they are dead, Gray. It sounds to me like you were doing your job in trying to stop a gunfight. When those Texans came out shooting, you had to protect yourself."

Turning to Lola, the Sheriff asked, "What did the Texans say to you?"

Lola shook her head and said, "Not much they could say. When they came in, I asked Betty what was going on. She said the foreman was looking for the new guy. Betty said she tried to tell the foreman that the man was down at Simpson Cafe. That's when the first shot was fired. The two Texans rushed out the doorway with their guns blazing."

The Sheriff grinned at Lola and said, "That is about what I figured happened. I saw Gray come out onto the walkway behind the Café. Then he disappeared into the dark. I didn't think too much about it until I heard the gunshots. Now, I've got to run along and finish checking the rest of the town. Lola, save me a spot at one of the poker tables. My fingers are itching for a good poker game. You a card player, Mister Gray?"

"I've been known to play some, Sheriff Brownie."

"Okay, then. I'll see you later. And, Gray, try to stay out of trouble." Brownie stood and walked around the table, kissing Lola before leaving the saloon.

For the few moments she watched him, I saw love for Sheriff Brownie written all over Lola's face. Then it was gone, and the fierce Saloon owner's face was back. Smiling at me, Lola said, "Gray, have you decided yet?"

I grinned and asked, "How many Texans do you figure are still out at their ranch?"

"Fifteen or twenty more. The next batch the owners send up from Texas will be more shooters than they have now. That would be my guess."

I nodded and said, "That would be my thinking, too. So, I'll take the job. But, before I do, I better play a little poker."

I looked around Lola's Place but did not see the lady Lola talked to earlier. And I didn't ask Lola about her either. Instead, I went over to a poker table. I looked at the dealer and asked, "Mind if I join you?" There were two empty seats at the table.

The dealer nodded, and I sat down. I bought a stack of chips, and for the next hour, I enjoyed myself. I was up a few dollars when I saw Sheriff Brownie come back into the saloon out of the corner of my right eye. He went over to Lola's table and started talking to her.

Although I couldn't hear it, I was sure I knew what the Sheriff was telling Lola. He was filling Lola in on what he had heard about me. I grinned at what the Sheriff might know. I'm sure Brownie heard that I was the law in all the towns I cleaned up.

"Cowboy, you grinning at me?" the guy across the table from me said. "You think my poker playing is funny? Well, I think you are a damn liar and a cheat."

The guy pushed his chair back and stood up. I stood up with him. He went for his gun, and a shot rang out. Someone had shot the guy in the right hand as it was closing over the handle of his pistol. The shooter was a hair faster than me. The sights on my gun were still in my holster when the lights went out for me. Something had struck the back of my head.

Chapter 4

The next thing I knew, I was waking up in bed. I learned it wasn't my bed when I took a small sniff. I could smell perfume. That smell, and knowing how hard the hotel bed was, this could not be my hotel bed. It was Lola's perfume. I could smell it on the sheets and pillow. A deeper breath told me someone else was in bed with me. Her scent was more pleasant smelling than Lola's.

I lifted my head and flopped back down with a loud groan. My head felt like it was going to explode. I shut my eyes and waited for the pain to subside.

The bed moved, and there was a movement to my right. I felt someone coming close to me. A soft female voice said, "Mister Gray, are you awake? My name is Norma. Lola told me to watch over you. The bump you got on your head might need some tender loving care. Lola had Doc Roth take a look at your head. He left some medicine for you."

I turned slightly to the left and said, "Can you kiss it? I bet your kisses will do more for me than all of Doc Roth's medicine. He's just a quack."

I sensed Norma was close and turned my head back to the right. Our lips collided. The jolt that shot through me chased all pain away and stiffened me up. My right hand shot out and caught Norma around the waist. I pulled her over on top of me. Our lips remained locked as she moved to where I wanted her. I heard Norma give out a soft, sexy moan.

I opened my eyes and looked into the most beautiful green eyes I had ever seen. I also found the lady Lola had been talking to earlier. I let my eyes smile and laugh at Norma at the same time.

Norma broke the kiss by pulling her head back a couple of inches and said, "Feeling better now, Mister Gray? I know I am."

I saw her glance down at my lips, so I said, "Go ahead. I know I want you to."

Norma kissed me, and her hands were all over me. I slid my right hand down her body. My hand stopped when it captured Norma's bare bottom. She was so small; my hand covered both cheeks. I had my left hand wrapped around Norma's back.

I think there was sweat coming off the top of my head when Norma ended the kiss. "My God! Where did you come from?" Norma said. "I want those kisses to go on forever. Who are you, Mister Gray?" She was looking down at me.

"I'm Charles Gray. Nice to meet you, Norma. I came from Missouri through Oklahoma, Northern Texas, and New Mexico, and finally, I'm here in Arizona. How about you, Norma? How did you end up with Lola? And, so you know, I also want those kisses to last forever."

Norma grinned at me and said, "May I call you Charlie? Charles seems like an older man's name. And you, my dear Charlie, are not old."

I laughed and pulled Norma tight against me. With a grin, I lifted my head and kissed the tip of Norma's nose. Norma giggled and said, "That was not where I expected those lips of yours to go.

I thought you just said you wanted the kisses to last forever. That was a short forever."

"If I kissed you like our first two kisses, I would end up screwing you to Lola's bed. I don't want Lola to come in and smell her sheets when we finish. Do you, Norma?"

After a long, loud laugh, Norma said, "No, my beautiful, sweet Charlie, I don't. What about my room? The bed is smaller, but it will hold both of us."

"Nope," I said as I shook my head. "I have a room in the Hotel. We can go there. I don't want anything to remind us of where we met. I checked so I would know the sheets were clean."

"Oh, Charlie, you do love me, don't you?"

"I have been with many women, but none of them compared to you, Norma. And, yes, I love you, Norma." I kissed the tip of Norma's nose and said, "Do you know where my clothes are?"

"Why? Where are you going, Charlie?"

"Maybe back to my hotel room with you tossed over my shoulder. Would you like that, my dear, beautiful, lovely, sexy Norma?"

Kissing the tip of my nose, Norma said, "I would probably laugh all the way there. Up until you dumped me on your bed and started kissing me."

"Am I hearing, 'I don't think so,' in what you are saying?"

"Yeah. I don't think Lola would approve of you carrying me away. She has made quite a lot of money off of me. How do we get around that?"

I shrugged and said, "I'll shoot her."

Norma laughed and said, "That is not the way to start a romance."

I drew in a deep breath and blew most of it out before I said, "Well, how about this? I put my left arm around your neck and hold my pistol to your head. As we walk down the stairs and out the swinging doors, I'll tell Lola that you now belong to me."

Norma shook her head and said, "Nope, that won't work. She would send a bunch of guys after you, and then there would be a gunfight. You would die, and I would have to kill myself. I can't live without you, Charlie Gray. My love for you is forever."

I rubbed my jaw in thought for a minute, and then my eyes opened wide. I kissed Norma, but it was a quick one before I said, "How about we walk down the stairs, dressed as we are, and tell Lola to find us a judge? We want to get married right now, and we can't wait 'til I can buy you a house. If I need to, I'll take the job Lola has offered me as her bouncer.'"

Norma laughed and tried to give me a quick kiss. My left hand caught the back of Norma's neck so I could hold her lips to mine. I kept the kiss for a long time. With almost a cry, I reluctantly let go of Norma.

Laying her head on my chest, Norma sighed and said, "I don't think I can move. Charles Gray, did you propose to me? If you did, I should warn you that I won't tolerate your chasing after any other woman while we are married. Lola will have to find someone else to take my place. Once married, you'll be the last man for me."

"Wait a moment now, Norma. We both said we loved each other, but I don't remember proposing. Besides, I'm on my way to California. We need to think about this a little bit more."

"What are you going to think on, Gray?" Lola said from the doorway.

Chapter 5

Norma and I stared at Lola as she continued to speak. "Both of you are getting up and going to work. Gray, I sure as hell am not going to pay you to lay around on your back, entertaining the womenfolk."

I opened my mouth to say something, but Lola said, "Save it, Gray. Some Texans came in, and James thinks he might need some help."

"How many are there?" I asked as I stood up. Lola got a grin on her face, and Norma said, "Oh, my God! He is beautiful. Boss, does he have to get dressed?"

I asked, "Where are my clothes, Lola?"

"On the shelf behind the curtain to your left. Come down when you get dressed. Let's go to your room, Norma."

Norma patted me and said, "There is way more of you than I thought there was."

Before the bedroom door shut all the way, I heard Lola ask, "Well, did you screw him, Norma?"

I didn't hear Norma's response.

When I stepped out of Lola's bedroom into the hallway, a young Indian lady came out of another room. She stopped when she saw me, and I said, "Hi. Is there a backway down from this floor?"

She nodded and said, "This way."

I followed and was quickly down on the main floor. The door from the back stairs opened at the end of the bar. I opened the door slowly and was glad I did. Two cowboys were between the bar and me. Both of them were in the process of drawing their guns.

Stepping up to them, I drew my two pistols and quietly said, "Leave that iron where it is, boys, and you might live."

Both cowboys froze, and when the barrels of my pistols touched their backs, their hands came up and above their shoulders where I could see them. I poked one of the cowboys a little harder in the back and said, "Why don't you tell them, other cowboys, to drop their iron before someone gets hurt? Namely, you two."

"Jake, Frank, Jess, drop your guns. He's got Dave and I covered."

I called out, "James, you got your scattergun handy?"

"Yeah, and it's pointed right at the middle one. Which one do you want me to take out?"

"You boys better drop your gun belts before someone is dead. And, just so you know, it will be you, boys. Now drop 'um. And I'm not telling you again."

I heard three heavy thuds and said, "Okay, now you two. And don't try anything stupid."

There were two more thuds.

"Now, let's all go out so I can meet your friends."

When all five men were in a group, I said, "Now, all of you lay on the floor and put your hands behind your backs."

"Now, why would we need to get on the floor?" the guy who didn't give his name said. "There are only two of you and five of us. I don't think you can take us all before we gun you down."

I holstered my pistol and stuck my second gun down in my boot. When I stood up, I said, "If you want to try for your knife, go right ahead."

"Why wo…."

The guy shut up when the barrel of my pistol was an inch from his right eye.

"Any more questions?" I asked.

The five cowboys got on the floor as if in a hurry. I said, "James, can you find some rope so we can tie their hands together."

"Josh, you hold my scattergun while I get the rope. It's got a real light touch, so keep it pointed at those boys on the floor and nowhere else," James said as he ran to the storage room.

James got the rope and tied the cowboy's hands behind their backs. With the help of some of the men in Lola's, the cowboys were put back on their horses.

While the boys did that, I went down to the stable and got my horse. On returning to Lola's Place, I ensured the five cowboys' horses were tied in a string.

Then I looked at the crowd on the walkway outside Lola's Place. Norma and Lola were at the walkway's edge, and I walked over to them. I reached up and lifted Norma off the boardwalk and into my arms. I kissed her quickly and said, "No time for a real kiss. I got to take these boys back home. I'll be back as quickly as I can. I love you, Norma."

"Hurry back," Norma said. "I love you too, Charlie."

I placed Norma back on the walkway and, looking up at Lola, said, "You heard what I told Norma, right?

Lola nodded and said, "Yeah. I get it. She is off-limits, so hurry back, and we'll work out something good for all three of us. And, Gray, take care."

James was standing beside Lola with the shotgun in his hands. I grinned up at him and said, "Mind if I borrow that hardware you're holding?"

Handing me the gun, James said, "They were trying to loosen the ropes, so I cinched them down tight. I just thought you should know."

I swung up into my saddle, and with a wave, I led the five cowboys away. As we headed out of town, I turned and looked at no name and said, "You better tell me which way to Broken Arrow Ranch. I will take the lot of you out into the desert and cut your cinches if you don't. Then I'm going to chase your horses away. I'll take your rifles and boots before I cut the cinch."

The guy said, "Two miles out, there is a track off to the right. Six miles down that road is the main ranch house."

We were in sight of their ranch a little over an hour later. I stopped the horses at the base of a small hill we had ridden over. I said, "You guys can stop at Sheriff Brownie's office at the Jail and pick up your iron as you leave town the next time you are there. You boys might want to change your attitude the next time you are in Lola's. And remember, she owns the other two bars in town. If she says you can't enter her establishment, all her places are gone. Oh, one other thing. Tell your boss to come in and see Lola. She wants to talk to him."

No name said, "Mister, what's your handle? I got to tell the boss who it was that ran us out of town."

I nodded and said, "My name is Gray."

One of the other cowboys coughed, gagged a moment or two, then said, "I heard of you. When you dropped those four guns, my brother was in White Deer, Texas. Brother said the fifth one raised his hands, fell to his knees, and dropped his revolver into the dirt. He said you kicked that boy's ass all the way to the Sheriff's office. Are you that guy?"

"Yes, that was me. In White Deer, you must turn your sidearms into the Sheriff when you come to town. You pick them up on your way out, just like we're going to do in Holbrook."

I cut the rope around no name's hands and backed up my horse. Then, I headed back to Holbrook and Norma.

Chapter 6

When I returned to Holbrook, I walked up the street from the Livery to Lola's Place when I got sidetracked. Sheriff Brownie was sitting outside his office and waved me over. From the look on Brownie's face, I knew he and Lola had talked.

I was shaking my head when I said, "You heard about the boys from Broken Arrow coming into Lola's Place, and you want to know why there were no shots fired."

Sheriff Brownie nodded, saying, "Lola told me about it. She said it smelled like a couple of them boys shit their pants. Do you know how that happened?"

I grinned and said, "The first one was one of the two boys I found in the storage room. Using the back stairs to get to the main floor, I ended up right behind those two when I pressed the barrel of my guns against their backs and told them to raise their hands; one of the boys shit.

"Then I corralled all five of them, cowboys, out in the middle of the floor. I told them to lie down and put their hands behind their backs. One of the guys thought the five could take James and me. I holstered my guns and told him to go for his knife. He stopped talking halfway through his first word. I don't think he liked looking down the barrel of my 45; it was an inch from his right eye. That boy shit and laid down."

The Sheriff was laughing by the time I finished talking. With a shake of his head, Brownie finally said, "How the hell can you draw your gun that fa…."

Brownie's face suddenly went white as he looked down the barrel of my six-shooter.

"…st? I would not have believed anyone was that fast. And your barrel wasn't even shaking."

I holstered my piece, saying, "Seeing as I just walked up from the Livery, I might have been a little winded and slower than normal. You want me to try it again?"

"No thanks," Brownie said as he held up his right hand with the palm facing me.

"Well, if there is nothing else, Sheriff, I guess I'll see if Lola needs me to fix any other problem. You have a good night now, Sheriff."

Before I could turn to leave, Brownie asked, "When do you think they are coming back for you?"

I shook my head slightly and said, "I assume Lola gave you the cowboy's hardware. I told them they could stop by your office the next time they are in town. And that they could pick them up when they were leaving. I also said that Lola wanted to speak to their boss. I expect he'll be in, but I can't tell you how many guns he'll have with him."

"Fair enough," Brownie said. "And thanks for the warning. Go see Lola and that cute little thing pinning for you."

When I left the Sheriff's office, I saw people in front of Lola's Place. I could hear plenty of hooting and hollering, but I couldn't tell what was happening—that is, not until I got to the edge of the crowd.

Norma and one of Lola's other ladies were in a catfight. They were in the middle of the street and covered in mud. While I was riding back from the Broken Arrow, the rain goddess dumped a couple of showers on this part of Arizona. The streets of Holbrook were a mess.

Lola stood at the walkway's edge, looking down at the fight. The other two ladies who had come looking for me at the café were standing beside Lola. From their looks, I figured Norma had already fought them. Both of those ladies appeared to have lost the fight.

As I started into the crowd, it parted, for me, as if by magic. I had a front-row seat to the fight. I looked up at Lola, and she shrugged her shoulders, so I turned my view back to the catfight.

It looked like Norma had this fight almost won from where I was standing. There was a sudden metal flash as someone threw a knife close to the other lady. The blade ended up a couple of inches from my foot, and I stepped on it before the lady could get ahold of it.

Norma saw what was happening and yelled, "You fucking bitch! I'll fix you." Norma yanked the lady up by her hair and slammed her face into the mud. She did it three times. The last time, Norma held the girl's face in the ground and moved it from side to side, burying the face further into the dirt.

I saw the girl was getting weak, so I stepped over to Norma and said, "Time to let her up."

Norma looked up at me, and I gave her my left hand. I helped her up to a lot of clapping and yelling, "Way to go, Norma, I knew you could whip all three ladies."

As Norma and I started to go into Lola's Place, I spun around and shot the knife out of the hand of the lady that Norma had just beat.

I looked around at the crowd and said, "Boys, whose knife was that?"

James pushed a young man forward. The man was fifteen at the most. "Gray, this man threw the knife into the fight. Before he threw the blade, he said he wanted to see more blood."

I grabbed the lady Norma had been fighting and said, "James, bring that idiot with you. We need to take these two down to jail. I'm going to have the Sheriff charge this one with attempted murder. And the same thing with that stupid kid you got hold of."

As we headed to Jail, I could feel a subdued crowd behind us. Sheriff Brownie must have seen us coming. He stepped out of the jail and waited for us. "Gray, what are all these people doing here? And why are June and Norma all muddy? Did I miss a good fight?"

"Sheriff Brownie, I want you to arrest June for attempted murder. And the kid James is holding for giving June the weapon she used."

"Who is June supposed to have tried to murder? You or Norma?" Sheriff Brownie asked.

"I don't know if it was meant for Norma or me; the fight was in the street. Norma had June's face in the mud so long that June's feet and arms quit beating and kicking the dirt. I told Norma to get up and that she had won.

"Now, Norma was holding June down so long because the guy James was holding threw a knife into the mud. June reached for it, but I stepped on it. The fight had been cleaned up to that point. Norma saw what June was going for and got mad. That's when she held June down."

The kid said, "I just wanted to see one cut the clothes off the other. As you can see, Sheriff, that one's tits aren't even hanging out. What fun is that?"

Sheriff Brownie said, "James, toss that guy in the first cell and lock the door afterward. And, James, I meant what I said about tossing him."

"Yes, sir, Sheriff," James said as he roughly took the kid into the Jail.

Turning to June, Sheriff Brownie said, "What do you have to say for yourself, June?"

June held up her right hand and said, "That bastard shot me, Sheriff. I want him arrested."

A man dressed in fine clothes stepped up to the Sheriff and said, "Sheriff, I have the knife in question right here. As you can see, there is still fresh blood on it. What Mister Gray is saying is the truth. I saw it all happen, and I couldn't tell you if June was going for Norma or Mister Gray."

"Thanks, Ned," Brownie said. "I appreciate what you did by bringing the knife to me and for what you just told me."

The Sheriff approached me and said, "Gray, I'll take June from you. And someone better get the Doc down here so he can patch up June's hand. Come on, June; you're going to Jail."

"But, Sheriff Brownie, that bastard shot me. Aren't you going to do something to him?"

"June, he didn't shoot you; he shot the knife out of your hand. There is a difference, you know."

Chapter 7

By the time Brownie took June into custody, the crowd had dispersed to just a few people. One of them was Ned, who told the Sheriff I was speaking the truth. Ned was heading over to say something to me when James came out of the Sheriff's office laughing.

I smiled and said, "What's so funny, James? Did June try to give herself to Brownie?"

"Naw. When Brownie put June in the second cell, her top finally came loose, and she was hanging out there for that kid to see. The sheriff shoved June into the cell. She stopped right in front of the kid. When I left, the kid's mouth was hanging open, and he was drooling. Brownie was going to get June a shirt to cover up with."

When James finished talking, Ned and I were laughing hard and loud.

Brownie opened the jailhouse door and said, "You guys go on and get out of here. There is nothing funny going on here."

Ned and I stepped up on the porch. I looked over Brownie's head, and Ned looked around him. We both saw a naked-chested June and the kid reaching through the cell bars to fondle June's left breast. Brownie started to close the door when we all heard June say, "Fuck, kid, be easy on them; they got feelings, you know." The kid was now squeezing both breasts.

"God damn it!" Brownie yelled as he spun around. "Kid, let go of June right now, or you will be sorry." Brownie slammed the door in our faces.

James, Ned, and I walked back to Lola's Place. As we walked, Ned said, "Mister Gray, I'm Ned Worthington, the town banker. I'm the man who convinced Lola she should move here from Saint Louis, Missouri."

I laughed and said, "From the sound of Lola's voice, I thought she was from Missouri. I'm from Jefferson City myself. I remember a few years back when my older brother told me about some trouble in Saint Lou with a couple of brothels. The owners disagreed on something. Wasn't one killed and the other blamed for the killing?"

Ned nodded and said, "Yes. I know that Lola could not have killed that other lady. Lola was snuggled up next to me when they said the lady was killed. We were at my house and not her brothel. The mob that went looking for Lola tore her place apart. Her entire inventory was destroyed."

I asked, "How did Lola end up here?"

"Lola stayed with me until things quieted down. Her attorney came to see me the day after the shooting. We talked for some time until I was sure he was looking to help her, not take her to jail. To make the story short, let me say this. The attorney arranged for the sale of both brothels. He was the attorney for both ladies, who at one time were good friends. According to the attorney, they both had wills, which stated that if the first one died, the other would take over the other's business. Since the mob never found Lola, both brothels were sold. The lawyer took his cut and gave the rest to Lola. About two months later, I sold my business to another banker. That's when Lola and I moved here."

"Thanks for telling me all of this," I said.

Ned grinned and said, "Heard you had a little run-in with some of the new hands at the Broken Arrow ranch. They are a rowdy bunch, even when they come into the bank. I also heard that the Ranch Foreman, a guy named Tim Ralston, used to be a gunman. So, Gray, be careful when Ralston comes looking for you."

"I guess Lola didn't tell you that the Foreman is dead," I said. "He was one of the cowboys I shot outside Lola's Place."

James said, "Gray, I will stop in the Country Mercantile and kiss my wife. I need to tell her what's been going on. Tell Lola I'll be there as soon as I can."

Once James was gone, Ned said, "It seemed like you and Norma were getting pretty friendly. What's going on there, Gray?"

I laughed and said, "Norma has the most beautiful eyes I have ever seen. The first kiss we had cleared up my aching head from where Lola clobbered me. Lola shot the gun out of the hand of the guy sitting across from me in a card game. He thought I was cheating."

"She hit you for her having to shoot a guy. I don't believe it," Ned said.

"No, she hit me to stop me from killing the man and wasting one of my bullets. Then, she had someone carry me up to her bed. Lola told Norma to stay with me until I woke up."

Ned laughed and said, "Damn, Lola is keeping all the good stuff from me. So, what happened when you woke up?"

"Norma told me the doctor left some medicine for me, and I told her that a kiss from her would do more good than his pills. I turned my head so she could kiss the bump, but before her lips could touch it, I turned back, and we kissed. That kiss took all the pain and aches away. Then Lola came barging in and told us that James might need help with the Texans who had entered the bar."

"And that's when you corralled those Texans and took them back to their ranch. That story is going to have to wait. I see my next client going into the bank." Ned stuck out his right hand, and we shook hands.

I continued walking toward Lola's Place. Before I got there, a woman stopped me and said, "Mister Gray, I'm Bella Wright. It was my son Tommy that they say threw the knife at you. He is only fifteen. That's too young to be in jail. Is there any way you could talk the Sheriff into letting Tommy go?"

"Ma'am, where's Tommy's father?"

Bella was winging her hands when she said, "He died in a gunfight. He wasn't even involved in the fight. A stray bullet broke the window of the Hotel and killed my husband."

"I'm sorry for your loss, Bella. I need to talk to Norma, the lady at whom your boy's knife was thrown. And then I'll talk to Sheriff Brownie. I can't promise anything, but I'll try to get Tommy out for you."

"Bless you, Mister Gray. That is all a mother can hope for; thank you, sir." I watched Bella drift down the walkway toward the jail.

Chapter 8

As I got close to Lola's Place, I figured something was up as no one was out on the boardwalk in front of the saloon. Day or night, someone was sitting in one of the chairs outside the bar or standing there, getting fresh air before returning to a card game or a drink.

The sounds I heard coming from inside Lola's Place seemed restrained. It was like everyone was not watching what they were doing but waiting for something to happen. I took a deep breath and pushed the swinging doors open.

When I entered the bar, the piano player stopped hitting the keys, and almost everyone stopped talking. I looked around and saw that Lola was holding court at her table. Eight ladies were standing behind Lola. Norma was sitting across the table from her boss. I could almost feel Norma's face light up in a smile as she turned to look at me. I could see excitement lighting up her eyes even at this distance, about thirty feet.

As I walked further into the room, I nodded to some men I had met after coming to Holbrook. I surprised many people when I didn't walk right up to Norma. I took a slightly different way to Lola's table, which took me between a few of Lola's ladies and Lola.

I walked over to Lola and kissed her on the lips. There was a loud gasp, which resulted from more than a dozen people making the sound simultaneously. I grinned down at Lola and said, "That was from Brownie. The Sheriff said to tell you he would be here as soon as he finishes the paperwork on those idiots he has in Jail."

"Okay. Now, Gray, about your job," Lola started to say something.

I put my hand up to stop her and said, "I had a nice chat with Ned Worthington when we returned from the jail. Oh, and James said he would be here as soon as possible. He stopped to kiss his wife. And tell her what was going on as if she didn't already know. I also talked to Bella Wright about her son Tommy. I need to talk to Norma about if we want to keep him in Jail. And with Sheriff Brownie, too."

I walked around the table to Norman and pulled her off her chair. I was holding her up high enough for our lips to touch. Then I sat down with Norma on my lap. As I was sitting down, I kept my lips glued to Norma's, and they didn't come apart for about five minutes. I only stopped the kiss because I could feel the natives getting restless. In other words, Lola wanted to talk to me.

I broke the kiss and saw that Norma's eyes had rolled back in her head. Her eyes fluttered and then fixed on me. She said, "Now that was a kiss."

"There are more where that came from," I said. "But first, we must finish a little business with our boss."

Turning my head, I grinned at Lola and said, "If June had hurt Norma with that knife, I would have killed her and anyone else who said a bad word about Norma. Right now, the safest place for June is in Jail. I still might shoot her on sight. Now, what did you want to say about the job?"

Lola laughed and stood up, saying, "Norma, Honey, would you please get off your man's lap? I need to hug and kiss him, and then you can have him back."

Norma gave me a peck on the lips and stood up. I also stood and, stepping over to Lola, hugged her. I turned the embrace into a swirl. I spun Lola around in a circle three times. When the spin stopped, Lola kissed me and said, "Gray, I like your style, and if I weren't in love with Brownie, I'd steal you away from Norma."

Giving Norma a grin, I said, "Lola, do you think you could do that? Didn't she whip three of your girls? Without hardly a scratch, I might add."

"You got a point there, Gray. Norma is a lot tougher than she looks. And Gray, you are going to have your hands full with her. Your way of living may end abruptly."

I smiled at Lola and said, "I was thinking the same thing while returning from the Broken Arrow Ranch."

Lola hugged me and said, "Norma, come over here by your man." When the three of us stood close together, Lola said, "Norma, have you seen that little log cabin down by Swan Creek?"

Norma thought a moment, and I could see when she knew the cabin Lola talked about. A slight frown was on Norma's face when she said, "Yeah. Why do you ask?"

Lola took Norma's right hand in her left and my left hand in her right and said, "Norma, while Gray was sleeping, I had Diego clean the place out. You two can live there if you want."

Norma grinned at me, and I could see she was so happy. Then, looking at our boss, Norma said, "Is there a bed in there long enough for Charlie to sleep on?"

Lola laughed and said, "There is a long mattress there. Stan Wiser said he had a long bed frame, but it would take a couple of days for him to get it here. Can you guys work with that?"

Norma gave me a questioning look, and I said, "Lola, I'm used to sleeping on the ground, so that mattress sounds like it will be a big improvement."

"I can handle anything as long as Charlie is with me," Norma said.

"There is one more thing," Lola said. "Norma, I understand you are as good with numbers as you are with your fists. Do you think you can be my accountant?"

Norma was holding my right hand and squeezed it hard once. Then she said, "Yes, Lola, I can."

I asked, "Lola, does that mean that Norma is no longer one of your girls?"

Lola nodded and said, "No more bar girl and no working upstairs. And Gray, Norma can become your wife once the traveling Judge arrives."

Norma all but jumped on Lola, hugged her, and kissed her. "Thank you, Lola; you won't be sorry about giving me this chance. When do you want me to start doing the books?"

"Listen to her, Gray; she sounds just like the accountant I used to have. You are going to have your hands full when you marry her. Norma, you know I don't like to get up much before midday. So, why don't you and Gray start your new jobs tomorrow afternoon? You two run along now. I have things to do, and you'll be in my way."

Chapter 9

As we walked away from Lola, I quickly said, "Norma, have you got something to cover yourself a little more? I want to check the cabin before moving our things there."

Norma grinned and said, "My coat is up in my room. Do you want to come up with me?"

I nodded, saying, "Yeah. I'll go up with you to look at your bed."

We rushed to her room, and while Norma found her coat, I looked at her bed and said, "That bed is way too small. The only thing we can do on it is curl up and sleep. Where's the fun in that?"

Norma giggled, then said, "Let's get out of here before you want to have your way with me on the floor."

On leaving the saloon, Norma took my left hand to lead me to the cabin. She went a different way than I had since getting to Holbrook. The further we walked, the quieter the town sounded. In a minute or so, I heard the soft rumble of moving water. Then, out of the darkness, the cabin appeared.

Norma unlatched the door and pushed it open. I scooped her up to stop her from stepping over the threshold. I grinned at my laughing Norma and said, "Let's go in together, shall we?"

Norma tried to wiggle closer to me and said, "Just like we are married. I like that. I was going to run in and holler, YES! But no, my sweetheart knows how to treat a woman. This is far more romantic than my way of entering our cabin. I love you, Charlie Gray."

Then Norma kissed me, and I stepped into the cabin while our lips were together. Someone had left a lamp burning and stoked the fireplace. Our lips parted, and both of us looked around. I stood in the center of the room and slowly turned in a circle. I wanted Norma to look around me without straining her neck.

"Oh, Charlie, this is going to be so good for us," Norma said before kissing me. She ended the kiss and added, "Put me down, Charlie. I want to ensure you won't hit that tall, beautiful head of yours."

I didn't do as Norma wanted. Instead, I walked over to the mattress and laid her on it. Then I dropped down beside her. Norma and I laughed when I wrapped my arms around her and pulled her tightly.

An hour later, we got up and dressed. I fixed the fire so it would not go out while we were gone. Then I went to check out of the hotel as Norma was going to get her things. I was ready to check out at the hotel when the clerk looked me over and said, "You're the guy they call Gray?"

I nodded and waited to hear what the man had to say.

It didn't take long before the clerk said, "A couple of fellas came in here looking for you. Their guns were hung about like yours is. Told them you were probably across the street at Lola's Place. They wanted to look at your room. Sheriff Brownie came in behind the men." The clerk grinned and continued, "The Sheriff had a scattergun pointed down at those boys' feet. Those two skedaddled across the street as quickly as they could. Those boys were scared the Sheriff was about to shoot their boots off. Sheriff Brownie and I had a good laugh over them gunmen afraid to get shot in the feet."

I grinned and said, "You can't be a gunman if you cannot stand up. What do those two look like so I know who I'm looking for?"

"Not too hard to miss. Both were almost as tall as you, Mr. Gray; both were wearing dusters cut, so their guns were clear of the coats. One has a scar from the corner of his right eye down to his lips. That one had dead eyes, if you know what I mean. He doesn't give a damn who he shoots. I think he kills people for the fun of it."

I nodded and asked, "Which way did Brownie go?"

"He went to the jail. If those fellas return, what do you want me to tell them?"

"If I were you," I said, "I'd hope I saw them coming over here so I could hide before they arrived. But I don't think they'll be back. I'll talk to you later." Turning around, I walked to the front door and stopped. I looked over my right shoulder and said, "If Norma comes looking for me, try to keep her here. I'm going down to talk to Brownie." Then I walked out of the Hotel.

At the Jail, I opened the door and walked in. Sheriff Brownie was sitting at his desk writing a report while June and Tommy were talking, or rather, June was talking. Tommy was squeezing June's right breast with his left hand. Brownie looked up at me, and I grinned at him. Then I said, "Tommy, I told your mother I would see about getting you out of jail. From what I can see, I think you would be safer right here, so maybe you should continue as a city guest."

Tommy jumped to his feet and tripped over his pants as they slid down his legs. We could all see what his right hand had been doing. The evidence stuck out from Tommy's body. Tommy pulled his pants up and said, "Mister Gray, you talked to my mom. What did she say?"

"Just what I told you. Your mother wanted to see if I could talk the Sheriff into letting you go home with her until your trial comes up. It doesn't look like you learned anything, so maybe you are better off right where you are."

"Please, Mr. Gray Ma doesn't have anyone else. Pa was killed, and I'm an only son. I need to take care of my Mom. I'll come back here every day and clean the jail. Sheriff Brownie won't need to worry about cleaning the place."

I said, "What about your love affair with June? Will that continue when you get out of Jail, Tommy?"

"No, Sir. June and I are just going to be friends. I can't have an affair with June because I ain't got no money nor a job. How am I going to take care of June and my Ma? Me and June we talked about it some, and she thinks we could make a go of it if she continues working at Lola's Place. But I told her I wouldn't like that very much. How would I know who pinched her bottom or felt her tits and other things men like to do to women? No Sir, Mr. Gray, I got to get me a full-time job which pays well enough for June and me to live together with my Ma."

I looked at June and saw her nodding at everything Tommy said. June grinned at me and said, "When Tommy gets a full-time job, I'd be willing to quit Lola's Place. His Ma and I could take in laundry to make a little extra. We could do some house cleaning too. I know it's not much, but I like Tommy. He is a good man, better than most of the men I'm around most nights. Of course, that would have to stop, maybe as soon as I get out of jail. Mr. Gray, are you planning on taking Norma with you when you move on from Holbrook?"

I grinned at June and said, "Yes. I believe Norma will go to California with me when I leave here. Tell me, June, who cleans Lota's Place when you ladies finish for the night?"

June stood straight and said, "We clean our rooms for Gentlemen callers. Lola has an Indian girl who cleans Lola's room. Two bartenders clean up the downstairs. The Indian girl also cleans Lola's office and washes our towels and linen."

Sheriff Brownie loudly said, "Gray, come over here and read this report I wrote up on June and Tommy. The Circuit Judge will want to read it before we take these two to court for trial."

I stepped over and sat in the chair next to Brownie's desk. "Let me see what you have so far, Brownie," I said, extending my right hand toward him.

Sheriff Brownie handed me some papers, saying, "I think I got everything in the right order. The Judge likes things done up nice and neat when he gets here. If something is wrong, let me know, Gray, and I'll make it right."

I skimmed the report while Brownie was talking, then reread it to ensure I read it correctly. I glared at the Sheriff and said, "This makes it look like Norma is the guilty party, not June. Why is that, Sheriff?"

The Sheriff sat back in his chair and said, "Well, you might be slightly prejudiced in this case, seeing as how you have become real friendly with Norma and Lola."

I took a deep breath and blew it out. I did this a couple of times before I said, "Sheriff, what I told you has nothing to do with how I feel toward Norma. I told you what I saw and what I did. Any fool with halfway good eyesight could tell that June was done and lost the fight. I helped Norma to her feet, and when we walked away, June got the knife and was ready to toss it at us. Which one of us she intended to hit, I don't know. I just shot the knife, and in doing so, I nicked June's hand. June is lucky as hell that I didn't shoot her. I would have been justified in doing so. Any damn jury would say the same thing."

Browning leaned forward and said, "Okay. I agree with you, Gray. I was trying to write it so that June would not have to spend time in prison. She doesn't need that. Now, how the hell do I write that up? Can you tell me, Gray?"

I grinned at him and said, "Brownie, why are you going to all that trouble? Norma didn't file a complaint against June. It was me. As of right now, I'm withdrawing the complaint and do not wish to file against either June or Tommy. Why not tear up this paperwork and let the two of them go? Give Tommy an idiot fine and tell him he will return to the jail at four o'clock every afternoon to clean up this pig pen you call a jail. Make it for a month. The same fine for June. That should make them happy unless you barge in on them."

With a hearty laugh, Brownie said, "You bastard! You made me write all this up, knowing you were coming back here to tell me to let them both go. Norma will have her hands full to keep you in line." The Sheriff tossed me the cell key and said, "You let them out and tell them what they must do. It will take me ten minutes to tear up all this paperwork."

I unlocked Tommy's cell and said before he could run out. "Stay right in the doorway there, young man. You need to make up to June for causing her to be in this Jail." Then I unlocked June's cell and caught her before she could jump on me. I said, "The fine for what you did, June, is that you and Tommy are to come to the jail at four o'clock every afternoon to clean the place. And it would be best if you did that for a month. Now I want to see you two make up for causing Sheriff Brownie to work so hard."

I was smiling when the two of them did their quick kiss. I said, "Tommy, you walk June back to Lola's Place, and then you run home and take care of your mother."

Sheriff Brownie said, "You two better be here at four tomorrow, or you'll be back in jail for a long time."

"Thank you both," June said. "Both of us will be here tomorrow. Even if I have to carry him."

Brownie and I watched the two lovers walk up the street, holding hands.

Chapter 10

As we watched Tommy and June, Brownie asked, "You didn't, by chance, see the two gunmen looking for you, did you, Gray?"

I shook my head and said, "No, but I heard they didn't like your shotgun pointing at their boots."

Giving a loud laugh, it took Brownie a moment or two to say, "Those boots are worth at least two hundred dollars, so yeah, those boys were trying to protect them. Did Jimmy, the hotel clerk, give you a description of the men?"

"Yeah."

"Do you know the one with the scar on his face?"

"Can't say that I do, Sheriff. You got a name for Scarface?"

Sheriff Brownie sighed loudly and said, "Dagobert Acadia and his partner is Cornelius Cameron. They are originally from Louisiana but now live in Huntsville, Texas. Dagobert is believed to have killed eight men. Cornelius claims to have killed seven. The killings were made in range wars, and the Sheriffs in those areas could never prove that either man killed anyone. I don't know if you know it, but when there is a range war, the law seems to take a vacation."

I laughed and said, "Most of the Sheriffs I know just stayed home. When they did come out, one hand held a shotgun, and the other held a forty-five. Do you know how Bert got his scar?"

Brownie said, "I've heard rumors about these two for a couple of years now. As I hear it, Dagobert got his scar from a woman. It seems he thought the woman was a whore, but she wasn't. She was a librarian. It is said that she sliced him and then walked away, leaving him bleeding. The bunch he was running around with witnessed the cutting, and they laughed Dagobert out of town. They say no man has ever tried to touch that lady again."

"I haven't seen the scar," I said, "but I thought it might have been from a saber, like some I've seen." I looked up the street at the Holbrook Hotel and saw Norma come out onto the sidewalk. She headed towards us at a fast clip, almost a run.

"Trouble coming," Brownie said.

"You got that wrong, my friend. Norma is no problem."

"Most women are trouble of one sort or another."

"When I kissed Norma for the first time, all my bad thoughts about women melted away to nothing. You can believe that or not, but it's the truth."

Brownie stared hard, then said, "I believe you, my friend. Now, I'll go get my shotgun, and you figure out what to do with Norma so she is not in our way."

I stepped down from the porch as Norma got close to the jail. I grinned at her and asked, "What are you doing here?"

"I was going to ask you the same question," Norma said. "And why is Brownie loading up his shotgun? What's going on, Charlie?"

Stepping right up to Norma, I pulled her into a hug and long kiss. Then, while still holding Norma, I said, "There are two gunmen over at Lola's Place, and they are looking for me. If I don't stop this right now, someone will tell them where we're staying. They'll come to the cabin and call me out. That would make me mad."

Norma kissed me quickly to shut me up more than anything else. Then she said, "What can I do to help? Give me a gun; I can shoot as well as most men."

I gave a short laugh and said, "Honey, I don't doubt that at all. But if you have a gun, I will have to have one eye on you when I need to be concentrating on the gunman. And that would probably not work out too well, don't you think?"

Norma leaned back and looked up at me for a few moments. She smiled at me and kissed me, which curled my toes. When she ended the kiss, Norma said, "Okay, sweetheart, I'm going to the cabin to wait for you. But I won't wait long. Then I'm strapping on my gun and coming looking for you."

I kissed Norma quickly and said, "Thank you, my dear, beautiful Norma. I promise I'll make this up to you later."

"I'm holding you to that promise," Norma said as she walked back up the street.

Watching Norma walk away from me distracted me; I never heard Brownie until he said, "Close your mouth, Gray, or you'll catch bugs."

I saw Norma enter the Hotel and come out a few moments later with two bags. Looking at Brownie, I said, "Let's see what these two guns want with me."

As Brownie and I walked up the street, I saw Norma head for our cabin. I relaxed a little and drew in a long breath of air. Brownie went to the back of Lola's Place, and I gave him a few minutes to get to the back of the saloon. Then I stepped up on the boardwalk before Lola's Place and pushed open the swinging doors.

I entered the saloon and saw the two gunmen standing at the bar. They were both looking at the mirror behind the bar. I said, "I understand you gentlemen were looking for me. Why don't you both loosen the gun belts and let them fall to the floor? Cornelius, if you think that little gun you have tucked into the front of your pants will do you some good, why don't you look over at the back door and see what's waiting there? Dagobert, if you think you are fast enough to beat me, slowly turn around. But first, tell Cornelius to move a few feet to your right. Wouldn't want the Sheriff's shotgun to take you both out."

Cornelius moved as instructed, and then Dagobert slowly turned to face me. Dagobert said, "Some people over in Eastern Texas say that a certain Mr. Gray has been causing some trouble here in Holbrook. Those same people sent word to me in Huntsville, Texas, that they wanted the trouble taken care of. Are you that, Mr. Gray?"

"I'm Gray. Shall we take this outside, or are you crazy enough to try for it in here?"

Dagobert's eyes flashed instantly at the word crazy; his right hand moved, but not fast enough. I shot his right hand before his gun cleared his holster. The shot also broke the gun.

There was a movement off to my right, then a shotgun blast that blew Cornelius back and into Dagobert. Both men fell to the floor, and I stepped over to Dagobert and relieved him of his other gun and a hunting knife. I also disarmed the dead Cornelius Cameron.

Dagobert looked at me and said, "I never saw your hand move. I didn't think anyone was so damn fast."

I said, "You need to get to a doctor so that he can take care of your hand."

"Naw, I'm just going to ride back to Texas. If I bleed to death on the way, so be it. I'm never going to be a gunman again. I know I wore two guns, which made men think I could shoot with the left hand. But I never knew where the bullet was going to go when I shot with my left hand. Now, if the Sheriff is not going to hold me, I'll get up and get my horse. Then I'll ride out of town. And Gray, don't worry. I'm not going to come back gunning for you. Those kinds of days are done for me."

Sheriff Brownie and I helped Dagobert get up, and then we watched as he went down to the Livery and got his horse. Brownie and I waved as the injured man rode by with his head held high.

The gravedigger stopped beside Brownie and asked, "Sheriff, is there a body that needs burying?"

Brownie and Digger went into Lola's Place as I ran to find Norma.

Chapter 11

I didn't get far as Norma came running around the corner of the Saloon and ran full-on into me. Luckily, my left arm was up to catch hold of her. I was knocked back against the building with Norma wrapped in my left arm.

"Are you all right, Charlie?" Norma asked. "I heard one pistol shot and then the shotgun go off. Oh! God! I was so scared I had lost you."

"It was the two gunmen that got shot. Not me or Brownie," I said. "I shot one guy in his right hand, and Brownie shot the other. At that close range, no one survives being shot by a scattergun. And I love you too, Norma."

Then we kissed, and the next thing I remember was waking up in Norma's arms. We were in our bed, in the cabin that Lola gave us. I smiled at Norma as she lay sleeping and whispered, "How did such beauty fall in love with me after only one kiss? I know I was in love with her when I first saw her talking to Lola. I know I'll always love her; if God permits, I plan to be with only her for a long time."

I felt Norma's arms tighten around me, and then she said, "What's with all the talking? You should be helping me make a baby. And, so you know, I plan to be with you just as long as you plan to be with me." Our lips locked and did not come undone until we collapsed back on the bed.

Norma was the first to move when she lifted her head off my chest and said, "I think it is time for us to get some breakfast. Do you want to go to Simpson Café?"

I grinned at her and said, "Yes, but only after you answer a question for me."

"Ask me anything. What do you want to know, my love?"

Norma started to get up, but I tugged her back against me and said, "How did we get to the cabin? The last thing I remember is kissing you after the gunfight. Then I woke up with this beautiful lady sleeping beside me."

"You don't remember carrying me down here? We stopped and kissed six different times, and you all but undressed me before we got to the cabin. You acted like you wanted to ensure it was me under my clothes. Have you had this happen before?"

I shook my head, saying, "No. When Lola hit me over the head to stop me from killing that card player, I don't remember how they got me up to her room or who undressed me."

"Lola's Indian maid undressed you. Once you were on her bed, Lola kicked everyone out, and she came out with us. When the maid came out and said you were in bed and sleeping, Lola sent me in to stay with you until you woke up. Tell me what you remember us doing," Norma said.

Taking a deep breath and blowing part of it out, I closed my eyes and said, "I remember catching you when you ran into me, and we ended up against the outside of Lola's Place. You said how scared you were after hearing the one gunshot and the shotgun blast. You were afraid that you might have lost me. I remember your arms around my neck and your pistol dropping out of your hand and onto the boardwalk. Then our lips met, and that is all until I woke up in the cabin."

"You don't remember my gun going off when I dropped it?"

"No, Norma, I don't. What happened after that?"

"Lola and Sheriff Brownie came out to see who else you shot. I explained that my gun fired when I dropped it as you kissed me with all kinds of heat and love. Brownie said, 'You mean like this!' He pulled Lola into a long hug and kiss. You saw them kissing and pulled me into another of our long kisses, which I love doing with you."

I asked, "What happened next?"

"When our kiss ended, Lola told you to take me to our cabin, and she did not want to see either of us until sometime after midday. Sheriff Brownie went for another of his walks around town, and Lola went into the saloon. Oh, Tommy and June stopped to see if we were okay. They had heard about the gunfight, but that wasn't one. They have both moved in with his mother, and June quit her job at Lola's."

"Well, good for them," I said. "What happened after June and Tommy left?"

Norma laughed and said, "I bent over to pick up my gun, and you grabbed my hips and pulled me firmly against your manhood. I said, wait until we get home."

"What did I say to that?"

"That you can't wait. Then I holstered my pistol, and you scooped me up and started walking to the cabin. We were both laughing loudly. As soon as we were away from the buildings, you turned me in your arms and kissed me. That kiss almost undid my desire to have you on our bed. But I finally talked you into taking us to the cabin. We barely got a dozen steps further, and you wanted to kiss me again. As I said earlier, we stopped six times, and our kisses got hotter and hotter at each stop. When we finally got to the cabin, I could barely breathe, and you tore my clothes off. I have to buy a new blouse."

"I'm sorry about the blouse. I'll buy you a new one. My not remembering doesn't make sense. There was nothing in what you said that would make me forget."

I ran the fingers of my right hand through my hair and gave out with, "What the hell?" I gently pressed the side of my head behind my right ear. It was sore and felt scabbed over. I looked at Norma and said, "I think the bullet from your dropped pistol ricocheted and grazed my head. Let's go out in the sunlight and take a look."

Norma slid her body across me, and I could see her grinning up at me as she did so. She looked where my fingers parted my hair and said, "Oh, honey, you're right. The skin is broken, and you're bleeding a little. Your hair is matted with blood. We better see the Doc and let him look at it. He'll probably shave your head around the broken skin and sew the skin back together."

"Okay," I said. "Let's get dressed and have breakfast before stopping by the Doctor's office. I better have some food before my head is sewn back together."

Simpson Café was already busy, but Cookie saw me when Norma and I walked in. I saw her say something to the waitress, whose back was to us, and then the waitress turned, smiled at me, and pointed to the table I had sat at before.

Norma saw what was going on and said, "So, Charlie. You know Cookie and the waitress so well that you have your own table. Most people grab the closest empty table. I bet we get better service than the rest of them."

When we got to our table, I pulled out Norma's chair for her and gently pushed it back in after she sat down. Looking up at me, Norma said, "Thank you, Charlie. You are indeed a gentleman, after all."

Taking my chair, I said, "And did you notice there are only two chairs at this table?"

Norma laughed and said, "I did notice. I suppose there is a story to just the two chairs."

"Good morning, Mr. Gray," the waitress said as she approached our table. She had two cups of coffee and two menus. She put things on the table and said, "Be right back for your order."

Norma and I chatted for a few minutes until the waitress returned and said, "Is it true that you two are living in the little cabin down by Swan Creek?"

Chapter 12

Norma looked shocked, and I grinned. Then I said, "Tell Cookie that it is true. Norma wants to know how you learned about us staying there."

The waitress laughed and said, "Diego stopped by the kitchen and got a bite to eat. He told us that he cleaned the place out for the two of you. Let me get your orders, and I'll bring the coffee pot around."

As we finished eating, Cookie drew up a chair at our table. She grinned at Norma and said, "I lost my bet when you and Gray walked through the door. I bet Nelda, your waitress, Gray, would come in today with one of those ladies. Nelda said if Gray came in with a woman on his arm, it would not be one of those three. Did Gray tell you what he did?"

Norma said, "He would do just that now that breakfast is over. I can't wait to hear the story."

"Well, let me tell you," Cookie said. "When Gray came in for dinner, he asked for this table, and when Nelda brought him some coffee and the menu, he asked her to take away two of the chairs. Gray said that three ladies of the night would be coming in looking for him. The ladies would argue over who would sit there first if only one chair existed. They would disagree, and they would leave. And, by god, that is what happened. The rumor is that you will be Lola's accountant, and Gray will be her bouncer. Is that true?"

"Yes," Norma said.

"And you two will get hitched when the Circuit Judge comes by. Is that also true?"

"Again, yes," Norma said.

"And, Gray, what this I hear you let one of those Texan gunmen ride away from here?"

"Yes, that is also true. I did that," I said. "I shot the gun out of his right hand. He'll never be a gunman again, and he knows that. He wouldn't let anyone take him to the doctor. He said he was going home."

Cookie nodded at me and said, "But, you think he is going to ride out in the desert, and when he falls off his horse, he'll just lay there until he dies."

With a nod, I said, "Yeah. Or he'll run into a war party, and they'll take his scalp."

Cookie stood up, saying, "I better get back to cooking. Norma, you can come back anytime now. You make sure to keep Gray happy. I think he has seen many deaths and unhappiness in his life. He needs a woman to watch over him."

Norma laughed, stood up, and gave Cookie a good hug. Grinning, Norma said, "Cookie, I plan to do just that. Your breakfast was excellent, and I thank you for that."

I paid for our grub, and Norma and I headed for the doctor's office. Norma stopped as we walked past the swinging doors to Lola's Place and said, "I think I hear Doctor Roth in the saloon."

We stepped into Lola's Place, and Norma nodded at the tall, skinny man talking to James the Bartender. Norma walked over to the men and "Doctor Roth, I would like you to meet Mr. Gray formally. He has a little problem that needs your attention."

Roth chuckled at Norma and said, "We met the other night, but you are right; we were never introduced properly." Looking me up and down once, Roth said, "So what seems to be your problem, Gray?"

I gently removed my hat and showed Roth where the bullet had sliced me. Roth looked and said, "Let's go to my office. I got better light there."

Roth had me lay on a table in his office area, and then he shaved and washed around the injury. When he finished, he said, "This will hurt a little when I pour some alcohol on the torn skin. Then I'll give you some stitches, maybe ten of them. Those will not be pleasant, but there is nothing else I can do."

I said, "Do what you need to do, but can Norma come over where I can see her? Her beauty will help me through this."

Doctor Roth laughed and said, "She can hold your hand if she wants."

Norma came into my view and smiled down at me. Then she took hold of my right hand and squeezed lightly. I saw her grimace when Doctor Roth poured alcohol over the cut. I didn't even flinch. There were tears in Norma's eyes when Roth finished stitching me up. When Roth stepped back, Norma asked, "Charlie, how did you not cringe when Doctor Roth put those stitches in? He did ten of them?"

"I know, Sweetheart. I counted as he did them. If you want to know the truth, I was hurting more from watching your face when he put in each stitch and poured the alcohol on the cut. I don't want to ever have you do that again. I'll hang up my guns before I let that happen. I love you so much, Norma, that when I saw you making those faces, I wanted to pull you up on the table so I could hold you tight."

"You're not telling me how you didn't feel it when Doctor Roth put that needle in your skin. And don't tell me it was my beauty that kept you from feeling some pain; I won't believe you. So, my dear Charlie, tell him, how does someone lay there and let another person put a sharp needle in them and not feel it?"

I briefly let go of a part of my mind I had somehow built around all pain, and that pain poured into my eyes until I could not stand it any longer, and I raised the wall to block the pain.

When my eyes cleared up, I saw that Norma had noticed the slight pain I had let go of. Her face was as white as a ghost. "Somehow, I can block the pain," I said. "I don't know how that works, so don't ask. Maybe Doctor Roth can explain it."

"I don't know how you do it either," Roth said. "Of all my patients, you and a man who called himself Bubba are the only two who can do that. I don't know if it is a God-given gift or the devil's torment."

Norma asked, "Doctor Roth, when Charlie is working out around our cabin, you know, cutting wood and stuff like that, should I go out and check him over to make sure he has not cut himself and not know it?"

Roth got a half-smile and said, "Norma, that would be an excellent idea, in my opinion. When he works as Lola's bouncer, someone should check him over after he has tossed a guy out of the saloon. He might never know when someone nicks him with a knife or, god forbid, shoots Gray. By the way, Gray. How many times have you been shot in your line of business? Just asking out of curiosity."

I laughed and said, "Ask Norma how many wound marks I have on my body. She has inspected my body very closely."

Norma was blushing when she said, "Not a one. I can't find where he has been shot at all. And that is unbelievable."

On that note, Norma and I left Doctor Roth's office.

Chapter 13

We were halfway to Lola's Place when I stopped and turned to Norma. I said, "So, by my recollection, this is the second time you have tried to kill me. What did I do so wrong to you?"

Norma gave me a stunned look for a moment, and then her face turned bright red with rage. The words she said were cold and hard. "I did not try to shoot you; that was an accident. If I had meant to shoot you, I would not have missed. And what do you mean the second time? When was the first time?"

Quickly, I lowered my head to the middle of Norma's body and wrapped my arms around her. I pulled her against my shoulder and stood up. Norma was screaming and laughing at the same time, and her hands were beating against my back as I ran down the center of the main street of Holbrook.

We laughed and yelled all the way to Simpson Café and then back to Lola's Place. Norma was across my shoulder the whole time. I slowed in front of the Saloon and called out to Lola, "We'll be back in about an hour, maybe a little longer. I need to cool off this green-eyed monster, and there is a creek with her name on it right by our cabin. We love you, Lola."

Then I was on the boardwalk, running to the back of Lola's Place and on the trail to our cabin. I carried Norma right to the edge of Swan Creek. "Are you ready to cool off?" I asked.

"You wouldn't dare!" Norma said.

I moved my hands to where I was holding Norma by her waist as she struggled to get down off my shoulder. I said, "I'll take that dare."

Norma yelled a long Noooo as I lifted her and slid her down my body to where our lips met. The kiss I gave her had us both breathing hard and sweating. I said, "Let's go get naked. We can cool off in the Creek later."

"Oh, you bastard, how I love you," Norma said. "You had me going there for a few minutes. I thought for sure you were going to toss me into Swan Creek."

I gave Norma a quick kiss before I said, "I love you too much to do that to you, my beautiful Norma."

Suddenly, a bunch of clapping came from up the trail to Lola's Place. Norma and I saw most of the townspeople clapping and laughing at us. I pulled Norma into my arms and gave her a quick kiss. Then she and I bowed to our audience and ran into our cabin, and Norma shut the door behind her. Then, she jumped on me with a laugh, and I carried her to our bed. Nearly two hours later, Norma and I walked into the saloon.

Lola sat at her table with Ned Worthington, the town banker, and Cookie from Simpson Café. Another man was there that I did not know. From the looks he gave Norma, I don't think I wanted to know him. He looked to be about my age.

Norma and I walked up to the Queen's Table, and Norma surprised me by giving the unknown man a kiss and hug. Then she turned to me and said, "Gray, I want you to meet Circuit Judge Clarence Moore. His last note said he would not be here for another two weeks. Clarence, this is my betrothed Charles Gray. He is the new bouncer for Lola."

Clarence stuck out his right hand to me, and we shook hands. Then he asked, "Mr. Gray, was that your brother John who was killed in Wichita a few months ago?"

I nodded and said, "Yes. John was shot in the back while walking to his home."

"Did they ever catch the killer?" the Judge asked.

"No, they did not."

"Mr. Gray, what are you doing here in Holbrook?"

"Passing through on my way to California. I heard it was a beautiful country with an ocean. Of course, I read about an ocean, but I've never seen one. Which way are you going when you leave Holbrook, Judge Moore?"

"From here, I head to Southern Colorado. You ever been married, Mr. Gray?"

"No, Sir, I haven't been hitched. Never thought about it much until I first saw Norma."

"I understand you handled a few problems while traveling around the country. I don't like paid killers, Mr. Gray. Are you one of those guys?"

"I got room and food when I cleaned up some trouble in a few towns. But I don't think that is what you mean, is it, Judge?"

"No, it is not Mr. Gray. So, you never received substantial money to eliminate a problem? Is that what you're saying, Sir?"

"Yes."

"I understand that a couple of paid killers from Texas came to Holbrook looking for you in particular. Is that correct, Mr. Gray?"

"Yes."

"That Sheriff Brownie shot one with a shotgun, and you wounded the other with a shot to his right hand. And then you let him ride away. Why was that, Mr. Gray?"

"His hand was shot up pretty bad, and he did not want to have Doctor Roth sew it up. The man wanted to go home to Texas and die. Sheriff Brownie and I watched the man ride out of town towards Texas. I have no idea if he got there or not."

"Are you and Sheriff Brownie worried the man might come back gunning for you or him?"

"No, Sir, we are not. His days as a gunman are over. He may never be able to pull a trigger again with his right hand, and his left hand was shaking so bad, I'm not sure he can draw a pistol with it without shooting himself in the foot."

When his interrogation started, Norma moved away from the Judge and stood by Lola, watching the Judge. I'm not sure she understood what was going on.

The banker put a stop to the Judge and my conversation. Ned said, "I propose we toast Norma and Gray for their engagement and forthcoming wedding bliss."

Lola looked around and said, "What a wonderful idea, Ned. James, a drink on the house and bring a bottle of champagne and glasses to my table."

Everyone seemed to be talking at once, and then Norma walked around to me and sat on my lap. She gave me a demanding kiss and said, "I think the Judge likes you. You stood up to him like no one I've ever seen."

I laughed and said, "Honey, I think we respect each other, which is not the same as liking each other. The Judge and I will never be friends."

Chapter 14

After several people toasted us, including a toast from Judge Moore, the Judge excused himself, saying he had to talk to Sheriff Brownie. When the swinging doors closed behind Judge Moore, there was a collective sigh of relief at Lola's table.

Norma was still sitting on my lap, and I kissed her and said, "Honey, you need to go with Lola into her office and get to work. You have been playing around long enough."

Before Norma could speak, Lola said, "Gray, I take it that you figured out that Norma was the only one of my ladies that the Judge wants to be with?"

I grinned at Norma and said, "Yeah, Lola, I figured that out when Norma told the Judge I was her betrothed. There was a rage in his eyes for a moment. If the Judge had been standing, he would have gone for the hog leg he is wearing on his hip."

Lola said, "I couldn't see his face, but I saw the rage in the corner of his right eye when it flared up. For a second, I thought the Judge would stand up and draw down on you, Gray. Instead, he tried to intimidate you, but you were having none of that. You stood up to him, and I knew I had the right man for my bouncer. And it is time for Norma and me to go over the books. So, Norma, let's go into the office. Oh! Gray, as of now, you and James are the only people who can come into the office when Norma and I are there. And that includes my ladies. Gray, how will you keep yourself busy while Norma is working?"

I grinned at Lola and said, "Is that space on the wall behind the bar where you will hang Brownie's head if he doesn't soon ask you to marry him? If not, that would be a perfect place to hang sidearms when customers come in. I thought you should require that all guns be handed over before they get a drink."

Lola and Norma laughed, and finally, Norma hugged me, saying, "You really must want to die. Can you imagine Brownie handing over his gun to you?"

I kissed her quickly and said, "Brownie is the law, so he can keep his gun on to enforce Lola's requirement."

Norma kissed me quickly and said, "What about you, my dear betrothed? Are you going to turn in your guns?"

I kissed the tip of Norma's nose and shook my head. Then I said, "Nope. I will have Brownie deputize me to enforce the requirement legally."

Lola called out, "James, when you get a moment, I want you to come over here. Gray has an idea I think you should hear."

While we waited for James, I gave Norma a lengthy kiss. When our lips parted, it was Lola who spoke first. "Shit! Gray, she will not be worth anything for at least an hour. Norma's eyes are glazed over, and I've never seen her that dopey before. You might as well take her back to the cabin and make love to her. I'll not get a lick of work out of her today, and she'll be dreaming of you, her new lover." Lola laughed, adding, "Maybe you can do that after you talk to James because he comes here with four drinks."

I explained my idea again for James's benefit, and when I got to the part about being a deputy, I added, "Brownie could also make you a deputy. That way, if you had to use your scattergun, Judge Moore would favor you just doing your job."

James laughed when I finished talking and asked, "Lola, how did Gray know what you planned to hang in that spot?"

"I don't know how he knew!" Lola exclaimed.

Norma kissed me and said, "He just knows things. Like when a man is going to draw his gun, and Gray draws his first. Gray can sense things before they happen."

Before I could speak, Lola said, "James, what do you think of Gray's idea?"

James nodded and said, "I think it is a smart thing to do. I've had a couple of cowboys ask me why we didn't collect their guns."

Lola smiled and said, "Good, I think it is an excellent idea, too. James, I wanted to make sure you were okay with the plan, as you will be helping to collect the guns."

In a low voice, I said, "James, get to your scattergun quickly. Brownie is coming in the back door, and I feel some boys are coming in the front door."

Before I had finished talking, James was moving, and Lola said, "Norma, let's go behind the bar and stay low."

As I walked over to stand by the swinging doors, the ladies were behind James. As I got into position, four cowboys stepped into the bar. Their guns were drawn and pointed at the ceiling. Behind them, I said, "Ease those guns to the floor, boys. There are three guns on you, and one of them is a scattergun."

Lola said before the cowboys could move, "Make that four guns pointed at you."

"Make it five!" Norma called out.

One of the cowboys softly said, "Ease them to the ground, boys, then stand tall with your hands up. Gray, is that you behind us?"

With a dose of hardness tossed in, I softly said, "It is."

The man asked, "How did you know we were gunning for you?"

I said, "Foreman, let's just say that sometimes I just know things. Like the man behind you thinks he can get his left gun out before I shoot him. He doesn't realize that if he goes for his gun, all of you will die. Sheriff Brownie has a quick trigger, as do the two women. The man holding the scattergun is shaking badly enough as it is. Those other guns will go off right after mine if I shoot your man. There will be carnage."

In a growling voice, the new ranch foreman said, "Josh, get your hands up as I told you to do."

I said, "You two in the front, take two steps forward and stand still." The foreman and another guy did as I said. I stepped over behind Josh and put the business end of my pistol at the back of his head, stating, "Josh, drop your gun belt, and if you try to draw that left pistol, your brains will be scattered around the room."

When I finished, all four men had dropped their gun belts. I said, "You boys see that big table off to the right? That is where Lola holds court. You boys go sit at Miss Lola's table because Judge Moore is about to step into the bar, and he likes his courtroom nice and clean."

The cowboys had barely sat down when Moore walked into the bar. He looked around and loudly said, "Lola, what's the meaning of all this hardware on the floor? You know I like a clean courtroom."

Lola said, "Well, Judge Moore, those cowboys sitting at the court's table came into my saloon with their guns held on high and ready for a gunfight. They were disarmed without a shot being fired and are now waiting for you."

Judge Moore walked back to Lola's table and sat in her chair. He took out his six-shooter and banged the handle on the table. "Court is now in session," he called out. "It looks like there is but one case before the court today. Sheriff Brownie, explain to the court what the case is about so I may render my verdict."

Brownie stepped over to the court's table and said, "Judge Moore, I was about to leave the Jail when I saw these four men ride into town. The man on your right works as an assistant Foreman at the Broken Arrow Ranch. I suspected they were looking for Gray, so I ran behind the buildings until I got to the back of Lola's Place. I entered through the back door and got to the bar area as these cowboys entered the front door. They each had a gun in their hand pointed upward. They were ready for a gunfight. Their guns should have been holstered if they were unprepared for a fight. Gray was standing to the side of the front door, and he got the drop on all four cowboys. James pointed his scattergun at the men, and Lola and Norma pointed guns at the cowboys. Gray made each cowboy drop their gun belts, which is why the floor was a mess when you got to court, Your Honor."

Judge Moore looked at the four men seated before him and asked, "Mr. Assistant Foreman, do you have anything to say before I pronounce a verdict?"

Chapter 15

The Foreman said, "This is not a court of law. It is more of a lynching. Your decisions wouldn't hold up in Texas, so do your worst."

Judge Moore sat up straight, and I saw anger in his eyes. He smiled at the four men, and only a blind man could see there was no humor in the smile. Moore said, "My area covers south to the New Mexico-Texas border at Ciudad. So, Mr. Foreman, I know how your courts work, and I travel up to Colorado, too. You four are now sentenced to two days in Jail and an eight hundred dollar fine. If you can't add, that is two hundred dollars each. The fine is to be paid before you are released from Jail."

"Sheriff Brownie, please deputize a couple of men, take the prisoners down, and lock them up in your Jail. This court is adjourned."

Lola said, "I think Norma would make a fine deputy, don't you, Judge Moore?"

We all laughed, and Brownie swore Norma and me in as his deputies. Then, the three of us marched the four cowboys down to the Jail. One of the cowboys called out, "Sheriff, do we get anything to eat or drink while we are in your nice jail?"

Brownie said, "I'll check with Judge Moore and find out how much we can charge you for food. You'll get water later on this evening."

"Sheriff…" that's as far as Josh got.

"Josh, shut the fuck up. You have gotten us into enough trouble as it is," the assistant foreman said. Then he added, "Sheriff, can you at least get a couple of us our bedrolls off our horses?"

"I'll see what the Judge has to say about that," Sheriff Brownie said.

I smiled at Brownie and said, "As Deputies, Norma and I will have to check those bedrolls for any kind of weapon that might be there."

The Assistant Foreman quickly said, "Sheriff, just forget the bedrolls; we can all get along without them. Okay?"

Sheriff Brownie, Norma, and I left the jail, and we were about fifty yards up the street when Norma began giggling. It wasn't long before we laughed hard and probably looked like three crazy people.

Norma finally asked, "Brownie, what do you think is in those bedrolls to make all four of those cowboys almost go crazy thinking that we were going to open their bedrolls?"

Brownie shook his head, saying, "I have no idea, Norma. Gray, what do you think they might have in those rolls?"

I rubbed my chin with my right hand for a few moments, then said, "Other guns, maybe a knife or two, and maybe a stick or two of dynamite. I hear them boys from Texas are kind of partial to the sound of dynamite when it goes off."

Norma said, "Gray, you're kidding about the dynamite, right, Honey?"

I shook my head and said, "I wish I were kidding, Norma. I have run into a few crazy Texans who would rather light a fuse on a stick of dynamite than draw a pistol and pull the trigger. But we have no right to check the bedrolls. Brownie will have to get the Court to approve their search."

Brownie said, "Norma, I will ask Moore if we can search the rolls. Those boys could throw a stick or two when leaving town if there is dynamite in them. There is no telling what they might blow up."

Judge Moore was standing at the bar when we entered Lola's Place. Betty was pressed up tight against the Judge, with his left arm wrapped around her waist. In the mirror behind the bar, anyone who looked could see where the Judge had his left hand buried. It was underneath Betty's skimpy blouse that barely covered her breasts. From the look of pain on Betty's face, I was sure the Judge was rough on Betty.

I walked up to stand behind the Judge and said, "Judge, we may have a serious problem in town, and we need your expert advice on handling the situation. Can we impose upon you to meet with us over at Lola's table? Thank you, sir, for your help."

As I walked away, Betty said, "You go right ahead and meet with them. I'll be around when you're finished." When I reached Lola's table, she grinned at me and quietly said, "Thank you, Gray. I was about to shoot him for hurting her that way."

Judge Moore stomped up to the table and sat down beside me. "Gray, couldn't you see I was busy? You could have waited a few minutes to get my advice. What the fuck is the rush?"

Sheriff Brownie said, "Judge, after we got them cowboys in their cells, one of them asked about meals and their bedrolls. We told them that the rolls would be checked for weapons or anything that could be used as a weapon. They backed off real quick and said they could get along without them. I told them I would check with you, Judge, and see what we could do.

"Walking back to Lola's Place, we talked about the bedrolls. We thought they could have extra guns or knives in the rolls and possibly some dynamite. We need your say-so to look in their rolls."

Judge Moore looked hard at Brownie before asking, "Why do you think they might have dynamite, Sheriff?"

"It was Gray's idea, Your Honor. He said he had encountered a couple of hardass Texans who preferred dynamite over a pistol. He also thought if there was a stick or two, those boys could cause all kinds of trouble when they left town."

I said, "I was just thinking about how to stop trouble before it started."

Moore looked back and forth between the Sheriff and me for close to a minute, then looked at Norma and said, "Norma, do you think there might be dynamite in those bedrolls?"

Norma nodded and said, "Yes, Judge, I think there might be a stick or two. The only one of the four cowboys I recognized was the Foreman. Those others look like they are hard ones, ready for a fight. Any one of them could have dynamite in their bedroll. I think they should be checked."

While Norma talked, Lola leaned down and picked up Judge Moore's carrying case. She set it beside Moore and said, "The Sheriff and his deputies need you to write an authorization to search the bedrolls for weapons and dynamite. The Town of Holbrook will pay for basic evening and breakfast meals."

Moore looked at Lola and opened his mouth to say something, then changed his mind, shook his head, reached for his case, and said, "Feed them two meals a day. And, Sheriff, you have my permission to check those bedrolls. Let me write this up so it is nice and legal. Norma, are you still a deputy for Brownie?"

Norma grinned and said, "No, Judge. That was a temporary thing. Besides, I don't think my future husband wants me to be a deputy. That may be too dangerous of a job."

Judge Moore quickly wrote a letter authorizing Sheriff Brownie to obtain meals for his prisoner for the next two days. Another note approved Brownie to have the bedrolls of the four prisoners now incarcerated in his Jail searched for weapons and dynamite along with any fuse material. The guns were to be returned to the owners after release from Jail. The US Federal Government would confiscate any dynamite through the Circuit Judge.

Brownie had his orders, so the Sheriff, Norma, and I left Lola's Place.

Chapter 16

Four horses were tied to the hitching rail outside the Hotel across the street from Lola's Place. We crossed the road, and Brownie checked the horses for the Broken Arrow brand. I stepped into the hotel lobby and asked the clerk, "Them horses out front, do you know who they belong to?"

The kid nodded and said, "It's them cowboys you took down to the Jail. They rode in here, tied their mounts to the rail, and walked over to the saloon. They had a mean way about them when they got off their horses. They never loosened the cinches or touched their horses. I was going to come over to the saloon and ask who would take care of the horses. I didn't want to touch them for fear of being shot."

I said, "Those cowboys are spending a few nights in jail, and we are taking the horses down to the Livery. You don't need to worry about the horses anymore. Thanks for keeping an eye on them."

Sheriff Brownie had already started taking one horse down the street when I left the hotel. I saw Norma talk to one of the horses with his ears laid back. While untying the other two horses, I saw Norma's horse move its ears forward and nudge Norma. She laughed softly, and we started making our way to the Livery.

Someone called Sheriff Brownie and said that he needed to settle a dispute. Norma stopped, took Brownie's horse in hand, and led both to the Livery. I was right behind her.

Chipper, the owner of the Livery, came out and helped us tie the horses to a hitching rail. I explained what was happening, and Chip said, "Yeah, Gray, I saw you two taking those cowboys to the jail. I wondered where their mounts were. You want me to store their saddles and gear until they get out of jail?"

I said, "Yes, Chip, the town would appreciate it if you would keep the gear safe. Norma and I will go through the gear, looking for any other weapons they might have brought to town."

Norma gave Chip a full-blown smile and said, "Gray didn't tell you, Chip, that we are also looking for dynamite. So we'll take the gear off the horses, one horse at a time. We'll take the saddles off after we have checked the gear." With another smile, Norma added, "Is that okay with you, Chip?"

True to form, I saw Chip melt before Norma's smile. He said, "Anything for you, Norma. If there is anything I can do to help, just let me know. I'll make sure there is a clear pasture of other horses so these four animals will have their own area and not get into a fight with one of the other horses."

Norma said, "That's good, Chip. We'll tell you when the horses are ready to be put out to pasture."

When Chip was out of sight, Norma and I quickly checked the bedrolls and saddlebags. I found an empty bag by the Livery's feed locker and put the four pistols, two hunting knives, and four sticks of dynamite, along with a coil of fuse material that were in the saddlebags, not the bedrolls. While I was putting things in the bag, Norma went to tell Chip we were leaving.

Norma and Chip walked out of the Livery, and Chip said, "Mr. Gray, just leave the horses right there; I'll take care of them. Where you guys put the saddle and the men's gear is good. No one is going to bother the stuff."

I said, "Thanks, Chip. I know you'll take good care of the horses. The horses have been standing outside the hotel for the last few hours; their saddle blankets are soaked in sweat. They need some water before you put them out in the pasture."

Chip nodded and said, "If that is what you want done, Mr. Gray, then I'll do it."

Norma and I said goodbye to Chip and headed for the jail. We were out in the middle of the road when I heard a horse galloping down the middle of the street. I reached out, grabbed Norma's right arm, and pulled her tight against me. She was walking to my left and slightly ahead of me. I took two steps back and pulled Norma to me. The horse flew by us, and I saw its hoofs hit right where Norma had been walking.

"Hey! Watch where you are going," Norma called angrily after the rider.

"You want me to shoot him, Sweetheart?" I asked Norma. "Too much further, and he'll be out of my range."

"Nah, he's just an asshole from the Broken Arrow Ranch. I've seen him around before."

I laughed and said, "He doesn't know how close he came to being dead. Let's get to the jail before some other asshole comes racing down the street."

As we got to the Jail's porch, Sheriff Brownie walked down the boardwalk shaking his head. Brownie said, "If you had shot him,

Gray, I would have called it a justifiable shooting. That guy was the reason I got called over to the Mercantile Store. It seems that he and the Store owner had a little disagreement about the price of bullets. The cowboy said he would only pay how much he paid in Texas for them. The owner told the cowboy to go back to Texas and get his bullets because he wasn't going to get them from him."

Norma said, "Brownie, I bet that cowboy backed down quickly after you showed up at the door."

"Yeah, it took him a little while to think about what he was going to do. He kept looking at the bullets behind the check-out counter and turning his head to look at me." That guy finally said, "Sheriff, it's just not right. A man ought to be able to buy bullets at a fair price and not have to pay such outrageous prices as this storeowner charges. In Texas, I can get a box of bullets for a quarter. This guy is asking for ten dollars."

I laughed and asked, "What else happened? The cowboy should have been heading out of town long before he did. What, or who spooked him?"

Brownie nodded and said, "I told the cowboy there was nothing I could do. The owner sets the price. I told that guy he had to leave without new bullets. The guy saw my hand was on the butt of my pistol, and he ran out of the store. I followed him as he ran up the street. He kept looking around like he was looking for someone. The guy went into Lola's Place, and when I got there, he was at the bar talking to Doc Roth. I sat at Lola's table and put my pistol up on the table. I wasn't sure what the cowboy was going to do. I saw Doc nod toward me, and the cowboy spun around really quickly. Doc said something, and I saw the cowboy look at my hand on the table. I held my pistol, and it was pointed at the guy. He hightailed it out of there and damn near ran you over, from what I could see from the Saloon's swinging doors."

We all had a long laugh, and then I handed Brownie the bag I was holding. "There are four sticks of dynamite, along with four pistols. You might want to put that bag in your safe and lock the damn thing."

Chapter 17

Brownie asked Norma and me to wait for him while he put the bag in his safe. It took him a few minutes to get back outside the jail. Brownie was shaking his head when he said, "Those jackasses were jawing so much I had a hard time remembering the combination for the safe."

Norma said, "You didn't let any of them cowboys see the combination, did you, Brownie?"

"NO!"

"What did they want you to do?" I asked.

Brownie gave a half-hearted laugh, then with a shake of his head, he said, "Two of them idiots wanted me to have Lola send down a couple of ladies to comfort them in their loneliness. I didn't acknowledge them at all."

We were on the boardwalk, almost up to the Saloon, when we heard the stagecoach coming up behind us from the west. We stopped outside of Lola's Place. We wanted to get a gander at who got off the coach in front of the hotel. Lola exited the saloon and stood beside Brownie, who put a protective arm around her.

Two cowboys, who appeared to be a little older than me, stepped down and turned around as if looking for someone. Next, two ladies got off and walked into the Hotel. Then, a man stepped down and turned to help another lady off the coach. One cowboy called out to the stagecoach driver, "Where's the Livery from here?"

The driver handed the cowboy a saddle and said, "It's on the other end of town; didn't you see it when we rode past?"

"I must have been busy looking at something else. How about you turn this coach around, take the saddles, and my partner and I back down there?"

Handing the other saddle down, the driver said, "Sorry, no can do. This here coach only heads east. Well, somewhat northeast, I guess, would be the right direction."

"How about if I put a bullet in your fucking head and drive the fucking coach down there myself?" the cowboy said.

Brownie moved away from Lola and called out, "Lonnie, is there a problem with the stagecoach?" I moved Norma behind me.

The cowboy spun around to face Brownie and said, "Well, look here, Ted, Josh was right. They do have a real sheriff here and a deputy. Man can't seem to go no place without running into the law."

I said, "Micky, you and Ted had best just get on that stagecoach and head out of town. Dag Acadia left town with a crushed right hand. I shot his gun out of his hand. The Sheriff dropped Cameron. Or, if you prefer, you can buy a couple of horses and head back to Texas. If you want to stay alive, those are your options."

Ted said something to Micky that I could not hear, but I knew what he was speaking. I saw Micky's dark face go ashen before he stated, "Is that you, Gray? You're in the shadow, and the sun is in my eyes. I can't make you out too clear, but Ted said it's you. Gray, you know I wouldn't shoot the driver. He's a good man and a good driver. He handled those six horses as though they were a part of him. Ted and I will carry our saddles down to the Livery ourselves. Maybe the Liveryman knows where we can buy a couple of horses. Is that okay with you, Gray?"

"That would be up to the Sheriff," I said sternly.

"Sheriff, what do you say? Oh, I'm Micky O'Rourke, and my partner is Ted Largess. We ran into Gray over in the northern part of Texas. Sheriff, you got a good man as your deputy. I've never known a man as fast on the draw as Gray. It's like he knows what you will do before you do. Ted and I were lucky enough to be on his side in Texas."

Brownie said, "You gentleman, carry your gear down to the Livery and tell Chip that Sheriff Brownie said he was to sell you a couple of horses. Then come back up to Lola's Place for a drink."

I watched Micky and Ted pick up their gear and politely say their goodbyes to the other stagecoach passengers. I kept my eyes on them until they went out of sight. I looked back to the stagecoach and saw another man was off the coach. The man was walking towards the Palace. He was holding a satchel in his right hand and keeping the left flap of his duster open so everyone could see he was a US Marshal. The man stopped before Brownie and said, "Sheriff, I'm Marshal Reed. Thomas Reed. I understand you're having some trouble here in Holbrook. The Governor of Texas sent me here to see if I could tidy things up a bit. So, to start with, do you know whom you got here as your deputy?"

I watched Brownie grow taller and taller as the man spoke. Lola took a couple of steps away from Brownie. In a tight voice, Brownie said, "Marshal, before you say one more word, let me tell you something. This is my town, and I don't give a damn what the

Governor of Texas says. He has no authority in Arizona. If I were you, I would get back on that stage and keep on going. You are not welcome in Holbrook, Arizona. If you have a problem with that, talk to our Governor. So, pick up your bag and move on."

Marshal Reed stepped back and said, "Sheriff, I'm a US Marshal. You cannot order me out of this town."

Brownie called, "Circuit Judge Moore, please step out here."

I saw Reed's face sag a little at Moore's name. He looked defeated.

Judge Moore exited Lola's Place and said, "Gentlemen, I heard every word you two spoke. And Marshal Reed, the sheriff, does have the right to remove you from his town. Yes, you are a US Marshal, and for you to come here too, as you say, tidy things up, that order would have to come from the United States Government, not the Governor of Texas. Even the Governor of Arizona does not have the authority to send you to Holbrook. The Arizona Governor would have to ask the US Government for your help. Marshal Reed, as you probably know, things like this take a long time. The problem in Holbrook will be long over when you get your government authorization. Take Sheriff Brownie's suggestion, pick up your bag, and get on the stagecoach."

Reed looked at Moore and Brownie for a moment, then reached down for his bag, but he went for his gun instead of the bag. My shot hit Reed in the right wrist just as his hand clasped the handle of his revolver. Reed glared at me and yelled, "You'll pay for this, Gray! What kind of trick do you have in that holster of yours? No man is that fast."

Brownie stepped down from the boardwalk and took Reed's gun, saying, "Reed, I didn't think Gray was that fast either. I started to ask him a question and got half of a word out before I stared down the barrel of his pistol. Now, let's see the Doc and get you patched up. Then you are getting on the stage and leaving Holbrook."

The Sheriff called Lonnie and said, "Lonnie, you might see if Chip down at the Livery has some fresh horses for you. It will take the Doc some time to fix the Marshal's arm."

Chapter 18

As the Sheriff took Reed to see Doc Roth, Lola and Norma went into the saloon to discuss something about Norma's work. I noticed the two ladies who got off the stagecoach together, heading towards Lola's Place. I heard Micky calling out for the ladies to wait for him; he wanted to get to know them better. Micky and Ted were hurrying up the boardwalk but not entirely running.

The two ladies stepped onto the boardwalk before me, and the tallest one asked, "Are you the owner of this Saloon?"

I shook my head and said, "No, Ma'am, I'm the bouncer. Lola, the owner, is inside. Would you like me to point her out to you?"

"That would be very nice of you, sir," the lady said without giving me her name.

I opened the swinging door and let the ladies enter first. Then I stepped in and led the ladies over to Lola's table. I said, "Lola, these two ladies wish to speak with you."

Lola looked at the ladies and said, "Hi, ladies, I'm Lola White. Welcome to Lola's Place. What can I do for you?"

The two ladies glanced around the room as Micky approached the tallest lady and said, "Miss, I think we got off on the wrong foot while we were caged up in that stagecoach. I'd kind of like to get to know you better, and my partner, Ted, would like to know your friend. What do you say? Can we be friends?"

"Cowboy," Lola said sternly, "step away from the ladies. We have a business to conduct here."

I said, "Ted, if your fingers get any closer to your gun, you might want to rethink what you have in mind. Micky, take Ted to the bar, and both of you cool down."

Ted's fingers moved to where they were, almost touching his pistol, and before he could say a word, the barrel of my pistol was staring into Ted's right eye. I said, "You don't want to be missing that eye at your funeral, do you, Ted?"

"No. No, Mister Gray, I don't," Ted said.

Micky grabbed Ted's left arm, saying, "Okay, Ted, let's get a drink."

The two ladies stood with their mouths open until I holstered my pistol. "Mister," the shorter lady said, "were you going to shoot that guy in the eye?"

Lola said, "I'm surprised Gray didn't shoot that cowboy in the hand as soon as it touched his gun. Why is that, Gray?"

I shrugged and said, "Ted is not a gunman; he is just a follower and is currently following Micky around the country. Hell, Lola, I think you're probably faster on the draw than Ted. Now, Micky is a different story. Micky's derringer up his sleeve is his first shot. Then he uses his forty-five. Neither man is an outlaw, but they both live on the verge of being one. If you want, I'll tell you more after you conduct your business with these pretty ladies. And, Norma, don't give me that look. You're by far the prettiest woman in Holbrook and all of Arizona. I'm going to go talk to Micky and Ted." I walked around the table and stopped beside Norma to lean down and kiss her. When I stood up, I'm sure everyone in the bar knew that Norma and I were together.

I stood beside Ted at the bar and leaned against it as James told Micky and Ted how I became the bouncer in Lola's Place. I waited until Ted finished drinking his beer and asked, "Did Chip sell you two horses?"

While looking in the mirror behind the bar, Ted said, "Yeah, Micky saw those horses that belonged to the men in jail, and he tried talking Chip into selling him one of those fine horses. Chip wouldn't even talk to him about it. All he said was they were not for sale."

"So, what are you two going to do now?"

Ted shrugged and said, "We was going to talk those ladies from the stagecoach into spending some time with us. Micky likes the taller one, and the shorter one is cute. She needs to put on some weight, but I wouldn't mind spending some time alone with her. What did they say to you outside of Lola's Place?"

I laughed and said, "They wanted to know if I was the owner of Lola's Place. I told them I was the bouncer and would introduce them to Lola. That's all; then I opened the swinging door for them and introduced them to Lola."

"That's what I told Micky you were doing, but he wouldn't believe me," Ted said—then added, "How did you draw your gun so quickly? I blinked, and when my eyes opened, I looked down the barrel. I about shit my pants."

I grinned at Ted and said, "You would have been the third person to shit their pants since I got to Holbrook."

Ted finished his beer and said, "I don't think I want to know about the first two."

"You are probably right, Ted. Let me buy you another round," I said, motioning for James to fill Ted's and Micky's mugs.

As James got the beer, Micky looked around Ted and said, "Thank you kindly, Gray. I've heard some tall tales of what has happened to you since you got to Holbrook. You have been a busy fella, scaring the shit right out of men. And what gets me is that you fell in love while scaring people."

I laughed and said, "Micky, you forgot one part."

Micky grinned and said, "And what part is that, Gray?"

I smiled over at Norma as she and Lola stood up to shake the hands of the new ladies of the night. Then I said, "Me getting engaged to be married to Norma, the lady standing beside Lola, the owner of this establishment."

Micky stuck his right hand out to me and said, "Well, good for you, Gray. She looks like a right, fine lady."

We shook hands, and Ted said, "Yeah, I wish you the best of luck. I understand a man needs much of that when married." Ted raised his hands and added, "But, I wouldn't know 'cause I ain't never been married."

Norma approached me and put her arms around me as Lola introduced her new ladies. "Gray, I want you to meet Betsy and Jo. You need to retrieve their luggage and bring it up to their rooms? The girls are starting tonight."

Micky stood straight and said, "Miss Lola, Ted, and I would gladly lend Gray a hand in getting the ladies' luggage."

Lola shook her head and said, "No, Mister O'Rourke. You and Mister Largess stay right here. James, another round for these gentlemen. The girls said there was not much luggage. Gray can handle it by himself."

Betsy, the taller of the two girls, said, "Mister Gray. That cute clerk over at the hotel has our things behind the counter. If the luggage seems like it was looked through, would you shoot the clerk, please?"

We all laughed, and I said, "Why I would be de…." That's as far as I got because Norma pinched my side real hard!

"He'll do no such thing," Norma said in a hushed voice.

Chapter 19

I gave Norma a not-so-quick kiss, but she had a different idea. Norma hooked the back of my neck with her left hand and would not let go until she was ready for our lips to part. As I walked from the bar, Micky said, "Gray, my friend, you are taking a chance leaving this beautiful lady here with Ted and me. You sure you want to do that?"

I kept walking and said, "Look around you, Micky, and guess how many men will be all over you if you even touch Norma."

My hand was on the swinging door when Micky called out, "It seems the whole town is protecting her; thanks for the warning."

"That was not a warning; that was a fact," I called out as I left the saloon.

When I got to the hotel, the clerk, Jimmy, was looking through a lady's carpetbag. He was so engrossed in handling the frilly garments that Jimmy didn't hear me walk up to the counter he was sitting behind. I watched Jimmy bring one article of clothing up to his face and sniffed it. I said, "Betsy said I should shoot you if I find you digging through her clothes. From the looks of it, maybe I should."

"OH, LORD! Mister Gray, I don't know what came over me to do this. You're not going to shoot me, Mister Gray?"

I laughed and said, "Jimmy, put the clothes back as you found them, or as close as possible. Then give me Betsy and Jo's luggage. If those cowboys who got off the stagecoach today were with me, like they wanted to be, you would be dead by now, Jimmy."

"I swear, Mister Gray, something took hold of me and made me need to look at their clothes and to feel and smell them. My daddy will kill me if he ever finds out what I did. He works hard trying to run the Hotel and the Livery. He had another man working here, but he up and left, so my dad gave me the job. He thought I was old enough now, I guess. My ma don't like it none. She says sixteen is too young to work unless there is no one else. My sister is two years older than me and could do the job but is too lazy to do any work. I swear, Mister Gray, I never did nothing like this before. What can I do to make it up?"

"Jimmy, just put the clothes back as best you can," I said. "I'm not going to say anything to anyone. But, if Betsy or Jo told Lola that someone was in their bags, I might have to say something. That is the best I can say right now."

I watched as Jimmy carefully put two garments he had taken out of the carpetbag back in the bag and closed it up. Jimmy put two bags and two frilly parasols on the counter. He then asked, "Mister Gray, are those two ladies going to work over at Lola's Place?"

"Yes, Jimmy, they are, and you can tell your dad that you helped them when they came in off the stagecoach. You know, kept their luggage behind the counter for them until I stopped by for the bags."

Jimmy had a big smile on his face when I left the hotel. I was about to step up on the boardwalk outside the saloon when the swinging door banged open. Norma came storming out with Micky right behind her.

"But Norma, it was an accident," Micky said. "I didn't realize you were so close to me. That man was coming at you so fast I thought he would tear your clothes off. My hands were coming up to protect you, and I looked over the top of you as you turned to stop me. My right hand hit your breast, yes. But I apologized for that."

Norma spun around and faced Micky, saying, "You didn't just hit me, Mister O'Rourke. You fucking punched me! And that hurt! Now you will find out how fast you are compared to Charles Gray."

I set the things I was carrying on the ground, keeping my eyes on Micky while I did. "Norma, what did I miss?" I said in a soft yet hard tone.

"The Judge had been upstairs, and when he came down, he was coming over to say goodbye to me. Your friend here thought the Judge was going to attack me. I was kind of in between the two men. Your friend swung at the Judge and slugged me instead."

"I didn't know he was a Circuit Judge," Micky said. "His hair was all messed up, and his clothes were too. I thought he was a madman about to attack Norma. I swung to hit the guy, and Norma got in the way of the punch. I know I was watching him and not Norma like I should have been."

"But, you slugged me, you idiot."

"And I apologized for that a couple of times."

It all struck me as being funny, and I could not help but laugh; I started laughing, and it ended up a belly laugh. I got control of myself when I saw Norma glaring at me. Micky was grinning, and Lola was behind him, laughing with me. Judge Moore was standing just behind Lola, and he was laughing too.

Shaking my head, I finally said, "Norma, it sounds like it was an accident. Micky didn't mean to slug you. He meant to smash Judge

Moore's nose. He didn't want to draw his weapon and shoot the Judge because too many people were around. Now come here and kiss me. Then, you can help me by carrying the parasols up to Betsy and Jo."

Norma leaped off the boardwalk, and I caught her in midair. I spun her around three times and set her down by the carpetbags. Norma said, "Gray, no one will hit my breast again except you. Those are for you alone. I was so mad that your friend hit me there before you could do that. But, as you said, there were too many people around, and someone else might get shot."

I cupped Norma's chin and tipped her head back to look up at me. I grinned at her, saying, "Norma, I will never hit you except playfully on the shoulder. Now, that is not to say I won't turn you over my knee and paddle your behind when you deserve a spanking. I don't believe in hitting women other than those times."

Lola said, "Norma, I told you you would never find a better man than Gray."

"I know," Norma called back.

"Damn," Judge Moore called out, "Sheriff Brownie is coming back with that US Marshal. The stagecoach is going to leave soon, so Norma Whitmore and Charles Gray, by the powers invested in me by the great State of Arizona, and in front of all these fine witnesses, I now pronounce you husband and wife. We'll fill out the paperwork when I come through Holbrook next."

Moore ran back into the saloon and came out with his bags. He kissed Lola and Betsy. Then Moore stepped off the boardwalk and offered me his hand. We shook hands, and he said, "Gray, you are far better suited to care for Norma than I am, so be good to her and name the first one after me." Moore quickly kissed Norma on the cheek and ran to the stagecoach. He barely made it inside the coach when Lonnie got the stagecoach rolling.

Chapter 20

Norma looked up at Lola and asked, "Did Clarence just marry Charlie and me?"

Everyone laughed at the shocked look on Norma's face. Then Lola said, "Yes, he sure did! We all heard it, so you do not get out of it. Or you either, Gray. And I've never seen a simpler wedding. I love you both."

There was a lot of whooping and hollering, along with best wishes from everyone. I picked up the carpetbag beside me as Norma picked up the other one and one of the parasols, which she opened and placed on her left shoulder. "Come on, husband," Norma said with glee. Let's take this stuff to the new girls' rooms."

I picked up the other parasol and followed Norma into the Saloon and up to the second floor. I stopped at the top of the staircase and said, "Norma, I'm a married man now, and I cannot go any further than this. I'll leave the bag and parasol here for you to take to the other girl's room."

"Charlie, you wait right there for me," Norma called as she entered her old room. When Norma returned, she stopped before me and said, "I'm having a hard time here, Charlie. Help me out on something, would you?"

I grinned at her and said, "That's right, sweetheart, I am not going to look at another lady's naked body. Your lovely body is all I'll ever need to look at."

With a laugh, Norma reached up, cupped the back of my head, and pulled me down for a scorching kiss. When she ended the kiss, she picked up the carpetbag and Parasol. She was grinning when she walked back down the hall. Norma walked past several doors, stopped, and looked over her shoulder at me. "I knew I found the right man when I first saw you, Mister Gray. I love you, Charlie. Wait for me right where you are."

I didn't even move when I saw a man enter the saloon and hurry to Lola's table. He said, "Lola, there is a herd of cattle a few miles west of here. They are headed right to the center of town. What are we going to do? They'll smash everything outside the buildings and probably break into some of them."

Do you know whose cattle they are?" Lola asked.

"Yes, ma'am. They are Broken Arrow cattle. It looked like about ten riders were herding the cattle," the guy said.

Lola asked, "Do you know where Brownie is?"

The man nodded, saying, "I think I saw him entering the Bank."

I saw Lola nod at James, and the guy ran out of the saloon. Norma put her arms around me and whispered, "Who are you looking at? What's going on, and should I know about it?"

I softly said, "Sounds like Broken Arrow wants to move cattle through the middle of town unless we stop them. Lola is the one that everyone turns to when there is a problem in town, right?"

"Come on, husband, let's see what she says."

I grinned and said, "Okay, little Missus Gray."

Norma laughed and grabbed my left hand to tug me down the stairs. We went over by Lola, and I was about to say something when Brownie, James, and Ned Worthington, along with several other men, came into the saloon.

Brownie went straight to Lola and kissed her. Then he said, "What the hell do we do to stop a herd of cattle?"

Lola said, "I was hoping you would have an answer."

When no one said anything, I said, "We block the road with every wagon or carriage we have in town. If we make it wedge-shaped, the cattle will turn off to the right or left, bypassing most of the town."

Brownie said, "The way the cattle are coming to town, there is Swan Creek to their right, so maybe we should make them go to their left. That would be out around the Livery. Hope they don't break down Chip's fences."

"Sounds good to me," I said. "How about you, Lola? Is there something else we should do?"

"Do you want men with rifles on this side of the barricade?" Lola asked.

Brownie grinned at Lola and said, "Every man and woman with a rifle meet by the Jail in a few minutes. Now, let's get the hell out there and build a barricade."

Micky stopped me and said, "Gray, our rifles are down at the Livery. Ted and I will meet you at the Jail. I'll tell Chip what is going on and help him move the horses he needs to move."

"Thank you both," I said.

It took three large wagons turned on their sides to block the center of the road. Smaller wagons were turned and moved into a line stretching past the Livery. Carriages were turned on their sides and pulled into the woods as far as the edge of Swan Creek. Then we strung rope three strands high to help stop cattle from entering the woods. We used wheel barrels and smaller carts to block the few holes we found. We tied those into place with more rope.

Brownie, Norma, and I mounted up and waited outside the barricade when the cattle finally arrived. We steered the first few cattle away from the creek and town. Sheriff Brownie stopped the first rider who got to the barricade and said, "Move the herd around Holbrook. There is no need for the cattle to come through the town."

The rider said, "Looks like you already got them heading that way. But Sheriff, our orders are to take them through town, which is what we will do. Now, you and your deputies best get out of the way before the big part of the herd gets here."

Brownie said, "And the forty rifles behind the barricade, how are you going to get through them without dying?"

I said, "Mister, if your right hand gets closer to your pistol, you'll miss a right hand. I'll blow it off at the wrist."

"Now, Gray, there is no need for gunplay," Brownie said. "This cowboy will take his herd around the Livery and on its way to wherever they are going. Right, Cowboy?"

The man I was looking at was not a cowboy. He was a kid who thought he was a gunman. It took him a moment to realize who I was, and I saw his face turn a couple of shades lighter before he asked, "You the guy who took Matt Diamond down?"

I nodded and said, "And a few others like him. If you knew that, you know what I say is fact, not fiction."

"Those assholes didn't tell us whom we are dealing with. Sheriff, I'm going to ride back and tell my brother that the cattle need to go back to Broken Arrow. Mister Gray, we are not going to bother your town. Was it your idea for the barricade? I didn't think a man who made his living with a gun would be involved in this sort of thing."

I said, "Ride on, Jack, and tell your brother I don't want to see him in town. If I do, one of us will be leaving in a pine box."

Jack nodded to me, turned his horse, and started moving the cattle away from the barricade. Another rider came up to him, and they had a little talk. I could tell it was Jim Fox, Jack's twin. I gave Jim Fox the limp he had when you saw the man walking. When I settled that town's problem, Jim was one of the lucky ones in Santa Ana, New Mexico. Matt Diamond was one of the unlucky ones. He was the first that I took down that day.

Chapter 21

When the herd of cattle was turned and headed back the way they had come, Norma asked, "Can we take the barricade down now?"

Brownie said, "That's up to the town council. I think it would be wise to leave it overnight, at least. Those two gunmen may get the idea to start a stampede and make it, so the cattle are headed right for our town again."

Norma said, "You think whoever is in charge of the Broken Arrow told them, gunmen, to shoot off some shots to make the cattle stampede through Holbrook."

Brownie chuckled and said, "I wouldn't put it past them."

I nodded at Lola, standing by the tongue of one of the large wagons, and said, "Brownie, you better go tell your lady that the barricade needs to stay up overnight. And don't forget to tell her why it can't come down. My wife and I will visit our cabin for a few hours. Oh, I wouldn't release them four you got in Jail until tomorrow afternoon."

"How the hell did you know I was thinking of releasing them?" Brownie said as he rubbed the back of his head. "I just had the thought that it might be a good gesture on the part of Holbrook."

I moved my horse beside Norma, leaned over, and kissed her before saying, "Yes, Brownie, it would be nice of the town to do that, but I have a feeling that those four would talk the Fox brothers into stampeding the herd of cattle."

"Shit! And the Broken Arrow owners would not know we let them out early. I'm beginning to see why Lola wants you around. You don't think like the rest of us. You two go home. I'll talk to Lola. She wouldn't get any work out of you two right now anyway."

Norma and I took our horses to the Livery, unsaddled them, and turned them over to Chip. Then we walked to our cabin. As we got close to the cabin, I stopped Norma and whispered, "Do you have any idea why the door is open a couple of inches?"

Her eyes opened wide, then shut down to squint when Norma said, "NO! I know it was closed and latched when we left this morning." Her voice was just above a whisper. "You need to peek in the window and see if you see anyone."

"Okay." I moved over to the side of the cabin and looked in the window. What I saw made me giggle, but not very loud. Stretched out on our bed was a large dog. One I had seen wandering around town since the night I first arrived.

I walked back to Norma and asked, "Are you ready to shoot the critter in our home?

"It's only an animal, not a person?" Norma asked.

"Yeah, and it is sure making a mess out of the place."

Norma ran up onto the small porch and threw open the door. I saw the dog's tail wagging like crazy. "Damn it, Butch, what are you doing here? Oh, God! I forgot to give you a snack last night, didn't I, baby?" Norma was over at the bed, petting the dog.

"Is that your dog?" I asked.

"No, it's the town's dog. Nobody claims ownership, but I've been giving him a snack every night for the last six months. Everyone feeds him, whether he needs food or not."

"Do you know if Butch bites people?"

"As far as I know, he never has. I know there was a run-away carriage one day, and a small boy fell in the muddy street in front of the carriage. Butch dashed out, grabbed the back of the boy's clothes, and carried the kid to safety. That's when everyone started feeding him. The boy's mother said she would take the dog home, but he wouldn't stay there. I don't think Butch likes the boy's father."

I sat down on a stool by the table, and Butch got off the bed and came over to me. He laid his head on my lap and gave me a sad-eyed look. "What's going on with you, Butch?" I asked as I petted him and ruffled the dog's fur.

Norma laughed and said, "I think Butch likes you, Charlie. We might have a new pet; I'll get him some water and set it by the door. We'll go to the Café, get dinner, and bring some back for Butch. As we leave, you can tell him to stay on the porch and guard the cabin."

We finished eating when Lola walked into the café. I saw several heads turn and stare at her. The waitress had put the last plate on the table closest to ours and moved a chair over for Lola.

Lola smiled at the girl and said, "Thanks, Nelda. I'll have a cup of coffee, please."

I grinned at Lola and said, "What brings you to the best Café in all of Arizona?"

Lola smiled and said, "I was looking for you two. I went to your cabin, but Butch would not let me get near the door. What's with him anyway? It was like Butch was guarding your place."

"He was in the cabin when we got home," Norma said. "It was like he wanted to make it his home too. I gave him some water, and when we left to come to dinner, Charlie told Butch to stay on the porch and guard the cabin."

Lola's head snapped back like she was hit. "Wait," she said, "are you saying that Butch is guarding the cabin because Gray told him to? That dog doesn't take orders from anyone."

Norma sat up and said, "Well, if Butch wouldn't let you close to the cabin, then that is what he was doing. Guarding the cabin as Charlie told him to."

"Gray, did you even know the dog before you found him in your cabin?" Lola asked.

I shook my head and said, "Oh, I'd seen him around town a few times. I didn't know who he belonged to, of course. He always seemed to watch any kids that were near him. It looked like he was trying to make sure the kids were safe. Norma told me about what Butch did to save that one boy. Has anything else like that happened with Butch?"

"No, it was just that once. But, you're right; Butch does try to ensure the kids are safe."

Nelda brought Lola her coffee, and when the girl took the coffee pot to another table, I softly asked, "Lola, what's the problem with your new girls that you want to talk about."

Chapter 22

Lola kept her face neutral, but I saw her body tighten like she was about to explode. She was smiling when, in a low voice, she said, "Now, Gray, what makes you think there might be a problem with Betsy and Jo?"

Keeping my voice low, I said, "From what I've seen of how you handle things, Lola, there is only one reason you would come looking for Norma or me. And that is when your gut tells you something is off with someone. You want to run it by someone you can trust. Since voices travel so well in your saloon, you thought the cabin would be the perfect place to talk."

This time, Lola's smile made it from her lips to her eyes when she said, "Gray, since we first met, I knew I could trust you not to say things to anyone. And that is the same with you, Norma. Shall we finish our coffee and go to your cabin, Norma?"

Norma's smile told me she was proud that Lola included her in this conversation. Norma said, "Lola, that would be our pleasure. I'm sure Butch will let you in the cabin this time."

When we got to the cabin, Butch was still guarding the place. I let Norma try to talk the dog off the porch. When Norma got close to him, Butch started growling at her. "Butch, what's the matter with you? It's me, your friend, Norma. You know me. Now, you have to get off the porch so we can go in." When Norma reached for him again, Butch's growl got louder.

I said, "It's okay, Butch. Come here, fellow." Butch thumped his tail a few times, stood up, and came to stand beside me.

"Dam," Lola said. "If I hadn't seen it with my own eyes, I would not have believed that Butch would listen to anyone. Gray, how the hell did you become his friend that fast?"

I laughed and said, "From when I was a little boy, I got along with all animals—far better than with people, that is for sure—with the exception of Norma."

Lola reached out and ruffled the top of Butch's head and said, "Well, I, for one, am glad that Butch has found a friend in you, Gray."

Norma opened the door, but before she could step in, Butch ran in front of Norma and stopped in the doorway to look around. Butch then moved out of the way. We all laughed, and Lola said, "Well, I can see you two are safe with Butch around."

Norma stopped by Butch and hugged him, saying, "Thanks for making sure there were no bad guys in here. I'm not sure that Gray would have thought to do that." Standing up, Norma added, "So, boss, what's the problem with your new girls?"

Lola shook her head as if trying to clear it, then said, "That's my problem. I don't know why I'm feeling uneasy about those two. I didn't get that feeling until after we stopped Broken Arrow's herd of cattle. Both of those ladies were out there, helping to move things where they needed. And they were tying rope as a man would. And maybe that is what is bothering me. I don't think I could tie rope as those two ladies did; they both moved like they were used to hard work, and I don't mean on their backs."

I asked, "Lola, did they tell you where they are from?"

"Yeah, they say they were from Bakersfield, California."

I frowned at Lola and said, "I think Brownie told me he was from Bakersfield when I told him I was heading to California. Does he know the ladies?"

With a shrug, Lola said, "I haven't asked him."

I said, "When they got off the stagecoach, they immediately entered the Hotel. Jimmy said they asked where they could find you, Lola, so someone has sent them here. Do you know anyone in Bakersfield?"

"No. That's the thing. When I asked how the girls ended up in Holbrook, they said they had heard about my place here and wanted to work for me. When I asked who told them about my place, they said they heard talk about the brothel they were working at in Bakersfield. It bothered me that I couldn't get a name out of them."

I wasn't sure what to do about this situation, but Norma seemed to have an idea. She said, "Lola, you know I'm new to this kind of business, but I think you should have Brownie and Gray sit down with Betsy and Jo. Both of them know how to get information out of a person."

Lola said, "You want Brownie and Gray to scare the hell out of the girls so they will tell who sent them to Holbrook?"

I asked, "Lola, did you see any scars on the girls when you interviewed them?"

Norma interjected, "Gray, sweetheart, do you mean a knife wound or a bullet wound?"

"Yes, honey, that is what I mean."

Lola said, "No, I did not see wounds or markings from being savagely beaten. They both seemed to have flawless skin."

Sitting on a stool with my arms resting on the table, I shut my eyes and raised my hands to cover them. Then I thought back to every time I saw either Betsy or Jo. I could see what they were doing and who they were with. I tried to determine where their eyes were looking. It didn't take much to figure out that the ladies looked at Brownie when he was around. They were also watching James and Lola, of course. They were trying to figure out who the real players were. I removed my hands and opened my eyes when I felt a cold nose nudging my neck.

"What do you think, Butch," I said. "Is there something wrong with Betsy and Jo? Or are they just trying to keep from stepping on the wrong person's toes?"

"Now, wait a minute, Gray," Lola said. "Are you thinking that this dog can tell if someone is a bad person or not? Does Butch even know a good person?"

Butch let out a few loud barks and ran over to the door. There was a loud knock on the door, and Brownie called out, "Lola, are you in there? James thought you were coming down here over an hour ago."

Before I could move, Lola was up and opening the door. Butch skirted around Brownie before Lola jumped into the man's arms.

Chapter 23

"Brownie, I need you to hold me," Lola said. "I don't care what these two, or their dog, has to say. I love you, Brownie, and I need you." Reaching down, Brownie scooped up Lola and carried her into the cabin. His lips were locked on hers.

I said, "It's getting a little crowded in here. Norma and I are going to find Betsy and Jo. We need to talk to them. Do you want me to leave Butch guarding the door?"

"Butch?" Brownie asked.

"Yes, let him guard the cabin. But will he let us out?" Lola said.

"How did Butch become a guard dog?" the Sheriff asked.

"I'll tell you later," Lola replied. "Now, kiss me, you beautiful man."

Norma pulled the door closed behind us as I put the food we brought home for Butch on the ground beside the porch. When Butch was done eating, I said, "Butch, you stay and guard the cabin. Norma and I will be back a little later."

When Norma and I got close to the Saloon, I said, "Why don't we take a walk around town as Brownie does? We can talk to the ladies later."

Norma laughed and said, "I just brought my jacket. I didn't bring my gun."

I brought Norma's holster from under my coat and handed it to her. "I picked it up when I grabbed the food for Butch. I thought you might need it to shoot your old beaus when they come near you.

Or maybe you would rather shoot the girls when they come up and kiss me."

Norma giggled and said, "I don't want to shoot anyone. I'll let you do that."

We walked around town and stopped at the barricade to listen for any cattle coming our way. We were standing in the shadow of one of the large wagons when I pulled Norma to me and kissed her. It felt like we had not kissed for at least a month or more. I was starving for my wife. When the kiss ended, I said, "I love you, Missus Charlie Gray, more than anyone, even my mother and grandmother."

Norma hugged me tight and said, "I will love you for the rest of my life. And Mister Charlie Gray, I will love hearing people call me Missus Charles Gray. Remember, I said that Charlie is for you and me alone. Other people can call you Gray or Charles Gray. Only I call you Charlie."

I sighed and said, "Okay, Sweetheart, I can live with that."

I stopped talking when I heard some horses heading to town from the west. Letting go of Norma, I held my left index finger to my lips. Norma nodded to me, and we stepped to the end of the wagon we were beside. Looking around the wagon, I saw two riders and a covered carriage coming our way. I whispered, "Norma, go get Brownie and Lola. Tell them that the owner of Broken Arrow has come to call."

Norma took off running, and I watched the riders. One rider called out, "Mister Thornhill, the road is blocked as Red said it would be. What do you want us to do?"

A deep bass voice called out from the carriage, "Toss a rope on that center Wagon and drag it out of the way. They can't stop us from coming into their town. This is a public road."

Chip walked up to me from the direction of the Livery and asked, "What do you want me to do, Mr. Gray?"

I glanced at Chip and saw he was carrying a lever-action rifle. "Are you any good with that rifle?"

"Yes, Sir."

"Good. If they throw a rope on this wagon, shoot the knot."

Even in the fading light of evening, I could see Chip smile, and then he said, "You got it, Mister Gray."

I called out, "Mister Thornhill, this is Gray. The rope will be shot if your riders put a rope on one of the wagons. The next rope will mean you have a dead rider. Is that what you want?"

The two riders pulled their pistols, and a moment later, Thornhill said, "Gray, I heard of you. What are you doing in Holbrook?"

"I was passing through on my way to California when one of your boys decided he didn't like me. He started liking me when I busted out a few of his teeth with the barrel of my pistol. The owner of Lola's Place offered me a job I couldn't refuse. Four of your boys are in jail for another night unless you pay their fine. When your boys or anyone comes to Holbrook, they must leave their sidearms with the sheriff."

"OKAY! OKAY!" Thornhill called out. "How do I get in to see this Lola lady you said wanted to see me?"

"Have your men holster their iron. Then, Mister Thornhill, you must borrow one of their horses and ride around the Livery. All the wagons and things will stay as they are until you and Lola agree. Is that clear to you and your riders, Mister Thornhill?"

"Yeah, it's clear. Holster those boys, Slim, I'll use your horse. And Chad, you and Slim stay here with the buggy. Men don't try to get over the barricade. We don't want any more bloodshed."

When Thornhill rode around the Livery, I called out, "Chad, are you the guy I put in jail over in Rockwood?"

"Yeah, but I don't hold that against you. It was your job. Is it true that you took down Dagobert Acadia and that asshole Cornelius Cameron?"

"That's partly true," I said. "I took down Dagobert, but Sheriff Brownie took out Cameron. Why do you ask, Chad?"

"Damn! Dag was as fast on the draw as I've seen, and you beat him. I got to quit this job before I'm forced to go against you, Gray."

As we talked, Chad moved his horse closer to the barricade. I moved over to the next wagon. Chip stayed where he was. Looking at Chad, I shook my head and said, "Chad, if that rifle comes out any further, you won't have to worry about quitting your job."

"Shit!" Chad exclaimed as he turned in the saddle to look at me. "I thought you were at the other end of the wagon, Gray. I can see your rifle, and it is still pointing at Slim."

"Can you see the two pistols pointing at you from here?" I asked.

Chad looked at my end of the wagon and, after a moment, said, "Oh yeah. I see the glint of metal in the shadow. Is your friend as quick on the draw as you, Gray?"

"Not quite, but just as good a shot, or maybe a little better than me. Why don't you take your hand away from the rifle and return to your boss's carriage? And stay there as he told you to."

"You're taking all the fun out of being a gunman."

"I'm just trying to keep you alive, Chad. Now, don't try my patience anymore."

"Jesus, a man can't have any fun anymore. I'm going, Gray, but I got a question for you."

"What's the question?"

"When the barricade is taken down, will we have to hand over our weapons to the Sheriff when we come to town?"

I said, "Either to the Sheriff or the bartender at any of the bars. And that will be before you have your first drink."

Chad rode back to where Slim was sitting in the carriage. Dismounting, Chad sat beside Slim to wait for Mister Thornhill.

I moved over to Chip and said, "Chip, if those yahoos decide to come up to the barricade again, shoot off one shot as a warning, not at them. You'll get everyone here in a hurry. I'm going to Lola's Place to determine what has been decided. I'll send some guys down to relieve you as soon as possible. Are you okay with that?"

"Will you stop by the hotel and tell Jimmy I'll be there as soon as you get someone to relieve me."

"Sure thing, and Chip, thanks for being here to help." I hurried up the street to meet Thornhill.

Chapter 24

I was on the boardwalk heading towards Lola's Place when Norma, Lola, and Brownie came out of the saloon. They started running toward the barricade when I called out. "You all stay there. Mister Thornhill should be here at any moment. He's not used to riding in a saddle anymore."

My three friends stopped running, and Brownie said, "Who is Thornhill?"

"Ask him yourself," I said. "That is him by the hotel."

Brownie and Lola returned to the saloon and waited by the door for Thornhill to get there.

Norma ran to me and threw her arms around me for a much-needed hug. "Why did you come back from the barricade?" Norma asked.

"I wanted to hear what Thornhill had to say. But I need to make one stop before going to Lola's Place. I need to tell Jimmy that his dad, Chip, will be there as soon as possible. Chip is watching to be sure that Chad and Slim stay by Thornhill's carriage."

Norma and I headed for the hotel, and she asked, "Who is Chad? I think I know Slim from Broken Arrow."

I said, "Chad is a young man who thinks he is a gunman. He has a fast draw, but you can draw faster than Chad, Sweetheart. I had a run-in with Chad in Rockwood, New Mexico. He was stealing things from a store owned by a friend of mine. The Sheriff of Rockwood had deputized me to handle a couple of things. The kid went into the store with his bandana wrapped around his face. When I arrived, Chad had pulled his iron and threatened my friend. Chad didn't like it much when I put the end of my pistol in the small of his back. The kid holstered his iron as my friend rebuttoned her blouse. Then, her pointed boot ended up right between the kid's legs. After I got done laughing, I dragged the kid to jail. The Sheriff laughed, then went and got the doctor to check and ensure that Millie didn't do Chad too much damage."

Norma was still laughing when we left the hotel after telling Jimmy his dad would be late. We were halfway across the street when Norma said, "I should have known your friend was a woman. How come you were friends with her?"

"I met Millie when she married my brother in Wichita. As I told Judge Moore, John was shot in the back and killed. John and Millie had a small ranch outside of Wichita, and when she sold it, I took Millie and their son back to her hometown of Rockwood. Some things were happening around Rockwood, and the sheriff asked me to stick around and help him. The sheriff is Millie's brother-in-law, so I stuck around. Millie bought her store with the money she got from selling her ranch."

"Oh!" Norma said.

I giggled and said, "You thought Millie was a wench."

"Well, what else was I supposed to think? You get to Holbrook, and one of the first things you do is end up in bed with me." Norma stomped up onto the boardwalk and into Lola's Place.

I was right behind her and still grinning. I watched as Norma went directly to Lola's table and sat beside her boss. I walked over and stood by the bar. James asked me, "What's the grin for?"

"I told Norma about how I knew Chad, one of Thornhill's men," I said. "When I mentioned that the person I helped out was a woman, Norma thought she was a whore. Millie was my dead brother's wife. I guess Norma has a point in that one of the first things I did was end up with her after getting to Holbrook. But, James, I've never thought of Norma as a whore, or lady of the night. She has only been the most beautiful lady I have ever known. And she will always be."

"Then you better tell her that," James said. "Do it before she gets furious enough at you that she shoots you down low, and I ain't talking about your feet."

"Yeah, I guess you're right, James. Thanks."

Lola called out, "James, bring me my bottle of whiskey, and Gray, get over here and meet Mister Thornhill."

I walked over to Lola's table and stood beside Norma. I said, "Mister Thornhill and I met at the barricade."

Thornhill nodded and said, "I've heard of you for some time now, Mister Gray. And most of it was much like tonight. When things might get messy, you say things that make sense, and the trouble gets settled. You have, on occasion, had to draw your weapon and take a man down. From what I hear in those cases, it was a fair fight. I like that in a man. Did Chad or Slim give you any trouble?"

"Naw. Chad did move his horse down to the barricade, but he kept his eyes on the end of Chip's rifle. He thought it was my rifle, and when Chad started pulling his out of his scabbard, I told him to leave it right there, or he'd be missing a hand."

Thornhill laughed and said, "I bet that made him happy."

I said, "Chad gave it a little thought about trying to outdraw me, but I asked him if he could see my two guns. He went back to your buggy and dismounted. What did you guys decide upon?"

Thornhill smiled at Lola and said, "My men will turn in all their weapons when they come to town, either to a bartender, the Sheriff, or his deputies."

I smiled and asked, "Does that also include their knives?"

With a nod, Thornhill said, "Yes, it does. If my men come to Holbrook for supplies, they will stop at the jail and turn in their weapons. Does that work for you, Mister Gray?"

I said, "If Lola and Sheriff Brownie are happy, then I'm happy. How serious are your bosses thinking of hiring Arizonians to take care of their herd rather than bringing more Texans up this way?"

Thornhill's mouth dropped open for a second or two, and then he said, "How the hell did you know they were thinking of doing that? I got a message today that they wanted to know what I thought. There is no way you would know."

Lola laughed, and Brownie smiled when Norma said, "Mister Thornhill, my husband just knows things. He doesn't know how that happens, but we have all seen it happen. It's kind of amazing."

Shaking his head, Thornhill said, "I'm going to tell my boss that it would be in their best interest to hire Arizona cowboys. And Gray, if you want a job, come see me. I better get going, or Chad will get antsy. Miss Lola, it was a pleasure meeting you. Sheriff Brownie, if you'd care to walk down with me and have some men move a wagon, I'll get my men and cattle out of your way." Thornhill looked at me and said, "Gray, you had me spooked there for a moment. I think I see why you are so fast on the draw; you know before your opponent does when he will draw."

Lola called out to four big guys and told them to go with the Sheriff and move the wagons. Then we all went to the barricade. Thornhill and the Broken Arrow men were soon out of our sight.

Chapter 25

Most of the barricades were gone when Lola approached me and said, "Gray, take your wife home. She says she misses Butch and wants to check on him. The guys we have working right now know where everything needs to go. I'll see you and Norma late tomorrow. If you want to, why don't you put up the gun rack you said would work where I was going to put Brownie's head."

"What about my head?" Brownie asked as he approached Lola and put his arms around her. "Miss White, I have a very fundamental question to ask you. And to be safe, I will ask it before Gray and his beautiful new wife."

Lola tried to turn around, but Brownie held her tight to him. "What kind of question has to be asked in front of Gray?"

I saw Brownie take a deep breath and let some of it out before he said, "Lola White, will you marry me? I know I don't have much to offer you, but…."

Lola shut Brownie up by putting her right index finger over his lips. She said, "Yes, you big idiot, I'll marry you. Your small house will be an excellent place to raise two kids."

Brownie spun Lola around, and their lips met before their arms could tighten around each other.

I pulled Norma into my arms and asked, "How long has Lola been chasing Brownie?"

Norma laughed and said, "She told me it has been since she got to Holbrook. He didn't want anything to do with her as she owned the biggest saloon in town. Brownie started spending time at Lola's Place when he saw that the townspeople accepted Lola. Lola said it was close to a year before she bedded him."

Lola pulled her head back to break the kiss and, with a smile, said, "Brownie, I could stand about forty years, or more, of those kinds of kisses. Now, where are we going to go to celebrate our engagement?"

Brownie smiled and said, "Well, I thought we could go to the jail, but all the beds there are taken. Then, we could use your room at Lola's Place, but we would be interrupted every ten minutes or less, so that won't work. So, it has to be my tiny house. My bed is not as big as yours at the Place, but I know you find it wonderfully comfortable.

"Gray and Norma, as my deputies, I leave the town in your capable hands for the rest of the night. Your first job will be to stop and tell James that Lola will not be back for the night and maybe not until early afternoon."

A few steps away, Brownie stopped and swept Lola up in his arms. They were both laughing when he carried her up the street. I kissed the top of Norma's head and said, "We'll stop and tell James, then go check on Butch. Does that work for you, Missus Gray?"

Norma pulled my head down for a quick kiss and said, "Mister Gray, I like that you asked me rather than trying to tell me what we will do. So, yes, that works for me. I'll pick up a couple of treats for Butch before we go home. Oh, how I love saying that."

I grinned and said, "What treats for Butch?"

Norma moved away from me a couple of feet and then slugged my right shoulder. She glared at me for a few seconds and then started laughing. I scooped her up and carried her to Lola's Place. Just before we arrived, Norma said, "You know what I meant, right?"

"Yes, sweetheart, I know what you meant, and I agree with you. I, too, like that we have a place we can call home. The word does have a lovely ring to it."

When we told James what happened to Lola, he laughed and said, "Damn, all the single men in town are going to be married off soon. And it's about time that fool-headed man got up the nerve to ask Lola. Norma, you know that Lola has been trying to get the man to marry her for a long time. Who's going to get Lola's room?"

I nodded and said, "It better not be Betsy or Jo. Otherwise, you will have a fight like you have never seen before."

"I agree with you, my dear husband," Norma said. "But it will be up to Lola who gets the room and when. Let's get a couple of treats for Butch and go home."

I was about to say something when James asked, "Wait! Norma, you sound like you are taking Butch home with you. I thought he was the town's dog that we all took care of him."

Norma said, "Last night, when Gray and I got home, Butch was sleeping on our bed. I petted him, but he got off the bed, went over to Gray, and put his head upon Gray's lap. When we went to dinner at Simpson's, Gray told Butch to stay and guard the house. Butch laid down on the porch and wouldn't let Lola even get close to the house. Lola came and got us from Simpson's, and when we got back to the cabin, Butch growled at me until my husband told Butch it was okay to let me in. Butch went into the house before us, looking around to ensure it was safe."

James was grinning by the time Norma finished talking. Looking at me, James said, "I would not have thought it possible that Butch would take to you, Gray. But, good luck with him."

I nodded at James and said, "I just hope that Butch continues to take care of the small children around Holbrook. I've seen him wandering from one group of kids to another and then to another. I think he was watching over those kids."

"Gray, I think you're right," James said. "About a week ago, when Fred Tucker left Lola's Place, I saw him grab hold of his son. Butch was there and had his ears back and growling at Fred. The drunk let go of the boy and staggered home. The kid and Butch followed Fred. The next day, Fred's wife told my wife that Fred was going to hit her, and Butch growled at him. The thing was, Butch first knocked Fred over and then stood on his chest as he growled in Fred's face. I don't think Fred has had a drink since that night."

I laughed and said, "Thanks for telling me that, James. Now I know I have a guard for when Norma comes home drunk."

Chapter 26

"What!" Norma exclaimed. "What did you say, Charlie? You better tell me, or I'll make Butch bite you."

James and I were laughing at the funny face that Norma was making at me, and James was finally able to say, "Norma, I think your husband has more control over Butch than you do. Before you interrupted us, I was going to tell Gray that I don't think you will ever come home drunk to the point that Butch will have to protect him."

Norma laughed, saying, "He thinks Butch will be his guard dog against me. Well, we'll see about that when we get home."

"Are you and Gray going to make the Sheriff's rounds tonight?" James asked Norma instead of me. I grinned, and I thought I was doing it only to myself. Was I ever wrong?

"Gray, what are you grinning about?" Norma asked.

"Honey," I said, "I was grinning at the thought that James asked a woman rather than a man if we would both do rounds. Since the Sheriff is a man, I thought James would have asked me instead of you, Norma. And don't get me wrong—I know that women work as hard as most men and that the lady of the households most families together."

"You got that right," Norma said, "It is the wife who holds a family together, and don't you ever forget it. Now, Sweetheart, we must go home and check on our dog. James, do you know if Lola has an old dish in storage that we can use for Butch's water dish?"

James said, "I know just what to get for Butch. I'll be right back."

I heard laughter in the street and looked out at the swinging door. I saw Betsy leaning over the hitching rail out front of the saloon, and a man was about to lower his pants. He was standing behind Betsy.

"The townsfolks won't appreciate what you two are about to do publicly. Betsy, take your gentleman back up to your room."

The guy said, "Hey! Do you know who I am? Oh! Mister Gray, I didn't know it was you. Betsy and I will go right up, and you won't see us again."

Ned Worthington, the town banker, pulled his britches off the ground and fastened his belt. Then he took Betsy by the arm and went to the back of the saloon. Ned opened the back door that led to the steps up to the second floor. As I spoke, I stepped out on the boardwalk, followed Ned, and saw them enter Lola's Place's back door.

I was grinning when I turned around to find Norma and James standing in the doorway to the saloon. Norma asked, "What are you grinning about now?"

I said, "Who in their right mind would bend over the hitching rail and let a man have his way like that in public? Fortunately for them, I stopped it before the deed could happen. They went in the back door and are probably up in her room now."

James asked, "Which one of Lola's girls was it?"

"It was Betsy," I said.

Norma asked, "Who was her gentleman caller?"

I shook my head and said, "I won't say until I have talked to Lola tomorrow. James, you might want to remind all the girls that sex or uncovering of body parts is to be done in their rooms only. Norma, if you got Butch's dish, why don't we take it to him and take the dog with us on our rounds?"

Norma hooked my left arm with her right and said, "See you later, James, and thanks for the dish."

When we got to our cabin, Butch was lying on the porch. Norma called to him, "Come here, Butch, I got treats."

The dog didn't move.

I said, "Butch, let's get some fresh water. Then I'll put the pan by the porch for when you are guarding the house."

Butch stood up with his tail wagging and gave out a loud bark. Then he ran over to me and nudged my left hand.

Norma loudly said, "Butch, you are a traitor. See if I bring you any more treats."

I started to the creek, and Butch let out a yelp and raced ahead of me. The dog drank some water from the stream and then barked at me. I picked up a stick and threw it back toward the cabin. Butch ran after it and caught the stick while it was still in the air. He brought the stick back to me and dropped it at my feet, and, looking up at me, he barked again. After the fourth time, I threw the stick. I told Butch, "That's enough; time to fill the dish and get Norma so we can make rounds as Sherriff Brownie does. Do you want to go with us, Butch?"

I saw some movement off to my right, and Butch saw it too. It was a rabbit, and the dog took after it, barking like mad. I filled the dish with water and carried it up to the cabin.

Norma was on the porch waiting for me. She was petting Butch and smiling at me. As I set the dish on the ground, Norma said, "It was amazing watching you play with Butch. It made me fall in love even more with you, Charlie."

I smiled at my wife and said, "Seeing you standing on the porch with Butch made me feel more in love than I ever thought I could. I love you, Norma Gray, and you too, Butch."

Norma jumped off the porch, and I caught her and swung her around once. We were both laughing. Butch was barking and chasing after Norma's booted feet. As I put Norma back on her feet, she said, "Come on, Butch, the three of us need to make a trip around town."

Butch barked once and started up the tail. "You see that, Charlie? Butch understands us more than we thought."

I let go of Norma, saying, "We better hurry and catch up with him. Sweetheart, do you know if Brownie has a set pattern of where he goes and when?"

We started walking as Norma thought about Brownie for a few moments. Then she said, "No, I don't know. I don't even know what he checks when he makes his rounds."

I grinned and said, "Then we'll stay on the boardwalk until it runs out. When that happens, we'll look for other buildings to check if they are locked up. Should we check both sides of the street before we look at any buildings that don't have a boardwalk, like the Livery?"

Norma said, "You're the man, so it is your decision."

"Oh, no!" I exclaimed. We are doing this together, so we need to agree on where we are going before we get to the boardwalk."

Norma asked, "Where did Butch get off to?"

Chapter 27

The trail from the cabin led us to the boardwalk outside of Lola's Place. I thought Butch would be waiting for us there, but no dog was in sight when Norma and I got to the trail's end.

Norma asked, "Gray, where do you think our dog went?"

In the light from the saloon's open door, I saw dog tracks in the dust. The tracks headed toward the other end of town. I laughed and, pointing, said, "I think Butch might be waiting for us down by the jail."

Norma shook her head, saying, "I guess you got better eyes than I got. I would not have seen those tracks. I guess Butch has made the rounds with Brownie for a time or two. Let's get our dog before Cookie or Nelda see him and take him home with them."

I reached out and stopped Norma as she started walking on the boardwalk. I said, "Let's walk in the street. I want a better feel of the town when most of the lights are off."

Until we got to the jail, Simpson Café was the only open place after leaving Lola's Place. Brownie had left a lantern burning on low, and I could see the light coming out of a high window but on the side of the building. There was also some light coming from around the front door. In that little light, I could just make out Butch. He was acting strangely, sniffing at the door and clawing at it. I stopped Norma and said, "Something is happening in the jail. Look at Butch. He doesn't like what he smells."

I was about twenty feet from the jail porch when Butch turned toward Norma and me. Butch jumped off the porch, ran over to me, and took hold of my left coat sleeve. He started pulling me to the jail. I said, "Okay, Butch, I'll go with you, so let go of me."

The dog let go of me, ran to Norma, and gave her a push from behind. "You want me to go into the jail with Gray? Okay, I'll go. Do you want us to draw our guns first?"

Butch danced around Norma and barked once.

We drew our weapons, and I pushed the door open an inch before Butch knocked it open as he barged into the jail. Butch stopped in the middle of the open floor and, with a shake of his body, let out a long, loud yowl that I was sure could be heard all over town.

The smell of blood hit me as I opened the door, and I could not believe what I saw in the jail cells. All four of the Broken Arrow cowboys were dead. It was carnage; all four had been shot and hacked to pieces. They had also been scalped.

I heard Norma throwing up outside, and I softly said, "Come here, Butch. We were too late. We have to get Sheriff Brownie. Norma is outside, and she needs your help, Butch."

The dog turned and ran out of the jail. I looked around and backed out of the jail, closing the door behind me. My last look in the jail scared the hell out of me. The safe with the dynamite in it was missing, as were all of Brownie's rifles. The shelf above the gun rack was also empty.

When I turned around, I found Norma was being comforted by Cookie and Nelda. I saw a string of people coming down to the jail to see what upset Butch.

James came running down the boardwalk, stopped beside me, and said, "I sent Diego to get Lola and Brownie. What's going on here? We all heard Butch sound the alarm."

I said, "The four Broken Arrow men were killed in their cells. It is a bloody mess in there. The men were scalped. All of Brownie's rifles are missing, along with his ammunition. We all better wait for Brownie before anyone else goes into jail."

James said, "I'll stand before the door while you check on your wife. I take it she saw what you did."

I nodded to James and walked over to Norma. The women hovering around Norma parted for me as I held my hands to her.

Norma said, "Gray, I thought I was stronger than that. I saw the blood and almost threw up in the doorway. I turned away just in time." She looked up at me and said, "Were all four killed?"

I nodded and held Norma close but not too tight. I did not want her to throw up on me, which was possible.

Norma whispered, "Were they all scalped?"

I nodded and whispered, "I had hoped you hadn't seen that."

Speaking a little louder, Norma said, "Who could have done this? Dear God, they were in jail and supposedly under the protection of Sheriff Brownie."

"Okay, folks," Brownie called out as he and Lola got to the back of the crowd. "With James guarding the door, I think it is safe to say the rest of you should go home."

"Sheriff! What did happen?" someone in the crowd called out.

"I don't know," Brownie called back. "I just got here and have not talked to my deputies. So go home, and we'll have a town meeting tomorrow morning."

Lola's stern voice rang out, "As the sheriff said, we'll let everyone know in the morning. It might take the sheriff a little while to figure out what happened. So, go home. Cookie and Nelda are taking care of Norma. Sheriff Brownie has to talk to Gray and Norma if she is up to talking." Lola put her arms out wide and shooed the crowd away.

Norma said, "Cookie, Nelda, thank you both. You, too, can go home as I am in the capable hands of Gray, my dear husband. I assure you that Gray can take care of me."

Ruffling Butch's head, Norma added, "And, ladies, if Gray can't take care of me, then Butch sure will." Cookie and Nelda were laughing when they walked away from the jail.

Brownie said, "Okay! What am I going to find in the jail, Gray?"

I had my left arm around Norma, and I gently squeezed her as I said, "All four of the prisoners are dead. They were shot and cut up, and they were scalped. All your rifles, ammunition, and the safe are missing. I couldn't tell if anything else was missing. We told Butch that we would do rounds tonight, and he ran ahead of us. When we got to the jail, the dog was on the porch sniffing the door and trying to get in. When I opened the door, Butch knocked it all the way open and ran in ahead of me. He stopped in the middle, looked around, and let out the loud yowl I thought everyone heard."

Lola said, "We were too busy to hear the dog. Diego almost knocked down the door to Brownie's house to get us to come here. Norma, where were you when Gray was in the jail?"

Norma said, "I was standing in the doorway. I saw that the acting foreman was scalped, and blood was everywhere. My stomach didn't like what I saw, and tossed everything I'd eaten today. Luckily, I did it off to the side of the porch."

Brownie took a deep breath and said, "James, thanks for guarding the door. On your way home, will you tell the undertaker he is needed here? He needs to hold four bodies until Mister Thornhill gets here tomorrow. Thornhill might want the bodies sent back to Texas for burial."

James nodded and said, "I'll let the Undertaker know."

Chapter 28

As Brownie reached for the handle of the jailhouse door, Norma said, "I'll stay out here with Butch; he doesn't need to see that again."

"Fine with me," Brownie said. "You coming in with me, Gray?"

I said, "Yeah. Something didn't seem right, and I wanted to take another look before Undertaker moves the bodies."

Lola said, "I'll stay with Norma for a few minutes. When she feels up to it, we'll return to Lola's Place and have a drink. I'll give Butch a treat for being such a good dog. You two go on in the jail and open the windows immediately. You need to air the place out."

I kissed Norma and stepped away from her before I said, "Don't get Butch so drunk he can't guard me when we get home."

Lola and Brownie gave me a blank stare as Norma started laughing, then Butch gave out some small barks like he was saying that Norma would be okay. With a shake of her head, Norma said, "I love you, Charles Gray, and I promise not to let our dog get too drunk. Now, go in there and figure out what happened to those men. Lola and I are going to the place to relax."

Brownie kissed Lola, and we watched the ladies walk up the boardwalk toward Lola's Place. Butch was walking beside Norma. Brownie finally said, "Let's get this over with."

When Brownie and I stepped into the Jail, he went to his desk, and I stepped carefully to the nearest cell. "Shit!" Brownie exclaimed. "They even took the spare pistol I had under the bottom draw. Those weapons are going to end up in the hands of some drunk."

"You are probably right," I said. Then I asked, "Brownie, have you ever seen a man who an Indian scalped?"

"Yeah. When I was an Army Sergeant, our company commander sent us to track down a band of Indians causing trouble in New Mexico. Our company came across a ranch where everyone was dead. It was a family of five and three ranch hands. All the men were scalped, and the two women had their throats cut."

I asked, "Did the scalp markings look like these men?"

Brownie looked at the four dead cowboys in his jail, and finally, he looked at me and said, "If you mean were they as clean and smooth of cuts as these, I will say hell no. They were quick, rough cuts, not as smooth as these guys. Gray, are you telling me that an Indian did not do the scalping?"

I nodded and added, "See those tracks in the blood over in the other cell? Those are boot tracks, not from moccasins. Someone went to a lot of trouble to make it look like Indians did these killings."

"Okay," Brownie said, "but knowing that, where does that leave us?"

"That leaves us checking out Ned Worthington's bank."

"Shit! The dynamite! You think someone will use that to blow open the bank's safe."

"It's been known to happen, yes."

Brownie grinned at me and said, "What are you waiting for; let's go."

"Let the Undertaker and his helper take the bodies, and we'll check the bank."

"Are you two done in here?" Undertaker said from the doorway.

Brownie looked at the man and said, "Yeah. I need to go out to the Broken Arrow Ranch and find out what the foreman wants to do with the bodies. He might want to take them back to Texas for burial. Can you store them somewhere?"

Undertaker said, "I'll take care of that, Sheriff, don't you worry. Do you want us to clean up as much blood as possible when we finish?"

"Yes. I would appreciate that very much," Brownie said. Undertaker gave Brownie a quick nod, turned to his helper, and waved him in.

Brownie and I headed for the bank. As we walked up the boardwalk, Brownie said, "Gray, take the right side of the bank, and I'll take the left. We'll meet in the back."

I stopped walking and held up one finger of my right hand, then I shut my eyes and thought of Butch. When I opened my eyes, I heard Norma call out, "Butch, you get back here! Where are you going, Butch?"

Butch came running down the boardwalk and stopped in front of me. His tail was flapping like crazy. I petted his head and said, "Butch, Brownie, and I need you to go with us to check out the bank. If you smell those bad guys again, you let us know. Okay?"

Butch gave out a loud bark and walked beside me when we crossed the street to the bank building.

With a bit of a laugh, Brownie said, "You think that dog will smell the guys that did the killings, right?"

I nodded and said, "It's worth a shot. Butch got their scent when they came out of the jail. Didn't he find a little girl that was lost?"

"Yeah, but the girl's mother let Butch smell the girl's blanket. Where would Butch have gotten the killer's scent?"

"From the doorsill and the porch. Your smell would have been strong there, but so would the last person who walked across the porch. I think Butch has the smell of at least one of the killers."

We were almost to the bank when I felt Norma was behind me. Without turning around, I said, "Norma, will you and Lola stay right where you are? I want Butch to snoop around a little. I got a feeling the killers might be after the money in the bank's safe."

"Gray, do you think the killer will use the dynamite on the safe?" Norma said, "Well, if you get yourself killed, Gray, I'll never speak to you again. I'll stay right here and wait for you. I love you, Charles Gray."

Lola said, "And I love you, Brownie, so I'll wait here with Norma."

Butch trotted on ahead as Brownie and I went down the left side of the building. The floor of the bank was about three feet off the ground. The safe inside the bank needed good support, and there were four posts under the floor where the safe sat.

Suddenly Butch stopped walking and lowered his nose to the ground. I saw him look under the bank and start to growl. I said, "Good boy, Butch. Come here." When Butch was beside me, I called, "This is Deputy Gray. Whoever is under the bank better come out now."

We waited in silence.

Chapter 29

James approached Lola and asked, "What's going on, Boss?"

"I'm not exactly sure. Gray had Butch sniffing around for something to do with dynamite, and now Gray told whoever was under the bank to come out. We're just waiting."

I called out, "James, bring me your scattergun."

James approached me and asked, "You want me to blast somebody?"

"No," I said. "Give the gun to Brownie. Then you and I are going to the other side of the bank. The Sheriff will give them a warning and then fire off one round. If that doesn't bring them out, he'll fire another round. If you have any extra shells with you, give them to Brownie."

James and I had just made it to the other side of the bank when the Sheriff called out, "On the count of three, I'm going to fire. ONE! TWO! THREE!"

There was the sound of crawling, and three men emerged from under the bank. I said, "Hold it right there, boys. Touch your iron, and you will be dead. I'm Gray, and I think you boys have heard of me. You three stay right like you are, on your hands and knees. I think Sheriff Brownie is going to want to talk to you."

Brownie walked up behind James and me and gave the shotgun back to James, saying. "Thanks for the use of it. So, what kind of snakes came out from under the bank? Shit, I just got a flyer on these three. They are wanted for bank robbery and murder over in New Mexico, Oklahoma, and Kansas."

I saw one of the outlaws reaching for something, so I put a bullet right next to his hand. All three of the boys stopped moving. Brownie took their guns and knives. A fuse was hanging out the back pocket of one of the men, and Brownie took that as well.

Then the Sheriff said, "You men stand up, and James, keep your scattergun on them while we take them to Jail."

I said, "Sheriff Brownie, can you hold up on that for a little while? I want to look behind the bank and see if their horses are tied there."

Norma approached me and said, "I'll go with you, Gray. Two sets of eyes are better than one."

I grinned at Norma and said, "Okay, and Butch can go with us."

We were at the corner of the back wall of the bank when Butch gave out a low growl. I looked around the corner and saw a man reaching out to untie his horse in the moonlight. I said, "Hold it right there."

The man spun around as his left hand drew his pistol. My gun was already in my hand, and I wasn't aiming for his weapon. My shot hit the man in the heart. The outlaw's gun had not cleared his holster, and he could still fire once. The bullet went into the ground.

Brownie called out, "What happened, Gray?"

I called out, "A fourth man was going to hightail it out of town. He tried to draw down on me but was too slow. I think I got him in the heart. His shot went into the ground."

"How many horses have got back there?" Brownie called out.

"Just four of them," I said. "Go ahead and take your prisoners to jail. Norma and I will bring the horses down there after Undertaker comes and gets this body. And Sheriff, I need a torch or lamp to see this guy's face. I think it might be our friend Dagobert from the way he moved. And the guy lied about being unable to draw and shoot with his left hand."

Lola said, "Gray, I'll bring you an oil lamp. Will that be bright enough?"

"That will work, Lola. Thanks." I called back.

I heard everyone leave, and at least two of them were limping. I grinned, and I guess my teeth showed up in the moonlight as Norma said, "Charlie, why are you grinning? There is nothing funny in a man's death."

"Sweetheart, you're right. But I wasn't grinning about this guy. Did you happen to hear that two of those outlaws are walking with a limp? Doctor Roth is going to have to remove some shotgun pellets from those two."

"Oh," Norma said. "I wasn't listening to the men walk away. I was wondering how Dagobert ended up with those other outlaws. Honey, do you have any idea?"

"I guess they could have found Dag on the trail and nursed him back to feeling like coming back to Holbrook to pay the town back for what I did to him."

Norma was quiet for a moment, then said, "That seems like such a waste. You are letting Dagobert go back to Texas only to have him come back here to die."

"Yeah, I see what you mean," I said. "Sweetheart, it might be God's way. He saw that Dagobert would not change his ways, so he brought him back here for me to finish my job."

Norma thought momentarily, then said, "I guess that's possible."

We suddenly stood in a ring of light as Lola came around the bank building with an oil lamp. She had the lamp's wick turned up so the flame was bright. I looked down at the dead cowboy and said, "Damn it, Dag, why the hell did you come back?" I could see his right hand was doctored up with a lot of white cloth.

Norma said, "Ah, hell, Charlie, I'm sorry for you. You tried to help the guy out, but he didn't listen. His death is not your fault."

"Mister Gray, that's the outlaw you let ride away," Undertaker said as he stepped past Lola. "I saw him ride out of town after you shot him. What do you want to be done with him?"

I said, "Get Digger and put him somewhere in the graveyard."

Undertaker and his helper put Dagobert on a wide plank while Norma and I gathered the outlaw's horses. Lola headed back to her saloon. Neither Norma nor I wanted to ride the horses, so we walked to the jail, leading two horses each. Brownie took all the weapons we found in the saddlebags and rolled in the outlaw's bedding. Then Norma and I took the animals to the livery. Chip was not there, so we unharnessed the horses and left everything besides the Livery building. We put the horses in the pasture.

Norma asked, "What happens to all the outlaw's things?" as we walked away from the Livery.

I put my arm around her and said, "Norma, I think Sheriff Brownie will try to find out if they had any kin, and if they do, he'll ask if they want any of it. At least, that is what I think will happen. Where did Butch get off to?"

Chapter 30

Butch was not outside the jail when Norma and I got back there. We went into the jailhouse and found that Sheriff Brownie was finishing up paperwork on his guests. The outlaws were all in one cell since a man was cleaning the second cell. The place still had the smell of death.

"Glad you two stopped in," Brownie said. "Are you ready to help take these guys to Winslow? It's about thirty miles between here and Winslow. So, I'm guessing it will take a week to get there and back home."

Norma asked, "When were you planning on going?"

"I'm sending a telegraph to the sheriff in Winslow in the morning. I need to make sure he has room for these three. I'll know more when I hear back from him."

I asked, "Have you discussed this with Lola? She is the Mayor of Holbrook, right? She might not want Holbrook without a sheriff or deputy for that long."

Brownie grinned at me, and Norma spoke up. "If you're not going to tell Lola what is going on, I will. Come on, Charles. We need to go talk to Lola."

"Now, Norma, give the man time to think. I think Brownie just came up with the idea of taking the men to Winslow."

"That's right, Norma," Sheriff Brownie said. "I thought of going to Winslow just before you entered the jailhouse. We can all see Lola. She is our boss, after all."

When we entered the saloon, Ned Worthington was sitting at Lola's table. Betsy was sitting on the chair beside Ned, draped all over him. I didn't see any of the other girls.

There was a commotion at the top of the wide stairs to the second floor. We all turned to look as a cowboy called out, "Lola, what kind of place are you running? The cowboy was holding onto Jo by her hair. He was dragging her behind him as they came down the stairs.

"Mister McCall, what has Jo done that's upset you? And why are you holding your pants and not wearing them?" The guy was wearing a union suit.

McCall was at the bottom of the stairs and marching Jo over to Lola's table. The crowd of men and women moved aside as McCall approached them. The women were staring at him, and the men were salivating over the sight of Jo's breasts. I know they were the biggest I had ever seen.

"When I was putting on my underwear, I caught this bitch going through my pants pockets. I saw her take a wad of money out of my pocket and stuff it down her pantaloon. Or whatever you call those things she is wearing. Now, Lola, you know I've been coming here a long time and never had any trouble with your ladies before."

Sheriff Brownie said, "McCall, let the lady go. We need to hear what she has to say.'

McCall glared at Sheriff Brownie a moment, then let Jo go, giving her a little push, so she bumped into Brownie. Then McCall started to put on his pants.

"Don't put those on just yet," Brownie said. "I may need to check them after I hear what Jo has to say."

"But Sheriff, I…"

"Mister McCall, you need to stuff yourself back into your union suit and shut up," Lola said.

"I…"

Lola raised her hand, palm out toward McCall. "Jo, what do you have to say?"

"He's lying, Lola. We had sex, and I got up to wash, but he wanted me to do something I wouldn't do. The guy got mad, and I thought he was about to hit me. I grabbed his pants and tossed them to him. I didn't take his money. I tried to run out of the room, but he grabbed my hair and brought me down here."

Brownie said, "McCall, give me your pants."

"But Sheriff, that is not how it happened," McCall said in an irritated tone.

Brownie motioned for McCall to give him the pants. The guy handed over his pants to Brownie, and the Sheriff patted one of the front pockets, then reached into it and pulled out some money.

"See!" Jo exclaimed, "I told you I didn't take his fucking money."

I saw that McCall was staring at what Brownie was holding. So, I asked, "Sheriff, is there anything in the other pocket?"

Brownie stuck his hand into the other pocket and said, "Nothing there."

Before anyone said anything else, I said, "Lola, you and Norma need to take Jo into your office and check her clothes." I added, "And do it now!"

With Jo protesting, the ladies went into the office and shut the door. I looked at McCall and said, Mister McCall, "You know she might claim that any money they find is hers. How will the Sheriff know any money they find is yours?"

McCall said, "Why would she have her own money stuffed in her clothes? I sure never felt any bulge of money when I was fucking her. That bitch took my money, and god damn it; I'm going to get it back from her.

While McCall and I talked, Sheriff Brownie counted the money he found in McCall's pocket. "Mister McCall, how much money did you have on you when you went upstairs with Jo?" Sheriff Brownie asked.

"There should be a little over two thousand dollars in that pile you have and another thirteen hundred in the missing pile."

Brownie smiled at McCall and said, "You got that mixed up. I got thirteen here." Sheriff Brownie tossed McCall his pants and told him, "Put your pants back on. I'll hold this money until this inquest is over."

"But that's my money, Sheriff. You just found it in my pants pocket. I want it back."

"You'll get it back after the ladies return to the table. Now put your pants on and shut the hell up."

McCall finished buttoning his britches as Lola returned to the table and said, "I had Jo take off her pantaloons, and the only money there was this three hundred dollars I have in my hand. As you can see, Sheriff, the money is all in small bills. There was no other money. How much is McCall saying is missing?"

"He said over two thousand dollars is missing."

"Will, I didn't take it!" Jos exclaimed.

McCall asked, "Well, where the fuck did it go?"

I said, "Why don't we all go to Jo's room and look for the money?"

There were five of us in Jo's room when we looked for the missing money. We searched as well as we could but with no luck. The money was not there.

Sheriff Brownie finally said, "I don't think your money is here, Mister McCall. What do you think, sir?"

"I got to agree with you, Sheriff, but I sure don't know where the hell it went," McCall said. "And, Jo, I'm sorry I mistreated you and called you a thief."

"That's okay, McCall," Jo said. "I forgive you, and next time you're in town, maybe we can discuss what I wouldn't do for you."

McCall laughed and said, "Thank you, Jo. I look forward to seeing you soon."

I saw a gun belt and holster on the floor, partly covered with a blouse. Something green was sticking out of the holster, and I asked, "McCall, is that your gun belt on the floor?"

"Yes, Gray, it is. Thanks for seeing it. Shit, I know where the missing money is. I stuck it down in my holster. I should have remembered where the money was, as I had difficulty hooking the hammer tiedown in place. I'm sorry, everyone, especially you, Jo. I was an idiot."

We all laughed, and Lola and Jo hugged McCall and kissed him. Then, we all went down to the bar for one last drink.

Chapter 31

We laughed when Norma and Butch, the traitor, came out of Lola's office. Norma came over and kissed me, then said, "Where did you find the money? In his boots?"

"No, Sweetheart, stuffed in his holster. I guess Jo is good enough to take all his memory away for a while."

Norma giggled, then whispered, "I bet I'm also that good."

I whispered, "You are way better. I can't remember anything for an hour or more after we have sex."

With a laugh, Norma looked over at Lola and said, "Boss, I have a couple of questions. Can we go to the office for a minute?"

Lola stood up, leaned over, and kissed Brownie before saying, "Sure, let's go."

The ladies entered the office, and McCall said, "I'm returning to the hotel and getting a few hours of sleep. I need to head back to the ranch tomorrow. Good night, everyone." He then pulled Jo to himself and hugged her. They kissed, and McCall walked out of Lola's Place.

Brownie said, "Gray, let's do a walk around town. I'll show you what I look for when doing rounds."

I laughed and said, "With all the excitement, I forgot all about doing rounds. I bet you start your rounds from the jailhouse."

"Yeah, but we can start here if you want. How did you figure out I started from the jail?"

"Norma and I found Butch waiting for us on your porch. He was going to go with us on our rounds."

Brownie petted Butch and asked, "Butch, are you ready to do rounds?"

With a yelp, the dog stood up, tail wagging like crazy. I said, "Okay, Butch, we will start from here and walk a different way. So, you be a good dog and stay right beside me."

As Brownie and Butch started to walk away, I said, "Wait a moment. I need to tell Norma and Lola that we are leaving." I dashed to Lola's office and opened the door without knocking. I closed the door behind me.

Lola looked at me and asked, "What's going on, Gray?"

I said, "Just wanted to let you and Norma know that...."

"WHAT DO YOU MEAN I CAN'T GO IN THERE? JAMES, I'M THE SHERIFF, AND I CAN GO WHERE I PLEASE."

We didn't hear James reply because the two ladies and I laughed too loud. Finally, Lola said, "Gray, you better let the sheriff come in."

I opened the door, and a sputtering Brownie came in. He was red from embarrassment. Brownie said, "Lola, your damn bartender pointed his shotgun at me. He said I wasn't allowed in here. What does he mean by that?"

Lola stood tall and, in a stern voice, said, "James is doing just what I told him to do. And Gray has the same orders, so he closed the door in your face."

The sheriff frowned and said, "I don't understand. What did you tell your men?"

Still standing tall, Lola said, "I told them that when Norma and I are here working, no one is to come in other than James or Gray when they need to tell me something important. My girls aren't even allowed in during that time. Why would you be any different?"

Brownie was silent for a couple of moments, then said, "So when you two are working in here, I can't come in and get a kiss from you. Is that what you're saying?"

"Yes, dear, it is. Norma is new at this job, and I want her to get it right. I hate bookkeeping almost as much as you do, Brownie."

"Oh," a sad Brownie uttered.

Lola softened her voice and said, "Now, come over here and kiss me. Then you and Gray go do your rounds."

"You can go only after I get my kiss from Gray," Norma said.

By the chime of the big clock out in the bar area, Brownie and I were in the office for fifteen minutes. I saw that Butch was sleeping behind the bar while waiting for us. The three of us did rounds.

Brownie checked or had me check the back door of each business in town. Behind the Hardware Store were two young cowboys asleep on their horses. Brownie knew the boys, and after rousting them, he sent them on their way back to the Crooked S Ranch. One cowboy tried to explain why they were there when he said, "Sheriff, we were waiting for Joe Shiner. He told us to wait here for him."

Brownie said, "Boys, I know you are fairly new to the Crooked S and probably not used to his pranks. I saw Joe and his wife leave town about four hours ago. If you hurry, you might get a few hours of sleep before breaking the new horses that Joe told me about."

The talkative cowboy said, "Thanks for waking us, Sheriff. When Joe finds out that we stayed right where he left us, we'll be laughed right off the ranch. If the cook doesn't see us, we should be able to sneak into the bunkhouse and get some sleep. Come on, Jeb, we got some riding to do. See you later, Sheriff."

When the cowboys were gone, I asked, "Does this sort of thing happen very often?"

"No, it's usually a couple of cowboys asleep between buildings. Once, Joe told a new cowboy to wait for him outside the hardware store. When the owner closed up for the night, he left the cowboy asleep in one of the chairs out front. When I woke that kid, he didn't know what to do. His horse was at the Livery but closed for the night. I had to wake Chip to go down and help the kid with his horse. That kid didn't stay at the Crooked S for more than a month after that incident."

As we passed an open field, we heard the baying of a donkey coming from the area. Brownie called out to find out if someone was there, but no answer. Brownie looked at me and said, "There shouldn't be a horse or donkey out there. We better check and see what is going on."

I said, "Okay, Butch, find that donkey."

The dog ran out into the field, and a bit later, he barked twice, and the donkey started baying loudly. Brownie asked, "You know anyone with a donkey?"

"The only donkeys I've seen around here were all with elderly Indians. Maybe one of them is out there, or it could be an old miner come down from the mountains north of here."

Brownie said, "We best check it out."

Chapter 32

When we got close to Butch and the donkey, I saw that it looked like a miner passing through Holbrook. He smelled like he hadn't bathed in quite a while. The donkey calmed down, and Butch quit barking.

Brownie said, "Looks like he is a miner, and it smells like he has been up in the country for some time. I should wake him and find out who he is and why he is sleeping here?"

"Can't a man get a little sleep without being bothered by a dog and fool people?" the miner said as he sat up. "Where are your horses, and why are you on foot?"

"Our horses are in the Livery, and I'm Sheriff Brownie of Holbrook, Arizona. You, my friend, are sleeping in the middle of town. We were doing our rounds, and your donkey started baying at us. Since there usually is nothing in this field, we came to see who's donkey was out here."

"Well, don't that beat all! I was on my way to Flagstaff and must have gotten turned around out there on the painted desert. Holbrook, you say! I'm way off course; it's no wonder I can't find any gold."

Brownie asked, "What happened that got you so far off course? You're a long way from Flagstaff."

"A few days ago, my damn donkey kicked me in the head when he was stomping on a snake that was about to get in my bedroll. Since then, I've been having trouble seeing in the bright light of day and traveling at night. The morning after I got kicked, I thought I saw mountains in this direction, so I've been headed this way since then. I see the mountains when I first wake up in the morning, and they are there for most of the day; then they haze over, and I'm not sure which way to go, so I let my damn donkey lead us by riding on him. I fell asleep this afternoon, and it was dark when he finally stopped walking. I must have fallen off of him cause the next thing I know is your dog barking."

Brownie said, "Well, I would let you sleep in the jail, but it is kind of full right now."

The miner said, "That's okay, Sheriff. If you don't mind, I would rather stay right here for the rest of the night. Is there a place in town where I can bathe and get cleaned up?"

"There is a bathhouse behind the hotel, but it is for paying guests of that establishment. I don't know if you can use it if you are not a guest."

I said, "Sheriff, I think Bella Wright, Tommy's mother, and June are taking in laundry, but I don't know if they are doing baths. If your friend has another set of clean clothes, he might want to try there."

"Shit, I plum forgot about them," Brownie said. "Sir, when it is light enough to see, follow the road to the left, and less than a mile down it, there is a small cabin that Mister Gray is talking about. You got any money to pay for the wash?"

"Yes, Sheriff, I surely do," the miner said. "Perhaps there is something I can do for the ladies instead of paying for the wash. I can do that if Tommy that Mister Gray spoke of, can't cut firewood.

I appreciate all the information, Sheriff; thank you, sir, and you to Mister Gray."

We left the Miner so he could get back to sleep and continued our rounds. Brownie and I talked about the miners as we walked around the town. We also talked about Jane and Tommy. When Tommy asked for a job at the Livery, Chip had him go out and bring in the horses for the stagecoach when it came through. It seems that Chip had just got a contract with the stagecoach to board six horses to be traded out when the stage came through Holbrook. It appears that Tommy had a way with the animals, and he had them in the Livery and harnessed up faster than even Chip could do. Tommy got his job. I also knew Tommy got up early to cut firewood for his ladies to use during the day. The miner was going to have his work cut out for him.

Brownie checked on his prisoners at the jail and moved one of them to the second cell. There was no complaining from the men, and Brownie turned the oil lamp he had off, and we left the jail. On the way back to Lola's place, I asked, "Brownie, do you know if those three had a larger gang of followers?"

Brownie shook his head and said, "From the posters I've seen, I would say not, but the posters were a few years old. I'm surprised they are still alive."

"I was trying to figure out why they were all so subdued. I think it might be the smell of blood in your fine establishment." We were outside the Country Mercantile, and I stopped dead, still in my tracks. The hairs on the back of my neck were on edge. As I spun around, I pushed Brownie out into the street. My pistol was out and trained on the two men behind Brownie and me.

"Gray, don't shoot. It's Mister Thornhill and me," Chad called out. "We just got back to town and saw Sheriff Brownie and you walk out of the jail. We wanted to turn our weapons in before we got rooms at the hotel. Thornhill is expecting some people on the stagecoach tomorrow, and he wanted to get here well ahead of them."

"Who are you expecting on the stagecoach?" Brownie asked.

Thornhill said, "I got a telegraph that said my boss and her friend would be on the stage. I was to meet them here. When I returned to Broken Arrow, the telegraph was waiting for me. Chad and I got fresh mounts and came right back here. But first, we washed the trail dust off and changed into clean clothes. Sheriff, do you want our weapons now, or can we bring them to you in the morning."

Brownie laughed and said, "Morning would be fine. I do appreciate that you took the time to let me know you were turning in your weapons."

Chad said, "Sheriff, I know it is late, but do you think Mister Thornhill and I could get a drink at Lola's Place? It looks like the lights are still on there."

I laughed and said, "Chad, the lights are still on because my wife is waiting for me, and Lola is waiting for Sheriff Brownie. I think I can talk them into letting you have one drink."

"But only one," Brownie said with a laugh.

Chapter 33

Norma and I didn't stick around to see how many drinks Thornhill and Chad had to drink. We took Butch and went to our cabin. To say that we went right to sleep would be a lie. I was still talking about the old miner sleeping in the grass when Butch put his head on my lap.

Norma laughed, saying, "I think your dog is trying to tell you it is time for bed."

So that is what we did, and I woke at first light to let Butch outside. As I turned around after closing the door, I found my wife curling her finger at me. Our lovemaking was fast and fun-filled. I didn't want it to end, but it did when Butch started barking like crazy. Then I heard a donkey loudly baying.

"Charlie, what's going on out there?"

I laughed and said, "My guess is the old miner has come to call. How he found out where we live, I don't know. Do you want me to go out and chase him away?"

It was Norma's turn to laugh, and then she said, "No. Let's get dressed and then go out to see what he wants. You can always toss him in the creek if he smells too bad."

Butch was barking while Norma and I were talking and getting dressed. Norma and I had another good laugh when we stepped outside. We saw what was disturbing Butch. The old miner and his donkey were both in the creek, and the miner was washing the donkey. It looked to me like the miner had also bathed himself. His long johns were all soapy and in need of a good rinse.

"Old Timer, what are you doing in my part of the creek?" I called out.

The miner stopped soaping his donkey and sat down in the creek. In doing so, he also pulled the donkey down with him. The animal quickly stood up and stomped out of the stream, where he shook off the excess water.

On standing up, the miner walked out of the creek and stood on the bank, looking up at us. "Mister Gray, I apologize for using your creek, but I didn't think you would be willing to talk to me when I smelled so bad. After you and the Sheriff left last night, I remember things I was going to do before my donkey kicked me in the head. Norma, the darn fool animal, didn't mean to kick me; it was an accident. He was killing a snake trying to get into my bedroll."

"Do I know you?" Norma asked.

"You'll recognize me when I shave off this beard," the miner said. "You may not recognize my voice, as it has gotten rather raspy over the years. Your mother, Isabella, was an amazing lady. And, I mean lady most wondrously. You two could have passed as twins. Even from this distance, I can tell your eyes are as green as hers were. I miss your mother every day. It was the itch of gold that drew us apart. I needed to search for the Mother Lode, but your mother finally put her foot down and told me that I could not return if I went prospecting again. Well, the itch got to me, and I left. When I returned two years later, your mother moved on, and I returned to prospecting."

Norma was standing to my left, and as the miner talked, she took hold of my left hand and squeezed it tightly. When the miner finished speaking, Norma quietly said, "It sounds like you are saying you are my father?"

The miner said, "Yes, I am. My name is Dalton Whitmore, and you are named after my mother, Norma Elizabeth Whitmore."

"Where the hell have you been for most of my life? I remember my mom with a very skinny little man. Mom said that he was my father. You filled out some and grew a few inches, if that was you. How do you explain a little man being almost as tall as my husband?"

Dalton said, "When I met Isabell, I was a skinny man, but I filled out toting my pack up in the mountains. After I left your mother, for some reason, I had a growth spurt in my height and my feet, arms, and hands. When it was happening, I stopped a doctor outside his office and asked him if it was normal for a man to have another growth. He said it sometimes happens that way.

"As to where I have been for all these years. Well, I was up in what they call Alaska for a good part of the time. Another miner I met talked me into hunting for gold in that godforsaken county with him. I came back almost a year ago and have been searching for you since then. I hear that Isabell died and that she had become a lady of the night. I had a hard time believing that could happen to her. I thought she had gotten remarried, and maybe to that teacher-man who was hanging around the house. Then I got word that there was a green-eyed beauty here in Holbrook. I'm here, wanting to talk to you. Norma, I know you probably don't believe me, but I loved your mother very much."

"Well, I'm not sure I want to talk to you," Norma said. Turning around, she went back into the cabin and slammed the door.

I looked at Norma's Father and said, "Sir, for what it is worth, I believe you. Now it looks like your long johns are about to dry. Why don't you get dressed in your cleanest clothes while I talk to Norma? I'm not promising I can get her to talk to you, but I'll try for both of you. The dog's name is Butch, but I don't know if he'll let you get close to the cabin without one of us out here."

"Thank you, Mister Gray. It is Dalton. I'll wait here with my no-name donkey."

I found Norma sitting at our table, crying. I hugged and held her in my arms while sitting on a stool. When the tears stopped flowing, I said, "Sweetheart, I'm going to take him down to Bella, Jane, and Tommy's place. Maybe he could cut wood for them instead of paying them to wash his clothes. Maybe they'll take him on as a border for cutting wood and helping the ladies with their work. Tommy has to get to the Livery fairly early to prepare for the stagecoach. I think you need to talk to him, but not right now. When I get back, you and I will have breakfast at Simpson Café."

"Don't take too long, my dear husband, as I'm getting kind of hungry," Norma said. "And I get cranky when I'm hungry."

I grinned at her and said, "Just like your mother."

Norma gasped and said, "How did you know? I never told you that was how she got."

I said, "Sometimes I feel things and know they are true, and that is what it felt like to me when you said you get cranky. The thought hit me just like your mother, and I said it out loud. Now I have to go if I'm going to be back before you're cranky. I love you, Norma. Take care of Butch while I'm gone."

Chapter 34

Dalton Whitmore and I walked to Bella's home and talked along the way. Dalton was several inches shorter than me, but I could tell he was strong enough. He had the weathered face of a man who had lived outside most of his life. His boots looked reasonably new, not worn over or ripped up. I said, "Dalton, I noticed your boots are much newer than the rest of your gear. Why is that?"

"Well, when I came through Cheyanne, Wyoming, my old faithful boots fell apart. I stepped over a log, and it was onto bare, hard rocks when my right foot hit the ground. The bottom of the boot just fell off. The left boot was no better. I forked over some good money for these walking boots, and they fit much better than my old ones. I didn't realize that leather rots away like that. Gray, how long have you had that hat you're wearing?"

I laughed and said, "Eight or nine years, I guess. It's just now getting to where it fits properly on my head. Dalton, I have to ask. How long were you planning on sticking around Holbrook? Not that I'm chasing you off or that you have to leave, but Norma will want to know."

"The question you have to ask," Dalton said, "is how long is Norma going to be working as a lady of the night?"

"That was taken care of before Norma and I got married. Circuit Judge Moore was one of Norma's steady clients, and when he got back to town, he was a little upset when he found out that Norma and I were engaged to be married. Norma is now the accountant for

Lola White, the owner of a good deal of Holbrook. Sheriff Brownie has appointed both Norma and me as his deputies."

"Wow!" Dalton exclaimed. "I didn't know that Norma was good with numbers. Of course, there is not much I know about her since I've been out of her life for most of it. Gray, do you know if Norma was ever married before you two got hitched?"

I shook my head and said, "No, I don't. We talked about her having a boyfriend when she was younger. She never mentioned being married before."

It was Dalton's turn to laugh, but it was more of a giggle. He finally said, "Sorry about that. It's just that you mentioned Norma's former boyfriend. Well, he was the fella who led me to Holbrook. I guess the man has been in love with Norma for years."

"So, whose place is this we're going to again?"

"Bella Wright owns the house. Her husband died in a gunfight that he was not even involved in. A stray bullet hit and killed him. Her son Tommy and his fiancé June live with Bella. Bella and June have opened a laundry business, and Tommy works at the Livery. Chip, the owner of the Livery, recently got a contract to provide horses for the stagecoach that comes through Holbrook. I was thinking that you could maybe talk Bella into doing your laundry, and for payment, you could cut firewood for the ladies and do whatever other work they might have."

"Does Norma know where you are taking me and why?"

"Yes, Dalton, she does. And the only thing she said about it was that I needed to hurry back to her so we could go to breakfast. She said she gets cranky when she is hungry."

This time, Dalton laughed long before saying, "Just like her mother used to get."

I chuckled and said, "Yeah, she mentioned that her mother got that way, too. Bella's house is right ahead of us. Let's go see what she has to say."

I introduced Dalton to Bella, Tommy, and June, and then Dalton started talking to Bella. When I left, they were all sitting down to eat breakfast. The donkey with no name was tied out back of the house. I fast-walked, almost a run, back to Norma and Butch. When I got to our cabin, neither one was home. Before going to Lola's Place to find Norma, I cleaned up the cabin and made our bed. I was going to put out some water for Butch when I heard a low growl outside the door. Then I heard Cookie say, "Now, Butch, what's gotten into you? And why are you lying on Norma and Gray's porch?"

The next growl was louder and more meaningful. I opened the door slowly, saying, "Cookie, you better stay right where you are."

Cookie asked, "What's going on with this dog?"

I said, "It's okay, Butch. Cookie is a friend."

With his tail twitching like mad, Butch got off the porch and went right to Cookie. He was rewarded with a hug from her. When Cookie stood up, she said, "From what I just saw, I take it that Butch has become your guard dog."

I grinned at Cookie and asked, "Why aren't you getting ready for your morning customers?"

"Because your wife, who would be Norma, stopped by the café and said that you two would be coming for breakfast after you returned from taking her father somewhere. I didn't know that Norma's father was in town, and your wife didn't stick around long enough for me to ask her. Gray, what's going on here? Your wife took off up the street like a hornet was after her."

I said, "Let me give you the short version of what happened. Last night, Brownie and I found a man sleeping in the open field in the center of town. The man was bathing his donkey and himself in Swan Creek right by our cabin this morning. He claims to be Norma's father, but she hasn't seen her father since she was a girl. He wants to get to know her, but Norma is unsure she wants to know him. I took the man down to Bella Wright's place to see if he could get his clothing washed. The man seemed to get along with everyone there."

Cookie frowned a moment, then said, "Okay. Now, what about Butch? I know you guys brought him some scraps, but I didn't know he was guarding your cabin."

I laughed and said, "When Norma and I got home the other night, Butch was in the cabin. We don't know how he got in. After Norma petted Butch and talked to him, the dog came over to me while I was sitting on a stool. He put his head in my lap, and his tail went crazy. I put some water out for him on the porch and told him to stay, which he did. Lola came by the cabin yesterday morning when Norma and I were having breakfast. Butch would not let Lola get close to the cabin. Lola came to the Café and got us, and we all went to the cabin. Butch wouldn't let Norma get in the cabin until I said it was okay. Norma opened the door, and before she could step in, Butch went in and stood in the doorway, looking around to make sure no unwanted callers were in there."

Cookie laughed and said, "Gray, you've got yourself a good dog. I'll see you and Norma at breakfast." Then she turned and walked back towards her Café.

Chapter 35

As we talked, Cookie gave me a few steak bones from the previous night. When she first got to the cabin, Cookie had tried to give one of the bones to Butch, but he ignored it and growled at her instead. I took the bones into the cabin while talking to Butch. "I think we can save these for later, Butch. What do you think? You want one now, or shall we go find Norma?"

Butch gave out a loud bark and ran out of the cabin, and I was right behind him. When I got to the boardwalk in front of the saloon, Butch was waiting for me. He had Norma's right wrist in his jaw.

Norma saw me and said, "Butch ran up to me as I talked to Lola and clamped his jaw on my wrist. He pulled me out here. What's going on, Charlie?"

"Did he break the skin?" I asked.

"No, at least not yet. I tried to pull free once, but our dog clamped down harder."

I said, "It's okay, Butch. Let Norma go. You were a good dog and found her for me. Cookie stopped by the cabin and said you had been by to see her. That's why I said we were to find you; our dog did that. Butch wouldn't even take a bone from Cookie, which I understand he always took from her."

Norma laughed, petted Butch on the head, and asked, "Are you ready for breakfast?"

Butch let out a loud bark and headed down the street toward Simpson Café. Norma chuckled and said, "I guess Butch told us where we are going."

When we got there, half the town was sitting in Simpson Café, and a line of people was waiting on the boardwalk in front of the Café. "Oh, my heavens," Norma said when she saw the line of customers waiting for a table. We'll never get a table now. Let's go to the Mercantile, and I'll buy some things and fix you breakfast."

I grinned at her and said, "I bet our table awaits us."

Norma laughed and then said, "I'll take that bet."

Someone called out, "Make way! The guests of honor are here."

Four people moved away from the door to give Norma and me room to enter the Café. Nelda was waiting for us when we entered the room. "Mister and Missus Gray, your usual table is ready for you."

At our table, I took Norma's chair from against the table and held it out for her. When she was seated, I pushed the chair in and went to my chair.

As she sat down, Norma whispered, "How did you know this table was for us?"

I shrugged and said, "Sometimes I just know things. For instance, everyone is here to find out about the man sleeping in their field. That would be your father, Norma. They want your thoughts about him showing up in town after all these years."

There was a ruckus at the front door, then people parted, and Sheriff Brownie and Lola entered. Nelda was quickly beside me and asked, "Mister Gray, is it okay if Lola and the Sheriff join your table?"

I said, "Nelda, they are the only two people allowed at this table when Norma or I sit here. So drag up two chairs."

Once Lola and Brownie were seated and Nelda had taken our breakfast orders, Lola quietly asked, "What the hell brought all these people in here?"

"They are all curious about the man Brownie and I found in their field," I said.

"Oh," Lola said, "Brownie told me about him last night, and then Norma filled me in on what happened this morning. Gray, do you think Norma's father will stick around for a while?"

I glanced around and saw that the occupants of every table were leaning our way, trying to hear what we were saying. I quietly said, "I'll answer that in a few minutes." Then I stood up and walked around the table to stand by Norma. I smiled and said, "Norma, why don't you stand on your chair and tell everyone who the man is."

Norma glared at me for a few moments, then, with a huff of air, she stood up and got up onto her chair. She looked around and saw that everyone was staring at her. "I think everyone has heard about the man that the Sheriff and Gray found in the Town's field," Norma said as she looked around again. "Well, that man claims to be my father. As I told most, if not all, of you, my father left my mother and me when I was four years old. He was a prospector when my mother married him, and he left us to go out into the mountains to try and strike it rich, as he put it. My mother could not pay the mortgage, and the bank kicked us out of the house where I was born.

We moved around a lot until I was fifteen, and my mother moved in with a nice man. At first, he treated my mom like a queen, which lasted until right after my sixteenth birthday. She caught him having sex with me. She started screaming and yelling at him, which was the wrong thing to do. By the time she passed out from the beating he had given her, I had had enough. I shot the bastard with his pistol, and the first shot was right between his legs. The second and third shots were into his other legs. I packed up everything that seemed worth selling. I put it in his wagon, along with my mother. I left the man on the floor where I shot him. Six months later, my mother died from the injuries caused by the beating. I moved a few more times before I came to Holbrook."

"Do I know the man who claims to be my father? No, I don't. Do I want to know him? I can't answer that right now. If he decides to stay in Holbrook, I guess I'll have to talk to him sometime.

"Now you all know why I'm a little hesitant in talking to the man who let what happened to my mother and me happen. You all enjoy your breakfast. I know I'm going to enjoy mine."

The crowd loudly clapped when I helped Norma step down from her chair. While we were eating, several townsfolks stopped by to tell Norma how sad they were for all she had to endure because her father abandoned her and her mother.

As we finished breakfast, Mister Thornhill and Chad entered the Café. They marched right over to our table, and Thornhill said, "Sheriff, there was no one at the jail, so we left our guns behind your desk. Don't you have a deputy on duty at all times?"

Brownie said, "Thornhill, what do you mean there was no one at the Jail? There should have been three prisoners in the cells."

"I was not counting them, as I did not think you would want us to leave our weapons with them."

"Were you two planning to have breakfast?" I asked. "You might want to rethink that. The stagecoach should be pulling in real soon. It will offload its passengers at the hotel and then go to the Livery to change horses."

"Damn," Thornhill said as he turned to leave. Then he added, "Come on, Chad. Let's go meet the stagecoach."

Chapter 36

After paying for breakfast, we left Simpson Café; Brownie kissed Lola while we stood on the boardwalk, and then Brownie went to work in his office at the jail. Lola, Norma, and I walked to the saloon, and the two of them went into Lola's office. It was too early to drink, so James and Diego restocked the liquor. I stopped James and asked him if Lola had an open account at the hardware store. "Yeah," James said. "You need to talk to Noddle, and he'll make sure that whatever you buy is put on Lola's account."

I had not met Noddle, but I quickly figured out why he went by that name. His head was big enough to make a ten-gallon hat look small. I told Noddle what I would make, and he pointed out where the wood and nails were.

When I was ready to check out, Noddle said, "We just got in a circular coat rack that I think might work for what you want."

He took me over, showed me the rack, and explained how it worked. I said, "Yes, Noddle, that might work until some drunk cowboy bumped into it and knocked it over. If one of the guns didn't go off, another cowboy would say we mistreated his gun, and we would have a fight on our hands. I don't need that kind of problem. Putting it on the wall behind the bar is better and safer for everyone."

It took the better part of the day to measure, cut, and hammer the gun racks to the wall. And that was with the help of two cowboys who knew how to use a saw and hammer. When done, there were five rows of hooks, with ten in each row. I left room for another row of hooks at the bottom and the top, which would be a reach for James or Lola to hang a gun belt high up on the wall.

With the last nail set, James said, "Gray, I got enough gun belts to fill two rows. But how will we know who belongs to which gun belt?"

Sitting at her table with four of her ladies, Lola said, "And I got the perfect answer for your dilemma, James. But first, I need Gray to send his two helpers over here. Betsy and Jo want to meet them, cowboys." The two helpers didn't take long to make it upstairs with the two ladies.

As we waited for the lovers to leave, Norma exited the office and stopped beside me. I hugged her as she looked at my handiwork. "You three did good work, Gray," Norma said as she looked at Lola. Out of the corner of my eye, I saw Lola give a little nod.

I picked Norma up in my arms and swung her around in a circle three times before saying, "My beautiful wife, that is a wonderful idea." Then I said, "James, we number the pegs one to fifty."

Lola stared at me with an open mouth, as did Norma. Then Lola said, "How the hell did you do that, Gray? I purposely didn't say a thing about numbers. I was waiting until Norma came out of the office so that she could tell you. Norma, go ahead and grab your husband and squeeze the information out of him. With all the racket out here, there was no way he could have heard us."

I felt Norma's right hand touch me between my legs, but she didn't squeeze me as Lola suggested. Instead, she said, "Honey, I won't do that unless, of course, you make me real mad at you. I understand that you have never figured out how you know what someone is thinking and say it before that person can. It shocks me sometimes when you do it to me, like now, but I'm getting used to it."

"Damn!" Lola exclaimed, "You got it right, Norma; it is a shock when Gray does his trick, and I am, like you, getting used to him doing his thing. There should be some black paint on one of the shelves in the storage area. Norma, why don't you and your husband go find it, then paint the numbers before James hangs the gun belts."

It took us much longer to find the paint than it should have. Norma had me tied up in her arms before the storage area door was completely closed. When that first kiss ended, I was ready to strip down and have my way with Norma, but that didn't happen. Norma had something else in mind.

Norma hoisted herself up my body with her hands clasped behind my neck until her legs went around my waist. "Walk us around like this until we find the paint." Then our lips met and locked in place. I could not walk for fear of stumbling.

When Norma ended the kiss, my eyes were open, and there was a bright flash of blue. I saw Norma's eyes were rolled back in her head as she said, "Did you find the paint?"

"No. I was afraid to move, fearing stumbling and having us both fall. I did not want you to get hurt."

"Thank you, my dear husband." Then, our lips met again. I still did not want to walk, but this time, my vision blurred when my eyes rolled back, and my legs were too unsteady.

"Shit, we are never going to find the paint like this," Norma said. "If I don't kiss you, can you walk us around until we find the paint?"

"If I shift you around slightly, I think I can walk." I moved Norma around so we meshed together better, and then I walked around the room. When we found the paint, I was sure that Norma knew I would be ready for her later in the night.

"What in blazes took so long to find the paint?" James all but shouted at us when Norma and I stepped out of the storage room. "I was about to come in there and see if a wild animal had taken you both away."

"One almost did," I said, "but it was not a wild animal; it was my wild woman."

There was laughter around us as I pulled Norma in for a long hug. Since I was the tallest person, it fell on me to paint the first row of numbers, which I did with a flourish.

James did the next row, and I did the middle row, as James had customers to serve. Lola did the fourth row, and Norma painted the bottom numbers. The wood in the wall was so dry that it sucked the paint right in, and it did not take long for the paint to dry.

I let James do the honors of hanging the gun belts. Lola called the gun owner's name out and said the number the gun belt was on.

When James hung up the last gun, the wall looked very impressive. Lola, Norma, and I were standing in front of the bar, looking at the gun rack, when the swing doors opened, and June, Tommy, and Dalton entered Lola's Place. The place got so quiet you could hear a pin drop.

Chapter 37

An older version of Norma was standing between June and Tommy. The three of us were looking in the mirror behind the bar when I said, "Sweetheart, without the bushy beard and scraggly hair, Dalton looks very much like you. Wouldn't you agree, Lola?"

Lola nodded and said, "Norma, you might hate him for leaving your mother and you, but you can't deny that you look too much like him for him not to be your father."

"Why did he have to shave?" Norma said, "Before that, all I could see were his eyes, and not too clearly. Now everyone knows he is my father. I suppose I have to talk to him. Lola, can we use your table? I want him on one side and me on the other, just as far from him as I can get."

Norma took a deep breath and blew most of it out. Then she turned around with a determined look on her face. In the mirror, I could see the relief on the faces of June, Dalton, and Tommy. I turned around and saw the three of them start across the bar toward Norma.

Lola turned and took Norma by the arm, saying, "No one is going to bother you at the table." Lola led Norma to the Queen's side of the table and pushed her into a chair.

I watched Dalton's face turn sad momentarily, and then he smiled again.   The trio started toward the table, and I saw they intended to go around it to Norma's side. I said, "June, you remember Lola's rules, right?"

The trio stopped, and June looked over at me and said, "Even for a family thing?"

"Don't make it any harder by circumventing the rule, especially for this meeting. People have died thinking they could break that rule."

Tommy asked, "June, what rule is Gray talking about?"

"Without Lola's permission, no one is allowed on that side of the table," June said, "The three of us must sit on this side of the table for now."

Dalton shrugged his shoulders and said, "That makes sense to me. I didn't think Norma would open her arms to me just because I talked you into cutting my hair and shaving me. June, this is not going to be one meeting, and then we are back to being a loving family. There have been some bad things that happened to Norma during her life that she partly blames me for, and I don't blame her for feeling that way."

I was surprised and proud at the same time when Tommy said, "Dalton, you go sit across from Norma. June and I will be at the bar with Gray and Lola. You and Norma need some time alone."

Dalton said, "Thanks, Tommy; I appreciate what you and June have done for me. If you want, you and June can go home. I'll find my way back to your place later."

"We'll stay here and wait for you, Dalton," June said.

Dalton nodded to June and turned to face his daughter. He walked up to the table and sat down across from Norma. Dalton said something in a low voice that I'm sure only Norma could hear.

His back was to the rest of the room, and he looked straight at Norma when he spoke.

Norma turned to look at me and, with a huge smile, said, "Yes, my husband has been wonderful to me since we first met. He makes me laugh and use my brain to think things through. Those are some of the reasons why I love him."

Turning quickly back to face her father, Norma said, "Yes, I know he has killed men, but he is not a killer. He shot the knife out of June's hand that she was going to throw at us. Gray also shot the right hand of an outlaw that had come to Holbrook to kill Gray. The outlaw's gun was still partly in his holster when Gray's bullet hit his hand and the gun. The outlaw didn't want any doctor touching his hand, and he wanted to go back home to Texas. The Sheriff and Gray let the man ride away."

Norma shook her head and said, "No, I'm not afraid of another gunman coming after Gray. Three other gunmen I know of left when they discovered it was Gray; they would be up against."

Something didn't feel right, and I was quickly beside Dalton when I said, "Touch that derringer in your pocket, and you'll be dead before the bullet hits Norma."

Dalton stiffened up and said, "No one is…" he was staring down the barrel of my forty-five.

"Now ease that gun out with two fingers and put it on the table," I said in a low, stern voice.

Dalton said, "How did you know I had a gun?" He slowly and carefully removed the derringer and laid it on the table.

Norma stood up and said, "That is what makes Gray special. He knows what a person will do even before that person does."

Norma got on the table, on her knees, leaned toward her father, and gave him a hard slap. The hit knocked Dalton off his chair and onto the floor.

I reached down and picked Dalton up by the scruff of his neck and marched him out of the saloon, saying, "Go pack your bags and get the fuck out of Holbrook. If I see you again, you will be dead." We were out on the boardwalk, and I gave Dalton a hard shove. Dalton tried to keep his balance but slipped and landed face-first in the mud. An hour before, a storm had passed through the Holbrook area, and the street was still muddy.

June came up beside me and said, "Mister Gray, I told that man he could not bring a weapon into Lola's Place, and he left his revolver and rifle at our house. We didn't know about the small gun. I'm sorry that happened."

"It wasn't your fault, June," I said. "That man is evil, and he needs to move on."

Sheriff Brownie approached me and asked, "Was that Norma's father that you just tossed out of the Place?"

"Yeah," I said, "He left his iron and rifle at Bella's, but he had a derringer that he almost used on Norma. I stopped him before he could use it. He didn't like looking down the barrel of my forty-five. Norma got up on Lola's table and slapped him so hard that it knocked Dalton out of his chair. I told him to pack his things and leave Holbrook. That if I saw him again, he would be dead."

June asked, "Sheriff Brownie, will you come back to the house with Tommy and me? I think that man is mad enough to shoot someone, and I don't want it to be Bella or Tommy."

Sheriff Brownie got an evil look on his face and said, "June, I'll go with you and Tommy. And I'll bring my two deputies with me."

Norma and Lola had stepped out onto the boardwalk, and Lola said, "Make that three deputies. I'm going too."

Chapter 38

The six of us stayed on the boardwalk until it ran out, and then we stayed on the side of the road. We watched Dalton as he sloshed his way up the middle of the road. He didn't seem to mind getting muddy. I could hear Dalton talking to himself, but I could not understand what he said. Later, Lola told us some of what she had heard.

When we got close to Bella's house, we saw Dalton walk over to a small corral and take down the poles that acted as a gate to keep their stock from getting out. Before Dalton could run the animals out of the corral, we all ran to the gate and lifted the poles back into place.

"Only you would stoop that low," Norma yelled at her father as she replaced the heavy end of one pole. "Now, get out of there and get your things before I tell Gray to shoot you just to end your worthless life."

Dalton said, "Now, Norma, you don't mean that. I'm your father, for god's sake."

"I will never acknowledge you as my father!" Norma screamed at Dalton. "My father died when I was four years old. Now get out of Holbrook, you dirty old man."

I said, "Sheriff Brownie, go with him and put his holster in his pack. He better not wear it when he comes out of that house, or there will be bloodshed."

As Norma and I talked, June and Tommy ran into their house. "We're going to let Bella know what is going on," June called out as she ran.

There were a donkey and three horses in the corral, and the donkey walked over to Dalton and gave him a head butt in Dalton's back. "You crazy donkey, what did you do that for?"

"Maybe to get your lazy ass moving," Norma yelled at Dalton.

Norma and I pulled the poles free again to allow just enough room for Dalton and his donkey to get out of the corral. As Dalton walked by me, I said, "There is a hitching rail in front of the Wright's home. Tie your mule there and load your stuff. It looks like the Wrights have piled your things outside their door. You are not going back in that house, Dalton."

Norma took a piece of rope off the corral fence and tossed the loop around the neck of the donkey. She threw the other end of the rope to Dalton and then slapped the donkey's rear. The animal took off at a quick walk, pulling Dalton with him.

Dalton got the animal stopped just before it got to the hitching rail. Dalton turned to us and called out, "Sheriff, who do I speak to about the rudeness of your two deputies?"

Before Brownie could say anything, Lola said, "Mister Whitmore, as Mayor of Holbrook, you would speak with me. And, just between you and me, I have not witnessed any rude behavior other than yours. Now pack your things and get the hell out of my town.

"Sheriff Brownie, if Mister Whitmore is not packed and on his way out of Holbrook within half an hour, arrest him and put him in the cell with the two outlaws. Those guys should be able to have fun with this asshole. Oh! Make sure that the outlaws know that this piece of shit tried to kill his daughter."

"JAIL? OUTLAWS? No, you can't do that to me," Dalton cried out. "Where is my pistol? I have to defend myself. Norma, you can't let them put me in jail with outlaws. I'm your father."

Lola said, "Whitmore, Norma has nothing to do with this. She cannot help you. The only person who can help is you. You better start moving because you have already wasted five minutes of your half-hour."

Dalton opened his mouth to say something, but nothing came out. The man just stood there in disbelief. It was Brownie who finally said something. "Dalton, you better get a move on it cause you just lost another two minutes."

Dalton spun around and glared at Brownie for a few seconds. Then, he hurried to get his donkey pack rack and harnessed the donkey. Dalton quickly tied three bags to the frame and picked up his backpack. The last thing he picked up was his rifle.

When I saw Dalton's right trigger finger touch the trigger of the rifle, I drew my pistol and said, "Move your right hand or lose it at the count of three. One. Two."

Dalton moved his hand and said, "I wasn't going to shoot anybody. Jesus, you're jumpy. A man can't touch his weapon without you drawing yours. Where did those bitches put my holster and gun? It wasn't on the porch."

I said, "I can see the outline of the holster in your backpack. For you, it would be best to leave the holster there until you are down the road a piece. Dalton, I wouldn't do that if I were you. I can kill a man from here to the bend in the road. So, keep the butt of your rifle away from your shoulder. You'll live longer that way."

"How…"

"I told you that my husband just knows things!" Norma yelled. Then she added, "Now get your donkey and get the fuck out of Holbrook. And don't ever come back. To me, you died a long time ago."

As we watched Dalton walk away from Holbrook, the Wright family came out of their house and joined us. June stopped beside Norma and hugged her, saying, "You need to take your husband home and let him cuddle with you. It can't be easy for you to lose your father for the second time. You said he was lost to you when you were a kid, but you can't deny that you two look too much alike not to be father and daughter. From my recollection, Gray has some rather broad shoulder you can cry on, and nobody will know you did."

Norma looked at June quizzically, then looked down the road and saw her father disappear around the bend. Turning to face June, Norma said, "Thank you, June. I think that is just what I need." The ladies hugged again.

Letting go of June, Norma turned to Lola and said, "Gray and I are going to our cabin, and he might not be back for quite some time. I have a feeling that I'm going to need to cry on his shoulders for longer than I first thought I would."

Lola started laughing, but we were soon all laughing. We said goodbye to the Wrights. Then, Lola had Brownie take her to his house, and Norma and I collected Butch from behind Simpson Café before going to our cabin.

Chapter 39

The next afternoon, Norma and I were getting dressed for work when we heard the first rifle shot, followed closely by several pistol shots. When we got our holsters and grabbed our rifles, it sounded like a war was being fought in Holbrook. Butch was out the door before we were, and after a quick look around, he waited for us. We headed for the back of Lola's Place.

At the tree line behind the Place, Butch gave out a low growl. Norma and I stopped and stayed still, waiting for whatever Butch had heard to show itself. Three Indians came from the ally between Lola's Place and the Haberdashery. Two of the Indians were holding onto Lola's cleaning lady.

Three quick shots later, we found out what happened. Someone had told a band of Indians that there was free whiskey at Lola's Place. Three Indians broke the swinging door when they went into the saloon. James tried to chase them out, but one Indian fired his rifle. James fired his shotgun, killing one of the Indians. The three I killed had grabbed her when she came downstairs to talk to them about why they were in the saloon.

The three of us headed for the backdoor of the saloon when it suddenly opened, and Betsy and Jo came running out screaming hysterically. Right behind them were four Indians. I was only able to shoot one of them. Norma still had her pistol out when the Indians came out. I had holstered mine. By the time I drew my weapon, Norma had fired three times. None of the Indians had time to sound any alarm.

I looked at Betsy and asked, "Do either of you know how to use a rifle?"

"We both know how to shoot to kill," Betsy said. "Can we use those rifles you two are carrying?"

Little Deer, Lola's maid, picked up two tomahawks and said, "I can use and throw one of these as well as any man."

I picked up another one and said, "I'll hold it for you."

We went in the back door of Lola's and made our way out to the door in the bar area. I cracked open that door and took a look at the situation. There were at least eight Indians down behind upended card tables. I opened the door a little more so the ladies could see. I said, "The tall Indian on this end is about to run to this end of the bar. James and two other men are behind the bar. I'll take the tall one when I open the door. Norma, crouch down by the door frame, and Betsy and Jo lie on the floor. I'll hold the door open until they start firing back at us. Are you ladies ready?"

As I talked, the women got into position, and I pulled the door open. The tall Indian was just rising to make his run. The sound of two rifles and two forty-fives going off almost together was deafening. My shot knocked the tall Indian into his buddy, who was already dead with half of his head missing. There was the boom of a shotgun as James shot an Indian trying to get into position to fire at us.

It was suddenly quiet in the saloon and out on the street. Then I heard some low moaning. I called out, "James, are you still with us, or did you go to meet your maker?"

James laughed and said, "Hell, Gray, you can't get rid of me that easy. My left arm will need tender loving care, but that's it. I want to know who told these crazy Indians to come here and demand free whiskey?"

I stepped out of the back area with my four ladies and my dog. James stood behind the bar, cradling his left arm. Two other men were also standing behind the bar. One of the men said, "I can hear that someone is still alive out in that mess; one of you needs to check who it is. An Indian or one of our boys?"

I turned, looked out the broken swinging doors, and said, "Brownie, you and Lola might as well come on in, but be careful. One of us can hear some moaning, but we don't know who it is: a friend or a foe. After all the gunplay, I can't hear much of anything."

Lola and Brownie stepped into the saloon, and I saw Lola look around and appraise the damage. Then she looked at Betsy and asked, "Where are the other ladies?"

"Oh, my heavens," Betsy uttered, "I got them all down the back hatch before Jo, and I had to run with four Indians on our butts. We made it out the backdoor and almost ran into Mister Gray. Before he could draw his gun, Norma shot three of the Indians that came out the door behind us. Gray did get to shoot the fourth one."

In my defense, I said, "I shot three of them when we saved Little Deer."

"Good job, Betsy, and you too, Jo," Lola said. "Now go let the ladies out. We have work to do around here."

"Sheriff, how many wounded do you have in here?" Doctor Roth asked from the open swinging door.

"I'm not sure, Doc. Lola and I just got here ourselves. What's the count out in the street?"

Doctor Roth said, "Seven wounded and two dead."

I said, "James needs his left arm fixed. He's bleeding all over the top of the bar. Pete, you look a little pale yourself. Were you wounded and too stupid to tell anyone but your wife?"

Lola stepped behind the bar and said, "Pete, let me see your wound. Doc, take care of James before his wife comes in here and faints at the sight of his blood." Lola moved Pete's coat out of the way and unbuttoned his shirt. When Lola moved the shirt aside, I saw that a bullet had grazed his right shoulder and about a foot down his right side. Lola said, "Pete, this needs to be stitched up, so you are going to Doc Roth's office along with James." Lola lifted her skirt, moved her petticoats around a little, and then ripped off a section of one, which she used to bind Pete's wound.

James's wife ran into the saloon and stopped cold when she saw the blood on his arm. She screamed out his name and ran over to him. "What am I going to do with you? I keep telling you to be careful with that shotgun. Now, look at the mess you made. When Doctor Roth gets you bandaged up, you come back here and clean up all this blood. And don't give me no excuse that your arm hurts too much to do a little work. Now lean on me, and let's go. Pete, is Doctor Roth going to patch you up, too? Come along then. I have another arm that can support you. Once I get you both settled, I'll fetch Angie and Pete; she can take you home when Doctor Roth finishes with you."

Chapter 40

When it was all over, the number of dead was unreal. There were fourteen Indians who died and three that were wounded. The townsfolks lost two men and one woman with seven wounded, four men, two children, and one lady.

Brownie talked to the wounded Indians and found out what I was afraid of what happened. Dalton had come across the Indian camp and told them the saloon had free whiskey. Dalton passed around two bottles he had absconded with to get them started.

Lola, Norma, James, Brownie, and I were sitting at the Queen's table discussing what to do about the dead Indians. We talked for nearly an hour when I said, "Lola, as Mayor of Holbrook, you need to send a telegraph to the nearest Army Post. I understand three Indians rode out of Holbrook when they saw we were winning. I don't know how far they have to go to get to their tribe, but there will be a war party here soon."

Lola said, "I'll have to tell them what happened and who gave them the whiskey to start. Does anyone have a problem with that?"

Sitting to my left, Norma reached under the table and squeezed my left hand. She took a deep breath and said, "Lola, if you're asking that question for my benefit, I say tell the army exactly who gave the whiskey to the Indians. He needs to be arrested and hung for doing that. I may look like that man, but he is not my father. My father died when I was a little girl."

The ladies who worked for Lola were all standing by the bar, waiting for word on what to do. Little Deer, Lola's maid, was there, and she finally said, "Betsy, can you and Jo go out back and get a fire going in the fire pit? We need to get some hot water and rags to clean up the blood in this place. You, other ladies, get some buckets, go to Swan Creek, and get water." Then Little Deer called out, "Lola, what else do you want the ladies to do?"

Looking over at the scantily dressed women, Lola shook her head and said, "Betsy, you and Jo do as Little Deer said and get the fire going under the pot out back. As for getting water, Little Deer, that was a good idea. But I think it would be better if Norma and Gray did that. The ladies are not exactly dressed for going outside. We need to move the chairs and tables to the side of the room as the floor needs a good washing. James cannot do much with his left arm in a sling, but he can sure as hell be here to make sure you ladies don't fight. Brownie and I will send a telegraph, and I'll be back as soon as possible."

Lola hired the two cowboys who helped put up the gun racks to fix the swinging doors and anything else that broke. She also included repairing the windows that were shot out. By the time Brownie and Lola left, the boys had half of the swinging doors rehung. They were ready to go to the Mercantile for more wood when Lola pushed the new half-door open as she walked out of her salon and said, "Boys, that works better than before the Indians tore it down. Thanks for the good work."

Lola returned to the saloon and said, "Little Deer, get as many mop buckets as we have and the mops, too. Somewhere in storage, there are a couple of long handle brushes. We'll need those for the spots that have already dried. Okay, that should do it. Now, everyone get to work."

When Lola went down the boardwalk with Brownie, I looked at all the ladies as they waited for directions from someone. I was about to say something when James said, "Ladies, get the furniture to the far wall and try not to drag it through the blood. Those skimpy shoes most of you wear will not do for this kind of work. All of you go up and put on boots."

Most of the girls headed upstairs, except for Betsy and Jo. I saw Betsy giving James a stern look that I did not like. I said, "Betsy, when Lola said that James would try to keep you ladies from fighting, she meant he was in charge. Am I making myself clear?"

Betsy shrugged and said, "Okay, if James is in charge of us, what will you and Norma be doing?"

I said, "Since you and Jo did not go up to put on boots, I assume you only brought what you are wearing. I suggest you take them off before they are ruined."

"Shit," Betsy uttered. "Are you really going to make us go out and start that fire?"

"It was not me who told you to go out and start the fire. Do you have a problem with doing that?"

"No, it's just that Jo and I will smell like wood smoke when we finish. No man will want to come near us. I didn't sign on to do this kind of work. Come on, Jo, let's pack up and get out of here."

"I'm not going anywhere," Jo said. "I like Holbrook and the people who live here. You have always done that when things didn't go to your liking. Well, I'm done with that. I'll work my ass off and get on Lola's good side, maybe even James. Gray has a good side, but it is only for Norma."

"Well, I'm leaving. Jo, stay here and enjoy your hard work," Betsy said and turned to go upstairs.

I said, "Norma, you and Jo go with her and make sure that Betsy doesn't take anything that is not hers."

The other ladies were coming down the stairs when Betsy stormed up them. Little Deer approached me and asked, "Gray, what is happening? Betsy gave me a dirty look. Have I done something to upset her?"

I grinned at her and said, "You did nothing wrong. Betsy said she was leaving and tried to get Jo to accompany her. Jo said no that she would work her ass off to get on Lola's good side. I told Norma and Jo to go up with Betsy to ensure that no one is missing anything when Betsy is gone. I don't know where Betsy will go; the stage doesn't come through for two more days. But then it is not my problem where she stays."

James said, "Okay, ladies, time to get to work. Gray is going for water, and a lot of things need moving before we can mop and scrub the floor."

I had a wooden bucket in each hand when I heard the gunshot.

Chapter 41

The sound of the gunshot came from behind me and inside the saloon. I dropped the buckets as I spun around to return to the building. Before I got partway turned around, my gun was out and cocked. Stepping into the back of Lola's Place, I heard screaming from the bar area.

As I started for that area, I heard Norma calmly say, "Betsy, now that you have stopped sounding like the baby you are, I'll tell you why I shot you in the arm. That little gun you had in your right hand was pointed at the back of Lola's head. She would be dead by now if I had not shot you, and I could not stand for that. Now, you, me, Lola, and Gray are going to Doctor Roth and get your arm tended to."

"Why, Gray? He's not even here!" Betsy said.

"He'll be here before I finish telling you why."

I stepped into the bar area and said, "And Betsy, I heard every word my wife said. And, just so you know, if I had been here, we wouldn't be having this conversation because you would be dead. Brownie will be here soon, and his prisoners are all okay. It will be up to Lola whether you go to jail or the hotel until the stagecoach gets here."

As he entered the Place, Brownie was talking, "Lola, what the hell is going on? Diego came into the jail and said you were shot." Brownie was at Lola's side before he finished talking.

"It wasn't me that got shot; it was Betsy."

"Then why did Diego say that you were shot?"

"He might have meant to say I was almost shot, or you misunderstood him."

Brownie hugged Lola as they spoke, finally letting her go slightly. He looked down at Lola and asked, "Care to let me know what the hell happened here?"

Lola hugged the Sheriff and, letting go of him, said, "Betsy has decided to leave us. As she was walking past me, Betsy drew that little gun you saw lying on the floor and was in the process of shooting me in the back of my head. Norma didn't like that idea and shot Betsy in the arm. We need to take Betsy to see Doctor Roth. Then, we need to decide if Betsy is going to jail or the hotel until she can leave Holbrook. You and Gray can escort Betsy to the doctor's office. Oh, Norma feels she should go along to make sure that Betsy doesn't try to shoot any of you men."

Brownie laughed and said, "Sounds to me like Norma is almost as fast on the draw as Gray, for which I am very glad." Looking over at me, Brownie added, "You two ready to take this bitch to see Roth?"

I nodded and said, "It might be best to take Betsy to jail after Roth fixes her arm. With Betsy in the hotel, she would have an opportunity to talk someone out of their gun, and then she could try to kill Lola again."

Brownie's eyebrows went up, and he gave out a little chuckle. "I'm glad you are around, Gray. I would not have thought about Betsy getting another gun."

Doctor Roth looked at the wound and said, "Gray, this is not your handiwork. Who shot this lady?"

Norma said, "I did when the bitch was about to shoot Lola. What's wrong with where I shot her?"

"You got me wrong, Norma. It was a perfect shot. The bullet missed both bones in Betsy's forearm. She'll have a scar on both sides of her arm from the shot and still use that hand. Let me get her patched up and in a sling. Then you can take her to the hotel. She needs rest and to keep the wound clean. Sheriff, that jail of yours is not very sanitary, and from the few times I've been called there, it is fairly noisy."

Roth pulled a curtain between his patient and us to work on Betsy's arm in some privacy. "Now, Betsy," we heard him say, "don't be reaching for my instruments. Some of them are very sharp and deadly."

"I'm not going to do something stupid," Betsy said. "I should have known that Norma was fast on the draw. She is Gray's wife, after all. Now, close the wounds and shut the hell up. I'm done talking to any of you idiots."

After leaving Doctor Roth's office, Brownie started across the street to take Betsy to the hotel. He held onto Betsy's left arm and almost jerked off his feet when she stopped walking abruptly. "What the hell are you doing, Betsy?" Sheriff Brownie said.

Betsy Glared at Brownie and, in a flat voice, said, "Just take me to your jail, Sheriff. I've lived in worse places than your jail could be. You can take me to Winslow when you take the other prisoners there. I'm sure your deputies would love to have a more pleasant person with them on the long trip to Winslow."

Brownie shook his head, saying, "Betsy, I'm sure you are right, but I hate to bust your dream of escaping from the deputies. When Lola and I sent telegraphs today, one was to the Sheriff in Winslow, and another was to the US Army Post in Winslow. The Sheriff has more than enough room for my prisoners and you. The Army is sending a large Detachment of Soldiers to Holbrook to help with any Indian uprising. A Platoon of Soldiers is going to take the prisoners to Winslow. I'll find out if the Lieutenant in charge of the Platoon thinks a female guard is necessary, then Norma will accompany you to Winslow. I'll send Gray along for her protection and his sanity."

As Brownie moved one of the prisoners back to the second cell, Betsy said, "What is that god-awful smell?" When we got to the jail, the smell was first noticed. In this case, it was the smell of blood. The floor had been mopped, but the smell was still there with the door closed.

Norma said, "Betsy, that is the smell of blood. These men Butchered four other men here, and now they are paying the price. Like the price you will pay for trying to kill Lola."

One of the prisoners called out, "Say, is that Lola White you are talking about?"

Brownie said, "Yes, it is. Betsy tried to put a bullet in the back of Lola's head. My deputy stopped that by putting a bullet in Betsy's arm. That's why the arm is in a sling."

Chapter 42

The outlaw said, "You mean that little lady is as fast as Gray is on the draw? I don't believe it?"

Norma was about to give the man a demonstration of how fast she was, but a commotion on the porch and the door being thrown open interrupted her. Norma spun around, pointing her pistol at two cowboys in the doorway. There were two other men out on the porch. All four of the men had their gun belts wrapped around their holsters.

"Hey, Miss, we just wanted to leave our weapons with the Sheriff. What's going on, Sheriff?"

Brownie laughed briefly before saying, "Sorry about the gun pointing at you, Jock. But Norma was showing one of these outlaws how fast she could draw her weapon."

Jock said, "Well, I've seen her draw and fire her pistol before, and I don't know anyone as fast. Is she going to be your deputy?"

Brownie said, "She is, and the man standing beside her is Gray. He is my other deputy."

"Shit!" The cowboy standing beside Jock exclaimed. "Everyone has heard of Mister Gray. Norma, are you as fast as Mister Gray?"

"No. And Dan, I am now Missus Gray. Judge Moore married us the other day."

I saw Dan kind of slump down as he said, "If that don't beat all. I should have just stayed out at the ranch."

Norma said, "Dan, when you get to Lola's Place, tell Lola that I would appreciate it if she saw that Jo takes care of your broken heart."

"Who's this, Jo? I never heard that name before," Dan said.

"Jo's new to Holbrook, and Dan, I think you'll be impressed by her," Norma said. Then added, "You boys go have your fun. Gray and I need to talk to Sheriff Brownie."

After the cowboys were gone, Brownie said, "Okay, Norma, what's on your mind?"

Norma grinned at him and said, "Not a thing, Sheriff. I just wanted to get them out of here. Dan will talk your ears off until the rooster crows, and we will get nothing done for the rest of the day."

Brownie and I laughed over Norma's comment, and then I said, "Well, I do have something I want to say. I'm taking a few days off to see if I can track down where Dalton met up with that group of Indians that came to Holbrook."

Brownie nodded and said, "What took you so long to go after him? And why are you telling me? It's Lola that you need to talk to."

Norma hooked her right arm around my left and said, "My dear husband, you should have first told me what you were thinking. Because, Charlie, I'm going with you on this trip. And you won't talk me out of going; Dalton is my alleged father, not yours."

"I didn't tell you, my dear wife, because I naturally assumed you were going with me. Where one goes, the other goes, right?"

Brownie laughed and said, "Take it up with Lola. I have paperwork to fill out, so get the hell out of my jail."

When Norma and I got to Lola's Place, we were almost ambushed by Lola. She stood just inside the new swinging door and to the right, where we did not see her.

From behind us, Lola said, "Am I ever glad to see you two."

"What's going on with you?" Norma asked as I re-holstered my gun. I had sensed someone behind me, and my weapon was out before Lola said one word.

"Dan came in and did just what you told him to do. He came right up to me as I was helping to put my table back in the right place. There were six of us lifting the table, and Dan started to pull me away, and the table fell back to the floor with a loud thump. Everyone turned and looked at us. I got right in Dan's face and was about to kick him out of the saloon. But he told me what you said for him to do, and I could do nothing but laugh. I pulled Dan into a hug and walked him over to Jo. The two went upstairs, and Jo was mothering him as they walked up the steps. Jock and the other two hands asked what they could do to help put the saloon back in order. They then helped with my table and a couple of other heavy things. I just sent those three upstairs and told the girls I didn't want to see them for at least an hour. Now, Norma, we need to do a supply order. We are running low on things that must be shipped from Albuquerque, New Mexico. Or further away if my supplier does not have what we ordered."

"How soon do we need to get that done?" Norma asked.

"Why? You planning on going somewhere?" Lola asked.

"Yes. Gray and I will track down my father and bring him to justice. Gray is leaving today, and I'm going with him."

Lola looked back and forth between Norma and me half a dozen times before saying, "I get the feeling I'm no competition with Gray. Norma, do not worry about the order; with James's help, I can handle it. You two get that bastard Dalton and bring him back here for trial. I'll message Judge Moore to get him back to hang that man. Now get out of here, and don't return without Dalton."

Lola hugged Norma and me, turned around, and called out to James. Norma and I went back to our cabin and packed. Butch was right there with us, and when we finished, Norma and I went to the Livery for our horses. We stopped at Simpson Café and got some bones for Butch. Cookie also gave us some treats she had made to give the dog.

It took me over a day to track Dalton to the old Indian campsite. Norma found two empty whiskey bottles and said, "That one Indian was telling the truth when he said the old man had two bottles to share. I might just shoot that bastard on sight."

"I agree with you," I said. "But doing that would deprive the town of seeing the man hang for what he did."

Chapter 43

When he left the campsite, finding Dalton's trail took me longer than planned. I had to circle the site more than a dozen times to find the donkey's tracks. Twenty unshod horses were messing up Dalton's tracks and the donkeys. Norma and I were about a mile and a half from the campsite when I found the right marks.

After figuring out which direction Dalton was heading, I knew he was returning to the mountains. The day we figured out where Dalton had gone, we pushed our horses until little light was left to see what was ahead. Norma laid our bedrolls out to where they were right next to each other, and it did not take us long to be in one bed. Our lovemaking started slow and tender, but it wasn't long before we were going like two animals.

We slipped our clothes back on and then laid down to sleep. A few moments later, Norma said, "I love you, Charlie Gray, and when we have that bastard back in Holbrook, I think we should head for California. I know that is where you want to go, and so do I, as long it is with you. You are the only man I will ever love, so don't you go getting yourself killed. That would be a damn waste as far as I'm concerned."

I said, "Norma Gray, I love you, and there will never be anyone else in my heart. I appreciate that you will be going to California with me, but we have a problem or two to take care of before we can go west."

"What problems might you think of, my dear husband?" Norma giggled and added, "I love calling you my husband. It makes our arrangement feel so real deep down in my heart."

"And I love calling you my wife, but that is when we are alone like now. When we are with others, I prefer to call you Norma. Or, I guess I could say, my wife, Norma."

"Then that is what we'll do. I'll call you husband when we are alone and Charlie with others. We know we are husband and wife, and we are who counts, not other people."

"When I introduce you to someone, I'll say this is Missus Gray, my wife. No, that is too formal. I'll call you Norma."

Norma laughed and said, "I'll just say, have you met Gray? I love to watch the men's reaction to your last name."

"Well, I can't say it is the same for you, and I thank God for that. The first problem is finding Dalton and returning him to Holbrook."

"That should be easy. We'll probably catch up with Dalton tomorrow. What else, my dear husband?"

"The second problem is Lola."

"What about her?" Norma said in a cautious voice.

"We both have jobs with her. And, my dear wife, I think she is planning to groom you to take over for her when she and Brownie get married."

Norma laughed and said, "Lola wants me to take over her whorehouse for her? You have got to be kidding."

"No. Lola took you on as her accountant, not knowing if you could do the job. She told me that you have started doing things that Lola wanted to be done, but no one could do them, and she did not have the time to do them. Haven't you noticed that she defers to your judgment when there is a problem?"

Norma was silent momentarily, then said, "Now that I think about it, you're right, my dear husband. But I didn't put it all together as you did. Why is that?"

I laughed and said, "I'm an outsider looking in; you needed someone like me to point it out to you."

I woke to the first rays of sunlight lightening the sky. When Norma woke up, I had some water brewing. "What will you do with that hot water?" a sleepy Norma asked.

"Throw you into it and cook you long enough to melt that cold heart of yours." I opened a pocket on my coat and, after taking them out of the pocket, threw a few coffee beans into the pot. "You better get up and feed Butch. I'll have breakfast ready by the time you are done."

"Yummy, something smells good. I need a little water to wash the grit out of my eyes. Husband, is that okay?"

"Yes. But remember, we will be in an area with little or no water between here and when we catch Dalton."

"Oh! I didn't think of that. I'll do as you did and rub the sleep away without water." I watched Norma get out of the bedroll and stretch to loosen up. I was about to comment, then thought better of it as Butch was jumping around Norma. "Down, Butch!" Norma exclaimed. "I'll feed you as soon as I get my boots on."

After we ate, Norma and I saddled up and left our campsite. I made sure the small fire we used was extinguished before riding away. It was not hard to follow the donkey tracks, but I was a little bothered by the unshod horse tracks alongside the donkey's tracks.

We covered a few miles before I called out, "Norma, I want to stop and take a closer look at these tracks."

"Do you think we are on the wrong trail?" she asked.

"No, Dear, this is Dalton's trail. His donkey's tracks are here, but there is also an unshod horse with the donkey. You can see two tracks in that sandbank just ahead of us. Let's dismount and walk over there to take a look. I'll have Butch guard the horses."

That is what we did, and from the look of the tracks, I told Norma that Dalton was riding the horse and leading his donkey. The donkey was still carrying Dalton's gear. When we returned to the horses, Butch would not let Norma get close to her horse. I laughed and said, "I guess you will walk to catch up with Dalton."

"You bastard!" Norma shouted after her fourth or fifth try to get to her horse. "Tell Butch it is okay that I am your wife and his friend."

"Come here, Butch," I said in a normal voice. When the dog was beside me, I added, "You are a good dog. It is okay if Norma gets on her horse. Now go show her that you're sorry for stopping her."

Butch ran over to Norma and almost knocked her down as he put his paws on Norma's shoulders and licked her face. Norma laughed so hard that she barely got the dog to stop before I approached them.

It took us two more days to catch up to Dalton, and we almost missed him after all the riding we did to catch him. At some point in the past, a landslide happened on the mountain Norma and I were going around. A large pile of boulders lay in our way, so Norma and I started around to the right. Butch stopped and gave out a low growl as he turned and headed to the left side. It was evening, and darkness was coming on fast.

Norma and I drew our pistols and followed after Butch. The dog suddenly sprinted around a boulder, and there was some barking and Dalton's squeaky voice calling for help to get the damn dog off him.

When rounding the boulder, Norma and I laughed at what we saw. Butch was standing on Dalton while the man tried to get out of his bedroll.

Chapter 44

It took us three days to get back to Holbrook, partly because Dalton tried to get away two times. I was almost at the end of my patience with the man when Holbrook came into view. His continued griping was getting to me.

Some changes were being made in Holbrook while Norma and I were gone. We were gone the better part of a week, and it seems the US Army had moved into one end of Holbrook while we were gone.

The prisoners that were in Brownie's jail when we left on our trip had been taken to the Winslow Jail to await trial. Some of the soldiers were busy adding to the jail. When finished, the jail would have four cells instead of two.

Dalton was put in the left cell, as the back wall of the other cell had been torn down to make room for the expansion. There was a lot of noise from the construction, and it did not take Dalton long to complain. Brownie came storming into Lola's Place the second day that Dalton was a guest of Brownie's jail. "WHERE'S LOLA?" Brownie shouted after looking around the saloon and not seeing her.

I was at one end of the bar, and James was busy pouring drinks, and he was halfway down the bar. I saw James look at me worriedly, and I nodded. Then I said, "Lola and Norma are working in the office. You know the rule, Brownie. No one is allowed in there right now. Why don't I buy you a drink, and you can tell me what Dalton has done to make you so mad?"

Brownie stomped to the bar beside me and said, "James, a glass of Lola's good whiskey, please."

James laughed and said, "Dalton must have pissed you off something bad for you to order a drink with the word please."

I chuckled and said, "Dalton's constant complaining will make any man take to drinking."

"How did you put up with him for that long?" Brownie asked. "I had to get out of there before I shot him."

The office door opened, and Lola came out with Norma behind her. "Brownie, what are you doing here?" Lola asked as she walked up to him and kissed her man.

"That idiot who claims to be Norma's father is causing me to have thoughts of murder. His whining and constant chattering have gotten to me. The man won't shut up."

Norma had come over to me and stood to my right, and we were both grinning at Brownie. Lola smiled and said, "Sheriff, I think our friend Norma has the solution to your problem."

"What!" Brownie almost shouted. "You want me to let him go so you can use him as target practice?"

Norma looked at me, and I nodded. "No, Brownie," she said. "Why don't you take Butch back to the jail with you? Then, when Dalton starts complaining about Butch being there, you can tell Dalton to shut up, or you will open his cell door. Dalton is afraid of Butch."

Brownie frowned at Norma and said, "Why is that man afraid of Butch?"

After a short laugh, Norma said, "We didn't tell you about how Butch was the one who found Dalton. By the time we got to the two of them, Butch was standing on top of Dalton as he was trying to get up. With Dalton yelling at the top of his lungs, Butch barking, and Dalton's baying donkey, there was quite a bit of noise. Gray almost fell off his horse; he was laughing so hard."

I said, "Well, dear, as I recall, you slid off your horse because you were laughing too." I hugged Norma, then, turning to Brownie, I said, "Sheriff, If you open the cell door, tell Butch to make Dalton stop talking. If Dalton stands up when you open the door, Butch will take him down. If Dalton lies on his cot, Butch will get on the cot with Dalton. In either case, Butch will stand on Dalton and drool all over Dalton's head."

"My so-called father," Norma said, "will stop talking, and you can tell Butch to come out of the cell. Then tell the idiot that you'll leave Butch in the cell if he says one more word."

When Norma and I finished talking, everyone in the saloon was laughing. James said, "Sheriff, you should do as Norma and Gray said. You could make some money if you let a handful of townspeople come into the Jail and watch Butch do his thing with Dalton. Let ten or fifteen in at a time, Butch would love the attention, but that bastard Dalton would not."

Brownie laughed, then said, "Wouldn't that be something the town is making money off of a prisoner?"

Lola grinned at him and said, "Brownie, get that look out of your eyes. You will do no such thing. As you said, he is our prisoner, and we must protect him, not ridicule him. But I also agree with Norma. You can take Butch to the jail and threaten Dalton. And do it without onlookers. Brownie, I love you, but you cannot do this, okay?"

Brownie gave Lola a hug and a long kiss. Then he said, "Okay, but the idea is surely tempting. Come on, Butch! I need your help down at the jail."

Butch gave a loud bark and ran to the swinging doors, where he bumped one open and was gone. He was barking all the way to the jail. Later, Brownie told us that half a dozen men were there waiting for him when he got to the jail. They wanted to know what was going on with Butch. The men had rifles in their hands, most of which were lever-action ones. Brownie told them about Butch and Dalton. One of the men said, "Leave the door open so we can see that shithead's reaction to Butch."

According to Brownie and a couple of the men I talked to later, when the Jail door opened, Butch ran in, and Dalton let out a scream and scampered up onto his cot, shouting, "Keep that animal away from me. It almost killed me a few days ago."

The men watching the show got a good chuckle, then they all went on about their business. Brownie told Dalton what would happen if he continued complaining. "And, Dalton, just remember, because Butch is not here with me, I can always go get him. Then the two of you can renew your acquaintance."

Chapter 45

A few days after we brought Dalton back to town, Sheriff Brownie was busy getting his paperwork to transfer Dalton to the Winslow Jail, so he asked Norma and me to take a trip around town. It was late in the afternoon, and we took Butch with us. Butch decided to chase a rabbit or two down past Bella Wright's house. The dog took off running and barking, and I saw three rabbits leap into the brush before him. I was about to whistle for Butch when he returned, making a low growl. He turned and faced down the road away from town.

"Riders are coming," I softly said to Norma.

In the quickly fading twilight, I could make out four riders who came to a stop about then. A man speaking in heavily accented English said, "I am Running Man, Chief of Navajo. I wish to speak to the Head Man of your town. You take us to him?"

"I am known as Gray, and my wife is Norma. Our dog is named Butch. We will take you to meet with our Mayor."

"Thank you, Gray. I come in peace; I am deeply saddened by what happened to your people and my braves."

"I am sorry for your loss as well. We have arrested the man who gave your braves the alcohol. He will be going to prison for many years."

When we were getting close to Lola's Place, I sent Norma to get Lola out on the boardwalk. Norma, Lola, and several other men were waiting outside the building when I stopped Chief Running Man and the other Indians. I said, "Chief Running Man, the Lady with my wife is Lola White, the Mayor of Holbrook. It is Lola that you must talk to. I know that might not seem right to you, but the men of Holbrook elected Lola as our Mayor. She is a fair and honest person."

Lola invited Chief Running Man and his braves to come into the saloon to talk without being interrupted. Lola added, "Chief, to make sure we are not bothered, Mister Gray and his wife, Norma, will be our guards. The only person they will allow near us will be our Sheriff. Sheriff Brownie is my man, so he is trustworthy."

Their meeting went well, and Chief Running Man and his braves were there for over an hour. Norma, Butch, and I walked the chief and his men out of town the same way we came into town. When I stopped, all but Running Man mounted their horses. The Chief said, "Gray, your name is known among Indians as one of the good and honest white eyes. If you come to our village, there will be a feast of honor in your name."

"I thank you, Chief Running Man. If there is some small thing I can do to help your people, have one of your braves contact me, and I will come to help you."

Running Man nodded, and we clasped right forearms in friendship. Once on his horse, the chief gave a wave and rode away. Norma and I watched the Indians until we could no longer see them. As I turned to head for our cabin, I said, "We need to make sure that Butch's food and water dishes are brought into the cabin tonight."

"Why in heaven's name do we need to do that?"

"Can't you feel it?"

"Feel what?"

"It's all around us. It's in the air. You must feel it?"

"WHAT!"

Butch let out a loud bark.

"What am I supposed to feel?" Norma asked.

"A major storm is coming our way."

"I don't believe it. Major storms are a couple of months from now."

"I think we need to bring them in along with a good supply of wood. I've been caught in a couple of storms like what I feel coming, and it is not pleasant. When we get home, a branch hangs over our roof that I want to cut down. Do you know which direction the storms that hit Holbrook come from?"

Norma pointed in a southeast direction, saying, "They seem to come from that way."

I said, "Well, it feels like this one is coming from the West, but I could be wrong."

When Norma walked around the cabin to the front, she broke out in a loud laugh. Pointing at the porch, she said, "That crazy dog of yours has his dishes on the porch like he knew what you were saying. Charlie, how can that be? Are dogs that smart?"

"This one sure is smarter than I thought he was. You better take his food dish in, or Butch will do it for you. It will be spilled all over like the water dish."

Butch had his empty water dish clamped in his teeth. He was waiting for Norma to open the cabin door. I took my ax from the cutting block and started cutting down half of the giant branch, almost touching the cabin roof.

Norma suddenly called out, "Butch, why are you bringing in that wood?"

There was the sound of a large piece of wood hitting the cabin floor and then Butch barking. It took a bit for Norma to understand what Butch was saying. Norma came out of the cabin and, looking across at me, said, "Your dog is bringing in uncut firewood. Did you tell him to do that?"

"No, dear, I didn't. He must have heard me tell you we needed to bring in the wood. Can you reach up and grab the branch that is touching the roof?"

Norma tried jumping up to grab the branch several times and finally exclaimed, "I'm too damn short!"

"You did well in trying. The branch is almost ready to split. I'll try pulling it away from the cabin; it might snap off. Why don't you show Butch which wood to bring into the place?"

I pulled the big branch away from the house when Norma was in the cabin. It broke with a loud snap and a thump when it hit the ground. Butch started barking, and the dog and Norma came running out of the cabin.

Norma ran over to me and said, "That branch didn't hit you, did it, Charlie? That thing is bigger than I thought it was."

"No, dear. It missed me by a foot or so. Were you worried about me?" I asked with a grin.

"Don't make fun of this, Charlie; you could have been badly hurt."

I pulled Norma to me in a tight hug and said, "I'm sorry. You're right; I could have been hurt. I need to cut up this monster and stack it by the back of the cabin. You could help me by carrying the smaller pieces or taking more firewood into the cabin."

Norma stood on her toes and, after kissing my left cheek, said, "Butch and I will take in firewood. Don't be too long; I started dinner."

As I finished stacking the last piece of wood behind the cabin, the first gust of wind hit the place. The rain got there as I got to the front of the place. It lashed the front of the cabin, and I barely got the door closed and latched. Before going into our home, I closed and latched the outside shutters.

I was glad we were in a log cabin during the storm. Norma snuggled up next to me that night, and Butch lay at the end of the bed.

Chapter 46

I got up during the night to add wood to the stove, and Norma and that traitor Butch stayed on the bed. One under the bedcover, with just his nose sticking out. The other was under our blanket, with her eyes and forehead showing. Getting back into bed was another chore. The dog did not want to move; I had to step over him and keep from stepping on my lovely wife.

My whole body was cold, so I stayed away from Norma as I pulled part of the blanket over me. Norma giggled and said, "Charlie, my dear husband, you can snuggle up to me. I know you got cold to make sure we had a fire going. Our dog will take your place if you don't get right next to me."

I moved, and I was glad I did. Norma wanted to climb all over me. We did not get much sleep that night, if any. The storm roared until well after sunrise. When we finally got up and opened the door, I found that our porch was no more. In its place, the storm left us a few inches of water.

Butch gave out a loud bark, leaped out the cabin doorway, and took off after a rabbit. Norma and I laughed at Butch, then she said, "My dear husband, you need to carry me up to check on our place of employment."

I stepped down into the water and turned to face Norma. I said, "You need to shut the door behind you, or we'll have all sorts of critters in there when we return."

Water was still running down the trail to Lola's Place, so walking was a little tricky, with Norma bouncing on my back. It didn't help to have Butch jumping up on me as he tried to play with

Norma. It also didn't help when we found that much of the boardwalk needed replacing.

James and Lola were standing on the portion of the boardwalk that remained in front of her business. "How did the cabin hold up?" Lola asked when she saw Norma and me. James asked, "Norma, why is Gray carrying you? Did you get hurt during the storm?"

Norma laughed and said, "I made Charles carry me because I did not want to step down into the water that is now our front porch. That thing is now scattered to some other place. Before the storm hit, which Charles knew was coming our way, he cut down that big branch above the cabin. And I'm sure glad he cut it down. Charles also made me bring in Butch's dishes and a ton of firewood. James, how would Gray know there was a storm coming?"

James laughed and said, "My dad could do that too. When I was a little boy, my mother would tell my dad we needed to go on a picnic, and he would look up at the sky and then take a few sniffs of the air. He would shake his head and say, not today; there's a storm coming. And he was right far more than he was wrong. I think Gray is one of those men who can do that."

As our friends talked, I set Norma on the boardwalk; then, I walked out into the street to survey the rest of Main Street. Butch tagged along with me. We were in the middle of the road when Butch began growling. I dropped to one knee as I drew my pistol and shot the man who had put a rifle bullet right where I had been standing. My first shot hit the man in the left chest. My second one caught him on the right side of his head.

Standing up, I walked over to the body and kicked the rifle away from him. I didn't need to do that, but it's just my way. Disarm the man, then check if he is alive or dead. I heard feet running behind me as I turned and said, "I think the storm damaged the jail. Dalton won't be standing trial."

Norma, Lola, and James were standing beside me, and when they looked at the body, all three gagged but kept from throwing up. Finally, Lola said, "When we got to the saloon, Brownie went to check on the Jail. I need to go see if he is okay."

I noticed that James had his scattergun with him, and I said, "We'll all go." From where I stood, I could see that a good portion of the new section of the jailhouse was blown over. The front door was wide open.

Lola took off at the run, but Norma caught up to her and slowed Lola down by catching Lola's arm and saying, "Do you feel that Brownie is dead?"

Lola shook her head and said, "No. But where is he, Norma?"

Norma said, "I don't know. Dalton might have knocked Brownie out and taken the Sheriff's rifle."

I saw movement in the jail doorway and said, "I think Brownie is coming out now."

Brownie was holding the left side of his head as he stepped out onto the jailhouse porch. Brownie was also petting Butch. Lola saw him and took off running, and Norma did not try to stop her this time. When Norma saw Butch was with Brownie, she said, "What's our dog doing there, Charles?"

I grinned at Norma and said, "If I were a betting man, I would say that Butch woke up the Sheriff by licking his face."

James and Norma laughed, and he said, "A dog licking my face would sure as hell wake me up!"

The three of us stopped before the Jailhouse and waited until Lola and Brownie finished their kiss. When that ended, Brownie said, "That bastard Dalton was waiting for me. He hit me as soon as I opened the door. I figured I was going to die. Did he get away?"

Lola said, "No, dear. Gray shot Dalton, and that bastard is still lying in the ally by the hotel. James, Norma, and I were standing outside Lola's Place, and Gray was out in the middle of the street looking at the storm damage. It was like Gray knew someone would shoot him, and he dropped to one knee. I was looking right at him, and I never saw Gray's pistol come up until he took two shots. I only know it was two shots cause I saw the bullet holes in Dalton. One was in the heart, blowing off half of Dalton's head. I didn't hear the shots because of the loud rifle shot that went off at the same time."

Brownie held Lola at arm's length and said, "Thanks for telling me that. I've been telling you that Gray just knows when someone is about to shoot at him. He doesn't have to think about it; he reacts. I'll say that Gray heard the bullet pass over him. The bullet was Probably right where his chest would have been had he not knelt."

Lola looked at me and said, "Gray, is that true? Did you hear the bullet?"

I nodded and said, "Yes, Lola, it's true. I would be dead if I did not get down on one knee."

"But how the hell did you know where Dalton was?" Lola exclaimed.

Chapter 47

I grinned up at Lola and said, "I cheated." Then I doubled over as Norma hit me in the stomach.

"What do you mean by that comment?" Norma asked before Lola could.

I said, "Damn, Norma, that hurt."

Without a smile, Norma said, "Well, the next one will be lower and hurt a lot more. Now answer the question."

"It was Butch," I said. "Our dog growled as he looked right at Dalton. Most men aim at the chest with a rifle, so I dropped and tucked my head to the right. Had I not moved my head to the right, that bullet would have given me a third eye."

Norma looked up at Lola and said, "Boss, I didn't look for damage to Lola's Place. Do you know if there was any?"

"There was none when Brownie and I dashed to his house. Before the wind hit, Jo said she could feel a storm coming and that we should shut and lock all the windows. We kicked all customers out and latched down the place tightly. Brownie and I went out the back door."

"Hey!" Norma exclaimed. "Jo and Gray are alike in knowing when a storm is coming."

Brownie said, "I'm not surprised Gray can tell when a storm is coming. He senses when a man is going to pull his pistol. I'm somewhat surprised he didn't know Dalton was drawing down on him."

"I might have had something to do with that," Norma said. "I had him carry me from our cabin to Lola's. I was on his back and laughing at Butch as he tried to knock me off."

Brownie chuckled and said, "Norma, are you saying Gray's mind was lost in love rather than watching what was happening around him?"

Norma nodded, pulled me tight against herself, and said, "Yeah, it was love for Butch and me."

I scooped up Norma and put her over my left shoulder. I said, "Let's go check with Cookie and Nelda. They might need some help mopping out the Café. I think the door blew open on Simpson Café."

Not to be outdone, Brownie scooped Lola up and said, "With this banged-up head of mine, I better just carry you in my arms."

Lola laughed and said, "I walked and ran in that muddy street to get to you, my beautiful man. I can walk just fine, but if it makes you feel better, I won't try to stop you from carrying me."

The door to the café had blown open during the storm. But the front window held, and the damage to the café was limited to the dining area. Many of the chairs would need fixing, and a good deal of dishes would need to be replaced. The café looked worse when you first looked in than it turned out to be. With our help and two other couples who said they stopped by to see if Cookie would open for business that day. Lola quietly talked both couples into helping clean. With all of us working, we soon had the café in good enough shape for Cookie to open for customers.

After eating, we all went to work, with Lola checking with James about liquor supplies and Norma working on the accounts of Lola's Place. Brownie went to talk to the Army Captain, who helped build the new jail. He needn't have worried. When the Sheriff returned to the jail, the Army Captain and his crew were already working. I went to Norma and my cabin to rebuild the missing porch.

As I got close to the back of the cabin, I heard Butch growling. There was also another sound that got my attention. Something substantial was being dragged on the ground. I walked around the corner of the cabin and laughed. "Butch, where did you find that?"

Butch let go of what he brought up from the creek and started barking loudly. The dog ran towards me, and I put up my left hand, palm towards him, and Butch stopped three feet from me and sat down. There was no dry spot on the dog.

Except for a few pieces of wood, Butch found our missing porch and drug the damn thing up out of the creek. "I don't know how you did it, Butch, but I know that Norma will be happy. Now, all I have to do is get it to the cabin. Butch, do you want to help?"

The porch was about twenty feet from the cabin, and Butch let out another few barks, ran over to the porch, took hold of it, and started dragging it again. I went to the back of the porch and pushed. When the porch bumped against the cabin, Butch gave out a loud series of barks. I moved the porch around and got it to where it would work best for Norma.

Butch and I went to the hardware store and got some nails and a good hammer. I also bought a handsaw and a couple of planks to replace the missing ones, a few heavier pieces of wood to use as bracing to keep the porch against the cabin, and some twine for measuring.

Butch and I left the hardware store with him, carrying the smaller things in a bag he held in his teeth. I hoisted the wood onto my left shoulder and headed for the cabin. Lola and Norma were on the other side of the street and returning from jail. I could hear female laughter coming from the backside of the jail. I was sure Lola's ladies had taken coffee to the army men working in the jail.

Norma and Lola were to my right, and I suddenly caught movement to my left. Then, a man's voice called out, "Norma, what are you doing wearing men's clothes?" Turning to the left, I saw a cowboy tying his horse to the hitching rail in front of Lola's Place.

"Hi, Red. What are you doing back in Holbrook?" Norma called out. "I thought you moved to Colorado," she added.

"I did move there," Red said. "I got word that there was some problem in Holbrook, so I came back to make sure you were okay, Norma."

"As you can see, Red, I'm fine. I am now Lola's accountant, and I'm also married. I'm Missus Gray. I'm sure you've heard of my husband, right Red?"

"The only Gray I've heard of is a gunman. They say he may be the fastest man there is with a gun. Is that who you're married to?"

Norma said, "Yes, it is, Red."

"Well, could I at least get a kiss for old times?" Red asked.

"My husband might object if that happened."

"Who's going to tell him? You or Lola?"

"Neither one of us. Gray is watching from the middle of the street."

Red spun to his right, and his hand did not move toward his pistol.

"Shit! You're taller than I thought you would be," Red said.

"And you're a lucky man," I said.

"Why's that?" Red asked.

"You didn't go for your gun," I said.

The color drained from his face as he said, "OH!"

Chapter 48

Norma walked over to Butch and me. She petted the dog and kissed me on my right cheek. "Gray, if you didn't figure it out, Red was a special client of mine," Norma said.

Keeping Red in my vision, I said, "You mean like Judge Moore was."

Red said, "Norma, don't tell me those two tangled?"

Norma shook her head and said, "No, Red, they did not. But Judge Moore married us just before he left town."

Red looked at me and said, "I heard two outlaws came looking for you and that you gunned them down."

"Not exactly true," I said. "Dagobert Acadia and his partner Cornelius Cameron came looking for me. I wrecked Dagobert's gun hand, and Sheriff Brownie shot Cameron with a shotgun. Dagobert's gun never cleared leather."

Giving me a wide-eyed stare, Red said, "I saw Dag draw, and I know he was fast, much faster than me. Just how fast are you, G…."

Red didn't finish saying my name because my gun barrel was between his lips. I said, "That fast. Is that fast enough for you, Red?"

The color drained from Red's face when the tip of my gun touched his lips. Once I removed the weapon, it took him a few moments to speak. "Yes, sir, Mister Gray, that is fast enough. I think Norma is in good hands, so I'll just go to the hotel and get a room for the night. In the morning, I'm going back to Colorado."

"Now, Red," Lola said. "You just march yourself into the saloon and have a drink on me. My ladies are returning from taking coffee to the soldiers rebuilding the jail. It got damaged during the storm we had last night. I'll send Jo over to see you when the ladies get here. Jo is the newest lady."

I shifted the wood on my shoulder and said, "Norma, our dog, and I need to finish building our new porch."

Lola and Norma laughed at me, and Lola said, "Gray, you can't build a porch with that little bit of wood."

The ladies laughed again, and I finally said, "This wood is to patch up the porch that the storm blew away. Butch, our wonder dog, found the porch in the creek and pulled it out of the water. Then the dog drug it up near the cabin. With my help, Butch was able to put the porch back where it belonged. My lovely wife, Butch, and I will see you later for dinner at the Café."

Butch lifted his bag of goods, and we went to the cabin and finished repairing the Porch. I peeled the bark off several branches that had blown down and set them aside to dry. The branches would become our handrail off the porch. Norma or anyone will not have to jump onto the porch to enter the cabin. I fashioned two steps out of a large chunk of wood and spiked the steps to the porch. Neither the steps nor the porch was going anywhere.

Several town folks were at the café when Norma and I got there. As Norma and I walked into the café, I saw a couple of ladies dressed all in black, and they were sitting at a table that was two tables away from ours. The ladies talked in low voices so their neighbors wouldn't hear them. One of them said, "Did you hear that the gunman had to marry that hussy he is with?"

The other lady said, "That's not right, Earline. He asked that old, and I do mean old, saloon owner to marry him, and she laughed in his face. Then she told him that the trollop was looking for a husband that she could do tricks that he had never heard of. You know what I mean by tricks, don't you, Earline?"

"Midge, I can only imagine what you mean," Earline said. "My daddy taught me never to think of those kinds of things. When my Harold was alive, he knew better than to step inside a saloon, especially ones where there were whores. Excuse my use of that word, but I don't know any other one to use."

"It's all right, Earline. Sometimes, I can't find the right word to use either. Oh my! They are going to sit at that empty table at the back wall. That must be why Nelda wouldn't let us sit there. How does a gunman get a table set aside just for him?"

Midge giggled and said, "Who's going to argue with him."

I grinned across our table at Norma and whispered, "Do you want to go tell them what happened? Or do you want me to go talk to them?"

Norma whispered, "If you went over there, it might give one of them a stroke. I'll talk to them. The folks in town need to know what happened and why we are married."

Norma got up, turned around, walked quickly to the lady's table, and sat down. "Good evening, Midge and Earline. My husband and I could not help but hear what you two said about Mister Gray and myself. Let me get something right out in the open. I met Gray after he got knocked out to keep him from shooting a drunk. The owner of Lola's Place is the one who hit Gray, and that was after she shot the drunk's gun out of his hand. Lola had me stay with Gray until he woke up. When he did, he kissed me for doing that. And that kiss almost stopped my heart; it was so magical. Gray and I fell in love, and when Judge Moore was in town, he married us. Yes, my husband is fast at drawing his gun, but he does not get paid to do that. He has done it to solve a problem in several towns, just like Holbrook. Now, you ladies saw the speed at which I drew a gun at last year's Holbrook Founders competition. I won that year. Let me tell you that my husband is probably three times faster than I am. You ladies now know what happened with Gray and me. Oh! Gray has his own table because he stopped having trouble here without doing anything, but he has two chairs removed from his table."

"Why did he do that, Norma? Or do you know the answer?"

Norma laughed and said, "After meeting Lola, Gray came here for dinner. Three of the ladies who work for Lola want to know who Gray is, and they all come looking for him. When they came in and saw only one chair at his table for the three of them, they could not decide who would sit with him, so they turned around and left without causing any trouble."

Midge and Earline were laughing when I watched Norma walk back to our table. Norma had her head held high when she sat down with me. Then she whispered, "Now the two biggest gossips in town know why this table is reserved."

We were ready to leave when Cookie came to our table. Only one other person was in the dining area, and Cookie nodded to him. Cookie grinned at Norma and said, "I would hug you, but my hands are all greasy, so I will sit here and tell you. I wish more people would do what you did tonight. Then, when those two mean old ladies said something, the town would know they were lying. They get things turned around to make a situation meet what they think is correct. And their thinking is all messed up. Thanks again, Norma, and I'm buying your dinners."

The other patron stood up and said, "How come you never buy me my dinner, Cookie?"

Cookie stood up and said, "Come with me, old man."

We walked outside and to our cabin when Norma said, "I think Cookie is going to have some fun tonight."

Chapter 49

We were getting close to our cabin when Butch was suddenly in front of us. He blocked our path and was growling just loud enough that we could hear him. It was dark out, with only a sliver of the moon for light.

Norma and I had our guns out, and we crouched down and waited with Butch between us. There was a slight movement at the side of the cabin. I could make out the shape of a man. The dull glint of moonlight off metal told me the man was holding a rifle.

I whispered, "Butch, is there more than one?"

The dog gave out two small huffs of air.

Leaning close to Norma, I whispered, "Do you see the person by this side of the cabin?"

"Yes." A whispered response came back.

I whispered, "Butch indicated there are two of them. My guess is the other one is on the other side. That way, they can watch this trail and the one from the saloon. I'm going to slip over to see if I can spot the second person. Butch will stay with you."

Norma whispered, "Go! And be careful."

I slowly worked my way around to see the left side of the cabin. I waited a few moments and got rewarded when the person moved slightly. He was standing still, and I guessed his legs were starting to cramp. In the moonlight, I caught a reflection off the barrel of his rifle. It pointed away from me and down the trail to the other end of town. I slipped up to the guy and used the butt of my revolver to knock him out.

I looked at the figure on the ground and saw it was a woman. I took her rifle as well as a pistol and hunting knife. Then I looked around to the front of the cabin, and no one was in sight. Staying as quiet as I could, I walked to the other corner in front of the place.

I stood there a few moments before I heard the man breathing. It sounded like he was standing right where I had seen him. Shifting my pistol from my right hand to my left, I reached around the corner, sticking the business end of the gun into the man's side. "Stay real still, and you will live to see tomorrow," I said.

"How the hell…" he said that much before I pushed the barrel harder against him.

I said, "Let me hear your rifle hit the ground."

There was a dull sound as the weapon hit the ground. I said, "That's good. If I feel you are moving to get your pistol or that knife in your belt, you will be dead. Do you understand me?"

"Yes," a quiet voice said. It was a voice that I had not heard in a long time.

Norma and Butch came up to my left, and she said, "Where's the other guy?"

"Taking a little nap at the other front corner of the cabin," I said.

"Why don't we take this guy out into the moonlight so we can see who he is?" Norma asked as Butch headed that way.

Suddenly, there was some loud barking, growling, and snapping of teeth. A female voice called out, saying, "Hey! Call your dog off. I ain't moving."

I said, "Norma, why don't you go get the lady? I took her pistol, rifle, and hunting knife. I don't know if she has any other weapons."

When Norma went to get the other lady, I nudged my captive to walk out into the moonlight. When he got out front, I said, "That will do right there. Now, undo the gun belt without undoing the tie-down lines."

"Shit!" was what I heard before two pistols and a hunting knife hit the ground.

"Now untie the holsters, Bill, and turn around slowly."

The man I was looking at was much older than I remember, but it was ten years ago. I thought he was a year or two younger than me then. This man had long gray hair and a beard. He was so skinny I would not have recognized him except for his voice. The Bill, I remember, had a large body with dark brown hair.

Norma brought over the lady, and I saw Maria Sanchez was still Bill William's partner. I didn't know Maria had taken Bill's last name when they married.

"This lady says she and her husband know you, Charlie," Norma said. "Do you know them?"

"Yeah," I said. "We met ten years ago, not long after I left Saint Louis. There was some trouble with missing cattle around Springfield, Missouri. Four ranchers hired Bill Williams to catch the cattle rustlers and bring them to justice. When I walked into a saloon in Springfield, Bill was recruiting men to track down the rustlers. I signed on, and Maria was right behind me. Bill took one look at her and said he didn't want women doing this kind of work. I asked Maria how fast she was with the iron she was wearing. She was pretty damn fast, and Bill hired her too."

"I was faster than Bill, and I still am," Maria said. "But, Gray, I was nowhere near as fast as you. So, this nice lady says she's your wife, Gray, just like I am Bill's wife. This is a good thing, right, Gray?"

I asked, "Which of you will tell me why you were hiding by Norma's and my cabin? And just how the hell did you find out where I was living?"

Bill asked, "Gray, can I put my hands down?"

I nodded, and then Bill said, "Gray, just about everywhere Maria and I have traveled in the last ten years, your name was there before we got there. You, my friend, have a reputation. When we got to Holbrook this morning, Maria stopped a couple of kids playing at being cowboys. One called himself Gray, so Maria asked how the kid knew you. The kids showed us where you live. They never said that you were married."

"That doesn't answer the question, why were you hiding," I said.

Butch, who was beside Norma, suddenly sprang at Maria, his jaw clamped down on her right wrist as a derringer came out of her sleeve.

"What the fuck! Let go of me, you stupid dog!" Maria yelled as the gun fell to the ground.

Norma's gun was up and pointing at Maria before either Bill or I could react. "You got anything else hidden up your sleeves?" Norma asked as she shoved the business end of her pistol into Maria's stomach.

"NO, I DON'T!" Maria screamed. "Call off your dog before he tears my skin."

Norma scooped up the Derringer and said, "Okay, Butch, you can let her go. I got her covered." When Butch let go of Maria, Norma said, "Sit down right where you are, bitch."

I had my pistol out again and said, "Bill, do you have any more weapons on you?"

"No. Maria has a throwing knife or two in her boots."

A gunshot was loud as Norma put a bullet between Maria's boots. Then Norma said, "Push one boot off with the other one, and then your bare foot can push the other off. If you reach for your boots, you will be dead."

"Maria, what the hell are you doing?" Bill called out. "Let me tell this in my way."

"Yeah! I don't think you dare to tell him why we were hiding," Maria said tauntingly.

"Yes, I do! Now shut the fuck up!" Bill snapped at Maria.

I calmly said, "How much were you going to get to kill me?"

"How…"

"He doesn't know anything!" Maria screamed.

"It's the only thing that makes sense to me."

"What makes sense?" Bill asked.

I shook my head slightly and replied, "The thought you were trying to send to Maria. Half is better than being dead. You took half of what someone offered, and when you had proof of my death, you would get the other half."

I saw Bill slump as though he was defeated. Out of the corner of my eye, I saw Maria's face turn into a snarling older woman.

"Bill, I don't know why I married you. You can't seem to think with the brains that God gave you. I told you Cray could read minds, but you wouldn't believe me. Gray will turn us over to the Sheriff, and we'll go to prison. For what? For nothing, that's what!"

Chapter 50

Butch gave out a low growl, and Sheriff Brownie stepped out of the trees, asking, "Who's going to jail?" Brownie was carrying his shotgun, and it looked like he was ready to use it.

"No one," I said. "Brownie, come over here and meet my friend Bill Williams and his wife, Maria."

The Sheriff didn't come any closer but said, "If they are your friends, why is their hardware on the ground?"

I laughed and said, "They were going to surprise me since they didn't know I was now married, but Norma and I did the surprising. Butch warned us that we had visitors at the cabin. It wasn't until I had Bill out in the moonlight that I knew it was him. Bill and Maria were waiting for us outside the cabin."

"So," Brownie said, "once he was in the light, you had Bill put his hardware on the ground and turn around. Is that about it?"

"Yeah."

"Will, the Sawyer boy, told me that your friends were here, but it was the single gunshot that made me come take a look."

"That was an accident on my part," Norma said. "Maria wanted to know how fast I was on the draw. When my pistol came out of the holster, I was in position, and my reflexes made me pull the trigger."

With a shaking of his head, Brownie said, "Since I now know that everything is okay here, I'm going to see if Lola is about ready to go home. Nice meeting you, Bill. And you too, Maria. Good night, all."

Sheriff Brownie was up the trail when Norma said, "Why don't we go into the cabin and talk this through? I don't think anyone wants to see any of us die. I know I don't."

Bill gave Maria a slight nod, and they slowly picked up their weapons. Bill grinned at Norma and said, "Do either of you mind if I put my guns back on? I feel naked without them."

I said, "Why don't you put the guns in their holsters and hold the belt in your right hand? I'm not comfortable with not knowing who paid to have me killed."

"Fair enough," Bill said, then complied with my request.

Maria glared at her husband for several seconds, then, with a huff, said, "Okay, I'll go along with you, Gray." She undid her gun belt, picked up her pistol, and holstered it. Grinning at me from about ten feet away, Maria said, "Gray, are you still as f...."

The barrel of my pistol pressed against her husband's forehead stopped Maria from talking.

Bill swallowed hard, then said, "Maria, honey, I think Gray has gotten faster on the draw since we rode with him. Honey, what say we take Clarence's money and keep heading west? Or, maybe we could go down to Mexico."

Maria walked over to Bill and hugged him, saying, "Sweetheart, what we have now will last us a long time, no matter where we go. So, yes, dear, we head west and not Mexico. I have too many bad memories from there. The Mexican Soldiers that came through our village were worse than any outlaw gangs I have been around in this country. The men in my village hid their women, but they came out of hiding when the soldiers shot their men. I was ten years old when the soldiers took my mother and older sisters. My mother returned four days later and never recovered from what they did to her. My two sisters were brought back a month after that. They were both naked and dead. One of the soldiers looked at me and said, "I'll be back next week for you, little one." That night, my father took my younger brother and me, and we rode until we were in what you call Texas. We stayed with one of his cousins. I have lived in this country since then, and I'll die here rather than go back to Mexico."

Norma said, "Charlie, put your gun away. Then, get the fire started. I think your demonstration about gave Bill a heart attack."

As Butch and I went into the cabin, I heard Maria say, "Bill is not the only one whose heart about stopped. I have never seen anyone that fast. It was a lot faster than I remember."

"Honey, I just told you he was faster," Bill said. "Usually, we slow down some as we get older, but as you said, Maria, I think Gray is one of the lucky ones in that he met Norma and is more relaxed. I think that being relaxed makes it much easier for Gray to draw his weapon."

"Bill, I have a question for you, but I'll wait to ask it until we are inside the cabin," Norma said. "There are two stools at the table where the boys can sit. Maria, you and I, along with the dog, will have to sit on the bed. I know there is little room, but it works for Charlie and me. If Charlie and I sat on the bed, it wouldn't take long for him to start wanting to get friendly."

Maria laughed and said, "Bill would be the same way. So, when did you two get married?"

Norma laughed and said, "Maria, I've only known Charlie for about a month. A couple of Charlie's old friends came to town and now work on one of the ranches hereabouts. Do you know Micky O'Rourke and Ted Largess?"

Maria said, "Yeah, we know those two. They are two gunmen. What do they know about ranching?"

"Well, from what I've heard of them, those two are guards out on the Broken Arrow Ranch. They are a lot more friendly than the Texans that have been coming up here since the Arrow was sold. The new owners from Eastern Texas were supposed to be coming in on the stagecoach the other day. I guess they took a train partway here, and the coach they were to catch at the railhead broke down, and it will be at least a month before they get here."

Maria asked, "How did you and Gray meet?"

Taking a deep breath and blowing part of it out, Norma said, "When Gray got to town, he checked into the hotel, got cleaned up, and came over to Lola's Place. Two Texan cowboys came out through the swinging doors and bumped into Gray when he stepped onto the boardwalk in front of the saloon. One of the cowboys made the mistake of drawing his gun."

"Oh, boy!" Maria said. "Did he kill them both?"

"No. The muzzle of Gray's pistol ended up in the cowboy's mouth, breaking a few teeth along the way. The cowboy had not cleared leather, and his shot went straight down into the boardwalk. Right after that, Lola offered Gray a job as her bouncer; Gray said he needed some food before making up his mind on the job. Later, Gray sat in on a poker game, and a drunk was about to draw down on him when Lola shot the gun out of the drunk's hand. Then she hit Gray over the head, knocking him out. He was brought to Lola's bed, and she told me to stay with him until Gray woke up. I did that, and when Charlie woke up, he kissed me. Now we are married, and I'm Lola's accountant and no longer one of her working girls."

Chapter 51

I was standing in the cabin doorway when I called out, "Are you going to stand out there talking all night or come in the cabin?"

Bill laughed and said, "Maria and I were getting an ear full on how you two met. Sticking that barrel into the man's mouth, through his teeth, must have been a first for you, Gray." Bill did another peal of laughter, then walked to the cabin as he wiped his eyes dry.

Maria and my wife followed Bill into the cabin. They were both giggling. Norma stopped, hugged, and kissed me before saying, "Maria and I are sitting on the bed. I just got to talking and couldn't shut up. Why don't you get out that bottle of Lola's whiskey? I know you got stashed away?"

I chuckled and said, "I should have known that now you're Lola's accountant. You would know when a bottle went missing—and right where it is." I got the bottle out and found cups or glasses for everyone.

Bill filled me in on some of what he and Maria had been doing over the last ten years. I told him some more about what had happened in Holbrook since I got here. We reminisced about some of the good times we had together. About then, Norma called out, "Bill, how much was Judge Moore going to pay you for killing my husband?"

Bill turned bright red with embarrassment. Then he said, "Ten thousand, with five thousand upfront. What Maria said earlier is true. With the five, we have enough to get us through for a long time. I'm not going to tell the Judge that you are dead and collect the other five. I'm not that good of a liar, nor is Maria."

I laughed and shook my head before saying, "Did the Judge tell you that he was Norma's only customer when he was in Holbrook?"

"No, Gray, the Judge never spoke about Norma. He told me, although Maria was sitting right there when he said, 'That bastard Gray did me a disservice and embarrassed me to no end in front of all my friends in Holbrook. I want him dead, and I hear you're the man to do it for me. I'll pay you ten thousand when you give me proof that that lying bastard is dead.' Maria said that we would need five right now. The judge took his wallet out of the inside pocket of his jacket and handed me five one-thousand-dollar bills. We were in a saloon in Durango, Colorado. Maria and I hit the trail right away after leaving the Judge."

I asked, "Do you know how Judge Moore knew about you, Bill? Had you ever met the man before?"

Bill shook his head and said, "No, Gray, I never met the judge before he came into that saloon. Maria and I saw him walk in and look around; you could tell he was looking for someone in particular. You know how it is when you make your living with a gun, you get to know people, or you'll be dead. He finally saw me, approached our table, and sat down. I had my gun in my lap and pointed at him. He said his name, and he had a problem that I could fix. The Judge never said who told him that I could be of help, so Gray, I don't know how he found me."

"Did you two come straight from Durango to Holbrook?" I asked.

Bill nodded, then said, "Yes, we did." I saw Maria nodding in agreement.

"Do either of you know if you were being followed since you left the Durango saloon?"

Bill shook his head and looked over at his wife. Maria nodded and said, "Gray, I have been able to sense when someone has been following me since I was a little girl. I would have known if there were someone behind us. I may not see them, but I can feel them. It is a warm feeling at first like someone is right next to you. If they are behind me, the itch begins at the back of my neck; in front of me, it's between my breasts. I can also feel when a person is watching me from the side. You don't want to know where that feeling is located."

I laughed and said, "Maria, I knew we were more alike than you want to believe. But right now, I have one more question, and I want a truthful answer from you, Bill. Does the law want you in any part of the country or Mexico or Canada?"

Without hesitation, Bill said, "No, and neither is Maria wanted by the law. There are a few Sheriffs who think we should be locked up, but I swear to you, Gray, we have not even been arrested."

"That is true, what Bill said," Maria said. "We have used our guns to settle problems much like you have done, Gray. Taking money from that Moore person was a first. Before this, we never got paid to kill a particular person. And for that, I am sorry we ever got involved with Moore."

My wife comforted Maria before saying, "Judge Moore may have married us, but that does not mean we love him. For a while,

I thought I was in love with him, but that was just the money he gave me and the presents, as well. Since I have been with Gray, I have realized that all I meant to Moore was a warm body where he could release his pent-up anger at the world he surrounds himself with. I was nothing more to him."

Butch, staying at the end of the bed, got up and went over to the door. We all watched as he put his nose under the door latch and pushed it up. Then he pushed the door open and went outside. The door stayed open. I said, "Now, that is a first."

"You mean that dog learned how to open the door from watching you do it, Gray?" Maria asked.

I shook my head, saying, "I don't know how he learned to do that. Butch may have known how before we got him."

"How did you end up with Butch?" asked Maria.

Norma said, "Everyone in town thought that Butch was the town's dog. But when Gray and I moved into this cabin, I forgot to give Butch his evening snack. The next day, a herd of cattle was going to be driven right through Holbrook, but Gray stopped that. Please don't ask how he did it. That is too long of a story for now. Anyway, when we returned to the cabin that night, the door was open a few inches. When Gray looked in the window, he said a critter was making a mess of the place in the cabin. I ran to the door and opened it wide. Butch was on our bed with his tail going crazy. I talked to him, petted him, and even hugged that dog. Do you know what that animal did?"

"What?" Maria exclaimed.

"He walked over to Gray and put his head in Gray's lap. Butch has been Gray's ever since then."

I said, "Bill, where are your horses? There weren't any tied in front of Lola's Place or the hotel across the street."

"We took them to the Livery and got a room at the hotel before we came here to wait for you. And it's about time we headed to our room. What time is breakfast? And where do we eat?"

"Simpson Café and Cookie usually opens around six. Norma and I need to talk to Lola so we can go to the saloon and introduce you to her before you go to your room."

Chapter 52

When we walked into Lola's Place, two cowboys were at the bar arguing with James. "Gentlemen, as I said, I cannot give you a drink until you hand over your weapons. As I also said, you can try another establishment, but the rule is the same in all the saloons and bars in town. Now, leave or hand over your weapons. I'm not telling you again."

The tallest of the two cowboys said, "I think you're bluffing and don't have a shotgun in your hand under the bar."

I said, "If either one of you touches your guns, it will be the last move you make."

The cowboys froze, and James said, "Thanks, Mister Gray."

At the sound of my name, I saw the smaller cowboy's hands move, and his weapons were soon on the bar. The smaller guy said, "Joe, that's the name we heard the foreman say. I'm not going to tangle with him."

Keeping his hands away from his pistol, the taller guy turned around and looked at me. He said, "NO one can be..." he was looking at the business end of my revolver.

"Care to wager on that," I said.

The cowboy's hands were shaking when he unbuckled his gun belt. The man slowly turned around and placed his holstered gun on the bar; his hands were still shaking. I walked up behind the cowboys and said, "James, put these boys' first drink on my tab. For which outfit are you boys riding?"

The smaller one turned his head and, looking at me, said, "Thanks for the drink, Mister Gray. We're riding for the Broken Arrow Ranch."

The taller cowboy said, "Thanks, Mister Gray. I thought our foreman was fast on the draw, but he any near as fast as you, Sir."

"Is your foreman named Chad, or is it Thornhill?" I asked.

"Chad is the working foreman, and Mister Thornhill is the overall foreman. Do you know them?" the taller one asked.

I laughed and said, "I met Thornhill when the Broken Arrow was going to run their cattle right up Holbrook's main street. I met Chad in Rockwood, New Mexico, when he decided he didn't want to turn over his weapons. He went to jail for a couple of days. Where you boys from?"

The tall one said, "Both of us are from Prescott. The Broken Arrow beats the heck out of any of the ranches around our hometown."

Both cowboys were studying me, and I grinned at them, saying, "I won't be the one who tells Thornhill that you refused to turn over your weapons, and neither will James. But neither of us can say what our boss will do when she finds out. Thornhill gave his word to Lola and Sheriff Brownie that the Broken Arrow hands would turn in their weapons. Since you boys are Arizonians, James and I will overlook it this time. You two are the only Broken Arrow hands that get this one pass; the next time, James will only ask once and then use his shotgun. Are we clear on this?"

Both of the cowboys swallowed hard and said, "Yes, Sir. Mister Gray." The shorter one said, "We'll be taking our gun belts off as we walk through the swinging doors. Is that okay, sir?"

I nodded and said, "That would be the safest way to stay alive. You two have a great night and perhaps enjoy a couple of the ladies here."

Turning around, I found that Norma had taken Bill and Maria to Lola's table and introduced them to Lola and Sheriff Brownie. When I got to the table, Lola said, "Brownie was about to talk to them cowboys when you got here. Gray, I'm sure you have figured it out that Brownie does not like confrontation, and I owe you one for being here at the right time."

I smiled at Lola and said, "How about sending two of your ladies to help the boys relax? I think the tall one might be having some trouble with his self-image. He thought he was fast on the draw, but when he was looking down the barrel of my six-shooter, he about shit his pants."

Bill laughed and said, "I know the feeling. I think Maria is right, and you are a hell of a lot faster on the draw than when we hung out together. Gray, I still don't know how you knew that Maria and I were outside your cabin."

Before I could say a word, Norma said, "I thought Charlie told you that it was Butch who warned us that you were there."

"Yeah, he did, Norma, but I still can't figure out how Butch would know we were there," Bill said.

I laughed and said, "Bill, a dog's nose is a hell of a lot more sensitive than yours or mine. He got two scents, yours and Maria's.

I waited until I saw you slightly adjust your position, and then I went over to the other side of the house. There was a small glare of moonlight from the barrel of Maria's rifle. I didn't know who I was dealing with, but I could not wait around to find out, so I hit her on the head and knocked her out. I took her pistol, rifle, and hunting knife. When I was taking her pistol and knife, I knew who it was I had knocked out. When I put the muzzle of my six-shooter on your side, I didn't think it was you. You have lost a lot of weight since I met you. But your scent was still there."

Maria reached down and petted Butch, lying between her and Norma. Then Maria said, "Norma, this dog of yours is one smart animal. When we came to town, I saw several dogs; how come Butch can come in here, and no one seems to care, and no other dogs even come close to this saloon. Why is that?"

I saw Norma puff up a little before saying, "This is Butch's territory, and the other dogs know that, so they stay away. It's the same at the jail. That is Butch's, and the other dogs better not mess with Brownie. Simpson Café, where we are going to breakfast, is Butch's. But he graciously lets the other dogs come close when it is time to be fed by Cookie."

Lola chuckled and said, "And each dog knows where they can lay down and stay until Cookie comes to feed them. When one dog gets into another dog's feeding area, Butch lets them know by growling at them. When Cookie goes to feed the bad dog, Butch stops Cookie, and that dog goes hungry for the night. As you said, Maria, Butch is a brilliant dog."

"Thank you for telling me that about Butch; it more or less answers the question of how Butch became Gray's dog," Maria said.

"They are both smart when it comes to reading other people and dogs. I don't know about my husband, but it is way past my time to sleep for me. I bid you all a good night."

Maria got up, and Bill did too, and he said, "See whoever is going to breakfast at that time. Good night."

Chapter 53

While talking at Lola's table, she sent Jo and Anita over to the two cowboys. When Bill and Maria were almost to the swinging doors, I saw the cowboys head upstairs. As I watched the cowboys, Norma leaned into me and whispered, "I'm proud of you, Charlie. You did them, cowboys, some real good. They will remember this day and you, my dear husband. I think I'll keep you around for another fifty years or so. What do you think of doing that?"

I grinned as I kept my eyes forward and said, "If you add another fifty years to your number, I could agree to that."

Norma laughed and said, "Let's go home and practice. Lola told me she was going home with Brownie. I think our sheriff is going to get lucky, too."

The following day, I woke when Butch let out a low growl next to my ear. I was instantly awake. I rolled off the bed, taking Norma with me. Grabbing my pistol and keeping low, I worked my way to where I could stand beside the window and looked out. I almost laughed at what I saw.

Jo and Anita were hanging onto the two cowboys who wouldn't give James their weapons. All four were naked except for the boots on their feet. The boys also had their gun belts on.

Norma looked out the window beside me and almost said something, but I covered her mouth with my left hand. I whispered, "Can you sound like a mad Lola?"

"Yes," Norma whispered. "What do you want me to say?"

"Tell Anita to get her ass back to her room, or she'll be fired. Or something like that."

Norma yelled at Anita and sounded just like Lola.

"Oh, God! That's Lola," Anita cried out. Letting go of the tall cowboy, Anita added, "Come on, Jo, we have to go!" then Anita started running, and Jo was right behind her. The cowboys looked at each other, and they ran as well.

The sight of what the boys had between their legs set Norma off in a peal of laughter. I put on my britches and opened the door for Butch to go out and check his area. Norma slipped one of my shirts on and was standing beside me when Butch came prancing back to the porch.

Norma hugged me and said, "Go get some fresh water. Make it enough for Butch's dish and coffee. It is too early to go for coffee at Simpson Café."

I got our wooden bucket, and Butch and I went down to the creek to get Norma's water. I went around a few bushes to ensure the water was clear of debris. As I came back around one of the bushes, Butch started barking. There was a pistol shot from behind another bush, and I saw two horses and riders coming up the creek. Both men wore bandanas, so I could not see who they were. A whizzing sound by my head made me drop the water bucket and draw my six-shooter. I had it tucked into the belt of my britches. I also fell to the ground as one bullet grazed my left shoulder. I fired twice, and my second shot caught one of the riders in the throat. I fired twice more. The second rider was lifted out of his saddle and onto the back of his horse. He sat there a moment before falling to the ground. Both horses raced by me, and a low-hanging tree branch knocked the first man I shot off his horse.

I watched to see if there were more men, but I did not see or hear anyone. What I heard was Norma calling, "Gray! Gray, answer me, Gray! What the hell is going on out there?"

"A couple of bastards tried to sneak up on us by riding up the Swan Creek," I said. "They didn't know I was getting water, and Butch gave out a warning. I have to find Butch because one of those bastards shot at the dog."

Norma laughed and said, "Your dog is fine. He came running into the cabin with his tail tucked between his legs. You better get back in here as well. And don't forget to bring in the water."

"Well, I know what one of those bastards shot," I called out.

"What?"

"Our water bucket. There is a hole on each side now. I'll bring in what water I can." I was bent over getting fresh water when a drop of blood fell into the creek. "SHIT!" I exclaimed.

"Gray, what is it this time?" Norma called from the other side of the bushes I was behind.

I stepped around the bush, and when I saw Norma and Butch standing there, I said, "One of the bullets grazed me. You want to kiss it and make it well?"

Norma grinned at me and said, "A simple bucket of water is what I asked you to get, and you go out and cause all kinds of trouble. Does trouble just naturally follow you around? Gray, what the hell have I got myself into being married to you?"

"Now, Norma, you know I did not cause this. I haven't even looked at the guys to see if I know them."

"But you have a hunch of where they came from and who sent them, don't you, my dear husband?"

"Yeah. So much for Maria's ability to tell if someone is following her. I'm going to catch their horses. Maybe we can tell something about these guys from their gear."

You better put a shirt on first. And you have to tell Brownie what happened.

We hurried up to the cabin, and I grabbed another shirt since Norma wore the one I had on yesterday. I looked toward Lola's Place and said, "James just went to tell Brownie about shots being fired. I should be back with the horses before they get here. If Brownie gets here before I return, have him see if he knows those outlaws. You want to put a temporary patch on my shoulder before I go?"

Norma tore one of her old gowns into strips and tied a couple around my shoulder. "You are going to see Doctor Roth before we go to breakfast," she said.

"I'll do that after I catch the horses and talk to the Sheriff and whoever else comes by. I love you, Norma, and I want to be with you for a long, long, long time. I got to go. Come on, Butch, let's go catch those horses."

Chapter 54

The reins of one of the horses I was after got snagged on some brush. That stopped the animal, and the one horse stopped beside the first one. It took me longer to return to the cabin since the reins were twisted so badly that I almost had to cut them.

When I was getting close to the cabin, I heard Digger say, "Sheriff, we can't leave these bodies in the creek. Their blood is going to draw a lot of unwanted critters looking for breakfast. Let me and my boy take them up to the Funeral Parlor." I stopped the horses and listened.

Brownie said, "Okay, Digger, you go on and take them. I may want a couple of Gary's friends to look at the bodies to see if they know the outlaws. So, don't be putting those bodies in the ground until I tell you can. Okay?"

"I won't do nothing until you tell me to, Sheriff," Digger said. I heard something heavy fall onto some wood, and I knew that Digger was taking the bodies away.

Sheriff Brownie said, "What the hell is taking Gray so long to find those horses?"

Lola said, "Honey, it can't be fun trying to catch those animals in the creek. The damn thing is so overgrown. Let's go into the cabin. There is nothing else to do out here."

I led the horses down to the front of the cabin and called out, "Brownie, these horses have a brand for a ranch out of Durango, Colorado. The saddlebags are full, and I have not looked through them."

Sheriff Brownie hurried out of the cabin and asked, "Where the heck did you have to go to catch them?"

I laughed and said, "Them animals went straight up the creek until the reins of one horse got caught in some brush. It took me forever to get them untangled. The horses initially did not want me close, and I had to convince them that I was a good guy."

By then, about half the town showed up in our front yard, what little there was. Ned Worthington, the town banker, finally called out, "Sheriff, who was shot, and who did the shooting?"

Brownie said, "Two outlaws rode up Swan Creek. They tried to catch Mister Gray, unaware that they were there. When they saw him getting the water, they started firing at him. Gray returned fire, and both outlaws were dead. I don't have any names yet, and Mister Gray does not know the outlaws. The horses the outlaws rode have the brand of a ranch outside Durango. That is all I know for now. Everyone go home or back to work."

I said, "Ned. I worked for the Durango ranch with the same brand these horses wear. The Crossed T is a small ranch land-wise, but they have a whole lot of Black Hereford cattle. The Sheriff has to go through the saddlebags on these horses to see if he can identify the two outlaws. Now, everyone go on home like the Sheriff said to do."

Brownie found a letter addressed to Cory Redding with an address of Durango, Colorado, in one of the saddlebags. In another, he saw a telegram. The sheriff went to his office with the name and looked through the wanted posters. Then, when he found nothing there, the sheriff sent a telegram to the sheriff of Durango.

While Brownie was doing that, Norma and I went to breakfast with Bill and Maria. After breakfast, we went by Diggers to see if Bill or Maria knew the two outlaws. At first, Bill seemed reluctant to even look at the dead men. Norma finally put her foot down, as they say. "Bill, you can look at the guys with us or do it with the Sheriff. Either way, the Sheriff will get an answer, so make up your mind and do it quickly.

"Okay," Bill said. "I'm glad it is you two and not the Sheriff; he makes me nervous."

"Hell!" Digger said. "Brownie makes me nervous, and I've known him since he got here—that's been ten or so years."

Bill looked at the bodies and started to shake his head when Maria asked, "Gray, what kind of horses were these two riding?"

I frowned for a moment, trying to remember which one was riding on which horse. I finally said, "The smaller of the two was riding an Appaloosa, and the big one was on a Strawberry Roan. Both horses are wearing the Crossed T brand of a Durango area ranch."

"Shit!" Maria exclaimed. "Bill, do you remember me asking you why two Crossed T horses would be in Gallup when we stopped there?"

Bill frowned momentarily, then said, "Yeah, but we wanted a drink so bad we forgot to ask who the owners were. When we left that bar, the horses were gone. But why would those two guys be in Gallup before us if they followed us?"

Maria laughed, saying, "That rotten Judge Moore sent those two to Gallup to watch for us. When we entered that bar, those two walked out a minute later. I was looking around for someone we might have known in Durango. I saw those two leave the bar."

I said, "They probably went to send a telegram to Moore. Then they waited around for an answer from him. He told them to come here and see if you had resolved his problem."

Maria asked, "So what do we do now? I don't like that Moore can send someone after us that easily."

"Neither do I," Bill said.

"Right now," I said, "We will see Sheriff Brownie. But we don't say anything about a telegram until we know what Brownie has discovered about the two guys."

We left Digger's place, and when we were out on the street, Norma said, "I need to get to work, or my boss is going to let me go."

Maria said, "I don't think that is going to happen. You and your boss are too much alike. I think she is looking for you to take over her business."

"Damn, that's what Gray thinks too. Well, whatever happens, I still need to get to work. I love you, Gray." With that, Norma kissed and hugged me, then ran to Lola's back door.

Bill frowned at me as he said, "You really think Norma may end up running that saloon? Don't get me wrong, but she seems a little young for managing that kind of establishment."

I laughed and said, "Bill, you remember how fast I drew my six-shooter on you? Well, think of a female who is less than half a second slower than me and shoots a hell of a lot straighter than me. Now let's go see what Sheriff Brownie has found on the dead men."

Bill looked at me in awe for a moment, then said, "Maria, I'm sure glad we didn't run into Norma before Gray found us. I think we both would have been dead."

Maria nodded and said, "Yeah. And, Bill, you let Gray talk to Sheriff Brownie unless the Sheriff asks you a direct question."

Chapter 55

I watched Norma push her way through the back door of Lola's Place. Then I turned and started for the sheriff's office. Bill, Maria, and I had taken about ten steps when I saw the sheriff come out of the telegraph office, so we turned to head Brownie off before he went to see Lola.

As we approached the Sheriff, I said, "Brownie, those two cowboys may have followed Bill and Maria to Holbrook. Maria remembers seeing them boys in Gallup when she and Bill went into a bar."

"Okay, let's go to my office, and I'll get their statements. And I've found out a thing or two about those cowboys."

Once we settled around the sheriff's office desk, Brownie said, "Okay, let's start with you, Maria. What makes you think those boys may have followed you to Holbrook?"

Maria nodded and said, "Sheriff, when Bill and I were passing through Durango up in Colorado, we noticed a couple of large ranches around there, including the Crossed T Ranch. Bill and I were sitting in one of the saloons in Durango when a man came in and sat down with us. He bought us a drink and joked with the waitress. The guy was well-known in the bar. Anyway, this guy finally started talking to Bill. The man offered Bill a few thousand dollars to come down to Holbrook and shoot Gray. Bill hemmed and hawed with the guy, finally settling on ten thousand. The guy didn't give Bill the name of who he wanted killed until after Bill agreed to do the deed. We got five thousand, and the other we would get after Bill provided the man with proof that Gray was dead."

Brownie asked, "Maria, how did this guy know Bill would do the job?"

"The guy said he talked to the Durango Sheriff, and that Sheriff gave him Bill's name. We don't know if that is true or not. But it sounded reasonable. Anyway, we left Durango and rode south. We stopped at the first bar we saw when we got to Gallup. We were both thirsty and dusty. There were two horses hitched to the rail out front of the bar, both with the Crossed T brand on them. When we entered the bar, I looked around for anyone I might recognize from Durango. There wasn't anybody, but I remember seeing those two leave the bar in Gallop after looking at the cowboys that Gray shot. Those Crossed T horses were gone when Bill and I left that bar."

Brownie said, "So if those boys left the bar before you, wouldn't they have gotten to Holbrook before you?"

Bill said, "Sheriff, that is what I thought too, but Gray said it's possible the men were waiting for us in Gallup, and they sent a telegraph to the man in Durango. They could have told the man we were there and then waited for a telegraph back from the man telling them what they were to do."

"And what do you suppose that would be?" Brownie asked.

Maria said, "We think they were told to follow us, and if Bill did not kill Gray, then they were to do it and also kill us. The cowboys could keep any money they found on us."

"By that, you mean any of the five thousand that was left, right Maria?" Brownie said.

"Yes." She said.

Brownie sat back, and I could tell he was thinking. I grinned and said, "Yeah, Brownie, it's hard to think of him that way, isn't it, my friend."

"What does Norma think of the situation?" Brownie asked me.

"She thinks the guy should be strung up and castrated for what he tried to have done," I said. "The question is, what if anything can be done?"

Sheriff Brownie shook his head, saying, "As a lawman, there is not much I can do because I don't see where the law has been broken. But Judge Moore better never show his face around here again. Bill and Maria, we have your word against a Federal Circuit Judge. Whose word do you think a jury is going to believe?"

Maria said, "Sheriff, what do you think we should do with the five thousand the bastard gave us?"

Brownie was silent for a moment, then said, "If it were me, I think I would want to have a change of scenery. You might want to head east, way far east, as far as a train will take you. Maybe keep in touch with Gray so he can let you know if something happens to your friend Judge Moore."

Bill said, "That asshole ain't no friend of mine."

Maria laughed and said, "Bill, the sheriff said that as a joke. He's figured out that Moore is no friend to anyone in this town, especially once they hear that Moore was behind the attempt to kill Gray. I think Gray has made more friends in Holbrook than he has anywhere else."

Bill nodded to his wife and said, "Yeah, you are probably right about all the friends he has here. Hell, even the dogs are his friends. But the question I have running around in my mind is, what the hell will Gray do when Norma takes over Lola's Place?"

We all laughed at the serious look on Bill's face, and Brownie finally said, "Well, I don't think I'm breaking any rules when I say that Lola and I have talked it over some. She thinks that Gray should take over as Sheriff of Holbrook when I retire. She doesn't think anyone in town would object to that arrangement."

There was a knock on the Jailhouse door, and a voice called out, "Sheriff Brownie, are you in there with Gray?"

"Yes, we are, Captain Flemming. We are in a meeting with two other people. What's up?" Brownie called back.

"I would like to talk to you about those two men that Digger has at the Funeral Parlor. Can I come in?"

Brownie opened the door, saying, "Come in, Captain, and meet Gray's friends."

The captain in charge of the troop of Army men camped just outside of Holbrook walked in, and when he saw Maria, he said, "Captain John Flemming, at your service, ma'am."

Maria smiled at him and said, "Captain Flemming, I'm Maria Williams, and this is my husband, Bill." She said this as she put a protective hand on Bill's arm.

I laughed and said, "Captain, I'm sorry if I spoiled your plans."

Chapter 56

Captain Flemming smiled at me and asked, "What plans are you talking about, Mister Gray?"

"The one where you planned to get back on track with your career in the Army," I said with a smile of my own.

Brownie said, "Gray, have you lost your mind? John is a Captain in the United States Army. He'll be a Major when word gets back to Washington that he stopped an Indian uprising here in Holbrook. So, from what I've seen, it looks like his career is already on track."

I said, "The two men in the funeral Parlor were Army deserters, and I believe they were under the command of Captain Flemming. Is that not correct, Captain?"

"Yes!" Flemming yelled. "But how in heaven's name did you know that? No one in my current company knows I fought in the Battle of Prairie Grove on December 7, 1862. Those two did not like the idea that a new Lieutenant was their commanding officer. I had been a sergeant, and our General promoted me to Lieutenant when our officer was killed in action with the South."

I said, "Captain, I'm not sure how it happens, but sometimes I just know things. Like, Captain, you want to take credit for killing those two deserters to clear the one blemish on your official record. Is that about it, Captain?"

Captain Flemming's posture slumped, and he said, "Yes. The Generals in Washington know that the two deserters were under my command. If I send General Hayes word that I had to shoot the two men, I think he would make my records show that I had tracked down the deserters. It would go a long way to ensuring that I got promoted to Major or even up to Colonel."

I looked around the room and said, "Does anyone in this room object to Captain Flemming taking the credit for killing two Army deserters?"

Bill said a loud, "NO! The two needed to be hung for what they did."

"I have no problem," Maria said.

Sheriff Brownie said, "Captain, if you are going to take those two bodies back with you to the Army Fort in Flagstaff, then I have not a bit of trouble with your reshooting them if you want to."

Captain Flemming stood tall and said, "Thank you all, especially you, Mister Gray. Based on what I have heard about you, I wasn't sure you would play along with my plan. They say you are a straight shooter and abide by or bend the law to meet the situation. What do you consider this to be?"

I laughed and said, "Captain Flemming, I say the two men broke the law when they deserted, so this is taking care of justice. The records are made right, and the bad guys have been punished. So, this is a good thing all the way around, wouldn't you say, Captain?"

Captain Flemming and I shook hands, and he said, "I agree with you, Mister Gray. Now, if Sheriff Brownie would kindly tell Mister Digger that the Army will be picking up the two bodies, we can get this ordeal over with."

Flemming bowed to Maria and said, "Ma'am, I bid you a good day, and all three of you gentlemen as well." The Captain walked out of the jailhouse with his head held high.

We were all standing when Flemming left us, and Bill looked at Brownie and asked, "Sheriff, how much money did you find on those two outlaws?"

"Now that's the funny thing here," Brownie said as he rubbed his chin. "I went through their pockets before I let Digger take the bodies to the Parlor. There was a total of ten dollars between them. I found no other money when I went through their belonging in their saddlebags and bedrolls."

Maria said, "Sheriff, that doesn't make sense to me. Moore must have paid them something, so where's the money?"

Brownie said, "They weren't wearing dusters of heavy jackets, and there was a lack of personal items, so I think they have a camp somewhere around Holbrook."

I grinned and said, "Or a room at the Hotel."

"Yeah," Brownie said. "I was heading over there when the three of you stopped me."

Bill said, "Well, what are you waiting for? Let's go see the clerk before he goes to the guy's room and checks their things."

A shower had passed through Holbrook while we were in Sheriff Brownie's office, and our boots were a little muddy when we walked into the hotel. Jimmy, the hotel clerk, saw us, and I saw him grimace. With the palm up, I stuck my left hand to Jimmy and said, "Jimmy, hand it over."

We could all see that Jimmy was shaking when he said, "I don't know what you are talking about, Mister Gray?"

"What you took from the room of the two dead outlaws. They didn't have it on them when Sheriff Brownie searched them. You don't want to be arrested, do you, Jimmy?"

Reaching under the check-in counter, Jimmy brought out a pouch and placed it in my hand.

Brownie said, "Jimmy, which room was theirs, and did you take anything else out of the room?"

"Room 105. It's the last room on the left, down that hall to your right, and no, Sheriff Brownie, I didn't take anything else, but Jo did."

I said, "By that, Jimmy, do you mean Jo, the lady from over at Lola's Place?"

"Yes, Mister Gray. She came in and asked me to show her which room those cowboys were in. I took her back there, and she found a stash of money. Then she opened her dress and said I could feel her breasts. They were sure big and soft. Then she left, saying that her being here was our secret. Then I picked up what you got in your hand, Mister Gray. I swear that's all I took. Are you going to tell my dad?"

I opened the bag Jimmy had given me and saw a razor, a shaving brush, a bar of shaving soap, and a deck of playing cards. Looking at Jimmy, I said, "No, son, I'm not going to tell your dad. And, Jimmy, you might as well keep all these things."

Maria, Bill, Brownie, and I left the hotel and headed for Lola's Place.

Chapter 57

When the four of us stepped into the saloon, heads turned and looked. Most of them then turned back to their drink or their card game. Lola kept her eyes on Brownie, and Norma had her eyes on me. Anita and Jo were also at the table with Lola.

Jo was sitting next to Norma, so I naturally walked around the table and stopped by my wife. I looked at Jo and asked, "So, Jo, how much money did the cowboys have on them?"

Moving a little away from me, Jo said, "What the hell are you talking about, Gray?"

After giving Lola a quick hug and kiss, Brownie moved to stand on the other side of Jo. He said, "Jo, when I asked Jimmy if he had taken anything other than what he had in a bag, Jimmy said he had not, but that you had. How much and where is it? The Army is taking over this case and wants that money back. I could tell Captain Flemming all of this, and he could come here and have some of his men strip search you. Is that what you want, Jo?"

Looking around Brownie, Jo said, "Lola, do you know what these gentlemen are talking about?"

Lola sat up straight, saying, "From the sound of it, Jo, I would say that they believe you took some money that does not belong to you. Can you prove that the money in question is yours?"

"If I had the money, how would I prove it is mine?"

Lola was quiet for a few moments, then said, "Jo, I believe you would need to have something in writing that says where the money came from."

"SHIT!" Jo exclaimed loudly. "That little rat, Jimmy, is lying, and after I let him see and squeeze my breasts. There is no fucking money in my room. Lola, will you come up with me and check the room for the Sheriff?"

I said, "We'll all go up and get the money."

"What? You don't trust me, Mister Gray," Jo said with a fake smile.

I chuckled and said, "I don't trust anyone other than Norma regarding money."

Anita approached the table to speak to Lola, but Norma cut her off, saying, "The four of you go on up to Jo's room. I'll stay here and take care of Anita's problem."

Lola reached over, squeezed Norma's arm, and said, "We should be right back. Anita, I need to go upstairs to help the Sheriff and Mister Gray with a major problem. Norma can answer any questions you have."

When we went up to her room, Jo stomped on every step. It looked like she was trying to break the staircase and maybe hoping that the sheriff would break his neck as well. We turned the room over but could not find any money.

Little did we know that Anita wanted to talk to Lola about the money and where it was hidden. When we came out of Jo's room,

Norma and Anita were in the hall waiting for us. Norma held the money bag behind her back in her left hand and out of our sight.

Lola asked, "What are you ladies doing up here?"

Norma asked, "Did you find the money?"

"No," Brownie said in an exasperated tone.

With a flourish and a smile, Norma brought her left hand to her front and said, "Anita and I, along with James, looked in the bag Jo hid when she hurried into the saloon. Anita was in the backroom, helping James stock some shelves. Anita saw where Jo put something through and opened the backroom door. That is what she wanted to tell you, Lola."

"Where did Jo hide that bag?" Lola asked.

"That is not essential right now," Norma said. "The important thing right now is the contents of the bag."

With almost a snarl, Brownie exclaimed, "What could be more important than the money in that bag?"

Norma pulled out a telegraph and said, "I think this ties Judge Clarence Moore to the would-be assassins now in the Funeral Parlor." She handed the telegraph to Sheriff Brownie, which read

I HAVE GIVEN THIS CONSIDERABLE THOUGHT, AND YOU ARE TO FOLLOW BILL WILLIAMS AND HIS WIFE TO HOLBROOK. IF BILL DOES NOT REMOVE MY PROBLEM, YOU ARE TO FIX THAT AND THE WILLIAMS. Signed C MOORE CIRCUIT JUDGE.

"Well, that sure does tie those two to Judge Moore," Brownie said. "Norma, what else is in that wonder bag?"

Norma smiled and said, "I'm glad you asked, Sheriff Brownie, because there are two other telegraphs—one from Gallup and one from the telegraph office in Gallup. The one from Gallup is addressed to Jo. It says he will be in Holbrook soon and had a wad of surprises with him: your loving husband, Cory. The one to Gallup says it better be more than the three hundred you told me you had for me to meet you in Holbrook. Your loving wife, Jo."

I asked, "Jo, was one of those cowboys your husband?"

"Yes. And you killed him, Mister Gray."

"I was defending myself, Jo. I would not have killed your husband if he had not been shooting at me."

"I know that," Jo said. "I knew he was an outlaw when I met and married him. I also knew that his life would probably end the way it did, so Gray, I won't hold a grudge against you. Do I get to keep the money?"

I said, "Jo, that is not up to me. Sheriff Brownie and Lola will have to decide where the money goes. But, if it were up to me, I would say you deserve the money."

Brownie asked, "Norma, did you count the money in the bag?"

Norma shook her head, saying, "No, Sheriff, I did not. James said, and Anita and I agreed that you and Lola should count the money. So, Sheriff Brownie, I'm handing you the bag of money and the other two telegrams. As Charlie said, it is up to you, Sheriff, to decide who gets the money."

Brownie took the bag from Norma and gave it heft. "I would say there is a little more than three hundred in here. I never realized how heavy paper money is. There must be about ten pounds here."

Lola said, "That is interesting, dear, but I think we need to take this all down to my table and have a drink. Anita, I am sorry that I didn't listen to you. It would have saved us some time, so Join me at the table; the first drink is on me."

Anita laughed and said, "All my drinks are already on you. But I will join you at your table. We don't get to sit with you that much."

We all went down to Lola's table, and James had her special bottle with enough glasses waiting for us.

Chapter 58

After discussing the situation and having a few drinks, Lola finally said, "As Mayor of Holbrook, I'm declaring that Jo is the rightful owner of the money in question. Sheriff Brownie, I hereby authorize you to hand over the bag of money in its entirety to Jo."

Brownie grinned and said, "It took you long enough to decide. I was ready to give Jo the money after Norma told us what Cory's telegraph said." Handing the bag of money to Jo, Brownie said, "Here you go, Jo. Sorry it took so long to get it to you. But we had to kind of document what we said and did with the money."

"That's okay, Sheriff Brownie. I understand this had to be done properly, and thank you for this money. And thank you too, Miss Lola. Who will walk me to the bank so I don't get robbed on the way there?"

We all laughed, and I said, "Jo, it will be Norma and my pleasure to guard you until the money is in the bank's safe."

Norma was sitting to my left and gave me a quick hug before saying, "Jo, we'll even take Butch with us to make sure no other dogs will try to snatch the bag from your hands."

"I thank you both," Jo said, "And I'm glad that Butch is coming with us. Shall we go now? This bag is burning a hole in my hands."

The teller counted the money at the bank; the total was twenty-three thousand and three hundred dollars. Jo cried at the amount of money and finally said, "Cory kept his word. He gave me the three hundred that he promised me."

On returning to the saloon, Norma and Jo discussed what she could do with the money. Jo finally said, "One of the things that Cory and I talked about was us moving to my hometown of Wichita, Kansas. I think I'm going to honor him by doing just that: moving back home. I know my dad died a couple of years ago, and I don't think my mother has remarried. Maybe we can become friends again. I don't have to tell her exactly where the money came from, do I, Norma?"

Norma was quiet for a few moments, then said, "Jo, I think that is going to have to be up to you. Does your mother know what you have been doing to make a living?"

Jo nodded, saying, "Yeah, I told her what I do, and that's where we kind of parted ways; my dad told me never to come home again, and my mother went along with him. My dad was ten years older than my mother, and she agreed with everything he said. If she didn't, he would beat the shit out of her, then take it out on me. I had a friend with me when I told my folks, and my dad couldn't hit him, so he kicked us both out. Maybe I can get together with that friend."

By then, we were back at the saloon, and the place was starting to hop. I went to the bar to talk with James, and then Norma and Jo went to Lola's table. Anita was still sitting beside Lola. Lola looked at Jo and said, "Jo, we'll talk about your leaving tomorrow. You and Anita get to work. Strike up a conversation with those two cowboys up at the bar. One has been eyeing Anita since they walked in."

After Jo and Anita were busy, Lola asked Norma, "Where is Jo thinking of going?"

"Jo talked about going to Wichita, Kansas, to be with her mother. Jo said there was a guy there she might get together with. She is good at what she does, and I would hate to see you lose her."

"Yeah, I've talked to her a few times since she got here," Lola said. "She told me that a guy named Cory hooked her up with Betsy. So, Cory must have been her husband. I wonder if Betsy was the wife of the other cowboy that the Army is taking away from here."

"Jo didn't tell me anything about Betsy," Norma said.

Lola looked sternly at Norma and asked, "When are you and Gray going after Moore?"

Norma looked over at me, and I knew she needed me by her side. Lola laughed when I got to the table and said, "Gray, I caught your wife in a swamp, and she knew just what to do. She called in the reinforcements, namely you, my friend. I asked when you and your wife are going after Moore. She didn't know what to say."

I grinned at Norma and said, "Lola, you know that was a damn tricky question to ask a lady who has not had sex in a few hours. She's so horny she is ready to burst. If you were to ask me that question, I would have to say I don't know. I say that because neither of us discussed the matter with Sheriff Brownie, and neither have my wife nor I. The Sheriff, good man that he is, maybe way over his head and needs to consult with his girlfriend and then the Governor or someone in that man's office. It may come down to asking the federal government to send the US Marshal to arrest Moore. The practical way of handling this is to say, Gray, you and Norma, get your asses going and arrest Moore if you can or shoot the bastard if you can't. Now that my wife has had time to think about your question, she may have a word or two to say on the subject of Moore. And, Lola, that is all I have to say at this time."

Lola opened her mouth to say something but shut it again when Norma kicked her shin.

"I do have something to say," Norma said. "My dear husband is right; we have not discussed going to Colorado and arresting that bastard Moore. We have not talked about going after him for a few reasons. The major reason is that we did not know for sure that he was trying to double kill us, once with Bill and Maria and the backup boys who thought they could surprise Gray. That didn't work out so well for them. I don't think Moore knew that Gray and Bill were friends. Someone, and we don't know who gave Moore Bill's name as someone who could take out Gray with no problem. A really important reason for not talking about Moore is that we have been discussing the possibility that you just might be grooming me to take over Lola's Place when you and Brownie get married. It's Gray's crazy idea, not mine, so if you want to yell at someone, yell at him, not me. And then all these other things have been going on around us. So, tell Gray and me to get our asses going and arrest Moore if we can. And that is all I have to say on the matter."

"Well," Lola said, "For your information, Norma, and yours too, Gray. Brownie and I have discussed Moore, and we agree. Why are you both still in Holbrook? Get your asses on your horses and take care of business. I'll see you both when you return from Durango, Colorado, with or without Moore."

Chapter 59

Norma and I, along with Butch, went to our cabin and started packing. I had both our saddlebags laid out on the table when Butch gave out a little warning growl. A tentative knock on our door followed this. I grinned at Norma and said, "Come on in, boss. We don't bite too much."

Lola opened the door and stepped in, saying, "Gray, how did you know it was me?"

"That's what I want to know?" Norma said.

I sighed and said, "Well, my first thought was that Jo wanted to talk to Norma again. But I knew she was busy right now; the same was true with Anita. The warning that Butch gave me was for a friend. Butch would have been barking long before she got to the porch if it were Cookie. That pretty well narrowed it down to you, Lola."

Lola and Norma came out with a long laugh, and finally, Norma said, "Charlie, you're telling us that you thought of all those things between the time Butch growled and Lola knocked on our door. How the hell does your mind work? It would have taken me five or ten minutes to think of that much."

Lola was standing beside Norma and said, "Norma, that is how your husband has stayed alive. His mind and eyes work together. Oh! I can't forget his ears. I believe that Gray hears things that you and I don't. Norma, I'm here to tell you that I am thinking of turning the Place over to you to manage, and sometime down the road, I might even sell it to you. That is if you and Gray want the place.

On your way up to Colorado and back, you two think about what I just said. Gray, I have a question for you?"

I smiled and asked, "What is your question, Lola?"

"Are you taking Butch with you?"

Before I could answer her, our dog did it for me. Butch let out one loud, sharp bark. Lola and Norma jumped back a couple of feet; the bark was loud enough to frighten most people.

I petted Butch on top of his head and said, "I believe that was a yes in answer to your question, Lola. Besides, we can't lock him in this cabin because he has already figured out how to open the door."

Lola came over to Butch and, bending down, hugged him and said, "I just wanted to make sure he was being taken care of if he stayed in Holbrook. You are a good dog, Butch." Lola stood up and hugged me, and then Norma. Letting go of Norma, Lola said, "You two, be careful on the trip, and remember that Moore is a sneaky one. He'll try anything to get away from you, Gray." Then Lola turned and walked out of the cabin.

After Lola left the cabin, Norma and I talked for a while, then she fed and watered Butch. When the dog was done eating, I said, "Butch, you stay and guard the cabin. Norma and I are going to get some dinner. Norma will see if she can talk Cookie out of some bones for you to eat on the trip."

I was standing beside the porch, and Butch leaned forward and licked the side of my face. I laughed and said, "I love you too, big guy."

When we got to Simpson Café, Norma gave out a low groan. Midge and Earline were again sitting two tables from ours. I leaned down to Norma and whispered, "Should I invite them to sit with us?"

"What a wonderful idea," Norma softly said. "Then you can tell them all about yourself. You know, the kind of stuff you don't want the whole town to know about."

I laughed, and, taking Norma's left forearm in my right hand, I led her to our table. I made sure to swing wide of the two busybodies. As before, I pulled out Norma's chair and pushed it back under the table when she sat down. This got a comment from one of the gossips, which Norma and I ignored.

Nelda brought us our coffee and something new: a menu with prices for each item, right down to the coffee. Holbrook had recently opened a print shop, and the owner helped Cookie with the layout and printing of the menu.

With her back to the old ladies, Nelda whispered, "Those old battleaxes tried to sit at your table, Gray. I didn't want to deal with them again, so Cookie made them move."

I put on my stern face, ensured the ladies in question could not see me, and said, "You tell Cookie she could lose customers that way. But in this case, Cookie is right. Everyone in town knows that Cookie reserved this table for me. The next time it happens, you tell Cookie, and she'll send you to fetch me. I'll make sure the old troublemakers stay out of Simpson Café for good." I was looking up at Nelda when I saw Earline look around Nelda. The look on Earline's face was one of shock and fear.

The old ladies did not stick around for a second cup of coffee like they usually did. They hurriedly finished their dinner, paid for it, and rushed out of the café. When the ladies were out of sight, Cookie hugged me from the kitchen. She grinned at Norma and said, "You better watch yourself, or I'm going to steal this man away from you. Gray, if those old biddies come in again, I don't think they will want to sit at your table. I got a small package of bones for Butch for you to take on your trip. Could you pick them up on your way out the door? I never did care for that Judge." Cookie went back to her kitchen.

We were returning to the cabin when Norma asked, "Charlie, do you know how Cookie knew we were going after Moore?"

I grinned and said, "I would say that Lola stopped by the café and talked to Cookie before going to Brownie's house."

Norma hugged me and, with a laugh, said, "I thought she went to Lola's Place, but not my wonderful husband. No, he knew that our boss had gone to see her boyfriend. I don't know how he knew, but that is what makes him so special to me. I love you, Charlie Gray, and don't you ever forget me."

"How could I forget you, Norma?" I asked. "Are you planning on running away?"

Vigorously shaking her head, Norma said, "No! It's just that you seem to have so much in that head of yours that you might one day forget that you have a wife and leave with another lady."

I stopped walking, turned Norma toward me, and said, "There is no way that could ever happen. Norma, my dear wife, you are the center of my life. And, one other thing. You will always be that center. I cannot imagine being with another woman. It has been that way since our first kiss. You remember that first kiss?"

Norma smiled at me and said, "In my mind, I compare that first kiss to all your kisses. So far, none have compared to it, but they have all come close. That first kiss uncovered something I thought I had buried for the rest of my life. You, my dear husband, changed that; I will always be grateful for that. I love you, Charlie Gray, and I always will. Can we check on Butch now? I think he knows we are close and is wondering why you haven't come and told him it was okay to move."

I laughed aloud and said, "Norma Elizabeth Gray, I love how your mind works. Yes, we'll check on Butch. Then I will turn you over my knee and give you a good paddling for forgetting something."

"WHAT?" Norma shouted!

"My kiss for being such a good husband," I calmly stated.

Chapter 60

The three of us headed out for Durango, Colorado, early the following day. A week later, we arrived on a bleak, dark, overcast day. The hotel that Norma and I checked into was a couple of buildings away from a very loud saloon since it was early afternoon.

Our room was on the third floor, and after putting our bags in the room, I went down the back stairs and waited at the back door. A few minutes later, Butch came up to me, and we both went up the back stairs.

"What took you so long?" Norma asked me after Butch had almost knocked her over in his hurry to be petted by Norma.

I chuckled and said, "I had to wait for Butch. Then I got the same treatment as you just got."

"Butch was not waiting for you. I'm surprised he wasn't there! Then where was he?" Norma asked.

I ruffled the top of Butch's head and said, "To tell you the truth, I don't know where our dog was. But from the way he acted when he got to me and you too, Norma, I think Butch knows where to find Judge Moore."

When I said the name Moore, Butch let out a low growl. It set the hairs at the back of my neck on edge. That growl was evidence enough for me that Butch did not like the good Judge Moore. Norma had the same thought as she said, "Gray, I don't think our dog likes the man we are after."

"That's what I was thinking. If the man we want is in that loud saloon," I stopped talking because Butch gave out two soft woofs.

"What'd he say?" Norma asked.

"I think he said our man is not in that saloon."

Butch gave out a louder woof.

"So, how do we handle this, Charlie?"

"You and I go for a stroll with our dog. When we get close to where the Judge is, Butch will let us know, and that is when we'll figure out the best way to take him. Alive if possible or not. Are you okay with that?"

Norma waited a moment, then said, "Yes, my dear husband, I'm okay with it as long as there is no other way to take him back to Holbrook."

I smiled at Norma, making sure the smile went to my eyes as well as my lips. I said, "Good. Do you want to go out the front door of the hotel or take Butch down the backstairs to the backdoor?"

Norma smiled and said, "I think I'll be safer with Butch, so go out the front and hurry around to the back."

Once outside, Butch led us away from the loud, noisy saloon to one that was much more sedate, at least from the outside appearance. The front of the building had a wide door and a four-pane window on each side of the door. I went up to one of the windows and looked in. Judge Moore was sitting at a table playing poker. Two dancehall girls were squeezed in next to him, one on the right and one on his left. I saw two bouncers watching the girls' action and not watching the game. We could hear someone playing the piano and a female singing along with the music. I counted six tables but figured there were probably two more over to the right of the door. The bar ran almost the entire length of the room. There was a staircase at each end of the place and a hallway at the head of the stairs. There was also a middle hallway between the staircases. All the tables had at least two players and a dealer.

Norma was looking in the other window, and I know she also got a good look at how the girls were dressed or almost undressed. While waiting for his turn to play, Moore's hands were full of bare skin. I saw him lose a round, and the girls paid for it. They both winched when the guy squeezed some flesh.

At the same time, Norma and I stepped back from our windows and headed back to the hotel. Norma took Butch up the back stairs, and I went into the front lobby. Norma glared at me in the hotel room when she walked in and said, "How are we going to handle this? There were more guns in that saloon than in all of Holbrook. And they are all that bastard's friends."

"We have to find out where he is staying and with whom," I said. "This may take longer than either one of us wants. The dusters and hats will help us fit into a crowd, but your voice puts you coming from the country's southwest part. My voice makes me from the middle of the country, but closer to the northern accent that is around here."

"I wonder if he is staying at this hotel?" Norma questioned.

I grinned at my wife and said, "There is a café downstairs. Why don't we go get something to eat?"

"So, you can flirt with the waitress and get her to tell you if the Judge is staying here. Well, my dear husband, that works for me. But what about Butch? Will he be okay here by himself?"

"Only one way to find out." I stood up from the chair I was sitting in and said, "Butch, you stay and guard the room while Norma and I go to dinner. She will see if she can find you something good to eat."

Our dog was lying next to the chair I had been sitting in. Butch lifted his head off the floor and looked up at me and then Norma. Butch gave out a small woof, and his head flopped back on the floor.

Norma grinned at Butch and reached down and ruffled his head, saying, "You're a good dog, Butch."

When we entered the café, the waitress said, "Sit wherever you want. I'll be with you in a second or two."

I led Norma to a table where we could watch who came in from the street or the Hotel Lobby. I held her chair for her when she sat down and gently shoved her up to the table. Norma smiled at me and said, "Thank you, dear."

As I sat down, the waitress came to the table and said, "Somehow, I figured you would sit here, just like Judge Moore. I saw you when you signed in at the hotel and when you left again a short time later. Our cook has done a great job on the chicken and dumplings. You both look like you need a little extra food. And, if you need it, I can get you a couple of steak bones for your dog. I was outside having a cigarette when you came back to the hotel. Your dog is lovely; what's his name?"

Norma smiled at our waitress and said, "My name is Alice, and he is Charlie. Our dog's name is Butch. When we left Shiprock, New Mexico, a friend told us Judge Moore might be up this way. Do you know him?"

Our waitress chuckled and said, "Some nights, he struts in with one of the dancehall ladies on his arm. On other nights, he is by himself. He always sits at this table. One night, he had me move the guy that was sitting there. He has been staying in room 37 since he got to Durango."

Norma asked, "When does he usually come in here?"

Our waitress shook her head and said, "It could be any time. My husband Frank came in for dinner about an hour ago and said the Judge was losing like crazy tonight. So, he'll probably be by himself tonight. If you leave before the Judge gets here, do you want me to tell him you are looking for him?"

Shaking her head, Norma said, "No. Charlie and I are tired tonight. It's a long trip from Shiprock, and we need to get up to our room and feed Butch. We'll meet up with the Judge sometime tomorrow."

Chapter 61

Our room was number 34, so Moore had to pass us before getting to his room. An hour or so after we returned to our room from dinner, Butch gave out a low woof. We heard someone stagger past our room, and I opened our door just enough to see who it was. Judge Moore stopped at his room and dug in his pockets to find the key. He was alone, and I almost took him out right there, but I wanted him facing me when I shot him.

When he got the door open, the judge stumbled into his room, leaving the door wide open. I waited a few moments to see if anyone had followed him to ensure he got to the right room. No one showed up, so I shut our door and softly said, "He left his door wide open, but I'm not sure why. Norma, do you think I should go close the door?"

"No," Norma said, shaking her head in disgust. "He may have left it open for one of the dancehall girls to come by for what he calls fun."

Butch gave out a little woof and then a low growl.

I returned to our door and pulled my six-shooter out of its holster. I cracked open the door and saw the two dancehall girls enter room 37. I waited for a while to see if they came back out. I was about to close my door when the girls danced out of the room. They were both giggling when they passed our room. When I could not hear the girls, I shut our door.

Norma approached me and hugged me, asking, "Do you want to go see what the girls did?"

I grinned at her and said, "I thought you would never ask. Let's do it!"

Judge Moore lay passed out on his bed. He still had his boots on, and it looked like his clothes were cut in two. His bed was four-poster, and his hands and boot were tied to the posters. His coat lay on the floor, and his wallet was sticking partway out of an inside pocket. I could see that it was empty of money. We left him that way for now and went back to our room.

We didn't laugh until we were lying on our bed. It was too comical to hold it all in. Finally, Norma said, "The only thing that would have made it perfect was if the girls had left his dick hanging out for the cleaning lady to see. However, it is so small she may not even notice the damn thing anyway."

I was silent momentarily, and I could feel Norma wondering why I was quiet. I finally asked, "Was our waitress named Mary?"

"What? That is not what I thought you would say. But the answer is yes, her name is Mary. But why do you want to know? What is it you're thinking, my dear husband?"

"I was wondering if she might know if the judge has a horse here in town. If so, we should cart him off in a couple of hours. What do you think, my dear wife?"

Norma smiled at me and said, "Go find out, but don't say we will kidnap him."

Before lying down, I removed my gun belt; now, I wondered if I should put it back on. Norma took care of my plight when she said, "Leave the gun. It might scare Mary into not saying anything."

I laughed and kissed Norma before putting my boots on and taking Butch with me down the back stairs. Butch took off running when we were outside, and I ran to the Café. Mary was about to lock the street door when she saw me coming. Instead of closing it, Mary opened the door and asked, "Why are you coming in from the street?"

"I had to let Butch out for the night. And I have a question for you?"

Mary shook her head and said, "He came in alone, but a short while after eating, two girls came in looking for the Judge. That's all I know."

"Do you know if he has a horse here in town?"

"I do know that," Mary said with a grin. "The hotel has a small livery out back, and I'm guessing that is where your horses are tonight. Did you see a buckskin horse in one of the stalls when you put your horses there? That's the Judge's."

"See, you did know something else," I said with a chuckle. "You don't like the Judge, do you, Mary?"

Shaking her head, Mary said, "What gave me away?"

"The tone in your voice, more than anything else. But, I'm rather good at reading people."

"So am I, Charlie. Where's that six-shooter you had on earlier? And why did you want to know about the Judge's horse?"

"I left the gun in the room. Alice thought it might scare you off from talking to me."

Mary got a smirk on her face as she said, "I was down in Santa Fe, New Mexico, when you came through there, Mister Gray. I recognized you when you walked in here, and I was going to say something to Judge Moore, but the way your wife made it sound as if you didn't want him to know you were here. So, what's going on?"

"Where do I start?"

"Give me the short version, okay?"

"Judge Moore sent a husband and wife to Holbrook, Arizona, to kill me. I know them both, and they decided to keep the five thousand the Judge gave them. That was half of what he said he would pay to see me dead. But, the judge tried to make sure his money would be earned; he sent two men to follow my friends and do the job if they didn't. The second two tried and failed. The Sheriff of Holbrook has a telegram that tells the men to take care of my friends and me. Any money they find on my friends, the two men could keep. Alice and I are taking Moore back to Holbrook to stand trial."

Mary said, "Wow! I wasn't expecting that. What can I do to help? That man tried to get me to his room and did it right before my husband. I was so mad that I would have shot the man right between his legs if I had a gun."

An hour later, carrying Moore on my back, Norma and I left the hotel. Mary was holding Moore's horse when I secured him to his saddle. Norma and I hugged Mary before getting on our horses and heading south.

The sun was coming up when we made camp the following day. Sometime during the night, Moore woke up and started yelling all kinds of cuss words, so I put a gag in his mouth. Moore was sleeping as he sat on his saddle, and the sun striking his eyes woke him up. I took the gag from his mouth and asked, "You want some water?"

"You can't do this to me! I'm a federal Judge. Unbind me and let me go. I'll forget this ever happened."

Norma said, "Like you forgot the men you sent to kill Charles?"

"What the fuck are you talking about, Norma? I never sent anybody after Gray."

"Do you want me to quote the telegram you sent to them?" Norma asked.

"I never sent a fucking telegram telling anyone to kill Gray. You are out of your fucking mind. You fucking bitch."

That was enough for me. I put the gag back in the Judge's mouth, which was not too easy either. I might have knocked a tooth out when I pushed the gag in with the barrel of my six-shooter.

It took a while, but Norma, Butch, and I got Moore to Holbrook. He had his trial the same day with a visiting Judge presiding. The jury said Moore was guilty, and the visiting Judge oversaw the hanging of Moore the next day.

The visiting Judge married Lola and Sheriff Brownie. Then, the newlyweds went to Amarillo, Texas, because Brownie had never been there. They took the stagecoach to Albuquerque, New Mexico, and then the train to Amarillo.

When she returned to Holbrook, Lola said, "Do you want to know the best part of the trip?"

Lola and Brownie were with us in our cabin, along with Butch, when Lola asked the question. In unison, the three of us yelled, "NO!" We had already heard that the train was the best thing ever invented.

A couple of months later, I was talking to Norma in the office of Lola's Place when Brownie knocked on the door and walked in before Norma could say anything. Lola was with him, and they both looked pleased. "What's up, boss?" Norma asked.

Lola handed Norma a stack of papers and said, "Don't read, just sign." Lola held the piece so that Norma could only see the spot for her signature.

"What am I getting into if I sign this sight unseen?" Norma asked with a smile. Then she signed her name.

Brownie said, "Gray, this calls for a drink. Norma now owns Lola's Place, The Cattlemen's Bar, the cabin you live in, the haberdashery, half-owner in the Holbrook Bank, and some other fine pieces of property."

I noticed that Brownie wasn't wearing his sheriff's badge, and I soon found out why. After Norma sputtered and cussed a few times as she read over what she had signed, Norma said, "Lola, I can't afford to buy all of this. I only have a couple of hundred dollars to my name."

"It's all spelled out in the paperwork that you and Gray can review later. Right now, I have one other thing to do." Lola said as she reached into her pocket and brought something out.

"Gray," she said, "The City Council met and decided they want you to be their new sheriff. Brownie resigned an hour ago. Every council member agreed to this." Lola handed me the badge and then hugged me.

I looked at Norma as she stood up behind her desk. I said, "As sheriff, I hope I can live up to Brownie's reputation."

Norma came around her desk to hug and kiss me. Then she said, "What are you two going to do now?"

Lola said, "We are moving to Amarillo. Brownie bought a cattle ranch while we were there on our honeymoon."

That was when we heard a lot of laughter coming from the bar area. The door opened, and James stuck his head in and said, "Boss, everyone wants to know what is going on. And so do I." He looked right at Norma and smiled.